I Walk Between the Raindrops

ALSO BY T. CORAGHESSAN BOYLE

NOVELS

Water Music (1982)

Budding Prospects (1984)

World's End (1987)

East Is East (1990)

The Road to Wellville (1993)

The Tortilla Curtain (1995)

Riven Rock (1998)

A Friend of the Earth (2000)

Drop City (2003)

The Inner Circle (2004)

Talk Talk (2006)

The Women (2009)

When the Killing's Done (2011)

San Miguel (2012)

The Harder They Come (2015)

The Terranauts (2016)

Outside Looking In (2019)

Talk to Me (2021)

SHORT STORIES

Descent of Man (1979)

Greasy Lake & Other Stories (1985)

If the River Was Whiskey (1989)

Without a Hero (1994)

T.C. Boyle Stories (1998)

After the Plague (2001)

Tooth and Claw (2005)

The Human Fly (2005)

Wild Child & Other Stories (2010)

T.C. Boyle Stories II (2013)

The Relive Box (2017)

ANTHOLOGIES

Doubletakes (2004), coedited with K. Kvashay-Boyle

I Walk Between the Raindrops

Stories

T. Coraghessan Boyle

ecco

An Imprint of HarperCollinsPublishers

I WALK BETWEEN THE RAINDROPS. Copyright © 2022 by T. Coraghessan Boyle. All rights reserved. Printed in the United States of America. No part of this book may be used or reproduced in any manner whatsoever without written permission except in the case of brief quotations embodied in critical articles and reviews. For information, address HarperCollins Publishers, 195 Broadway, New York, NY 10007.

HarperCollins books may be purchased for educational, business, or sales promotional use. For information, please email the Special Markets Department at SPsales@harpercollins.com.

Ecco® and HarperCollins® are trademarks of HarperCollins Publishers.

A hardcover edition of this book was published in 2022 by Ecco, an imprint of HarperCollins Publishers.

FIRST ECCO PAPERBACK EDITION PUBLISHED 2023

Designed by Angela Boutin

Frontispiece © Luria/Shutterstock

Library of Congress Cataloging-in-Publication Data has been applied for.

ISBN 978-0-06-305289-5 (pbk.)

23 24 25 26 27 LBC 5 4 3 2 1

Grateful acknowledgment is made to the following magazines in which these stories first appeared: *Esquire*, "What's Love Got to Do with It?" and "The Thirteenth Day"; *The Kenyon Review*, "These Are the Circumstances"; *McSweeney's*, "The Apartment" and "Dog Lab"; *Narrative*, "Big Mary"; *The New Yorker*, "I Walk Between the Raindrops," "Asleep at the Wheel," and "The Shape of a Teardrop"; *Playboy*, "Not Me"; *Zoetrope*, "The Hyena."

"The Apartment" also appeared in *The Best American Stories, 2020*, edited by Curtis Sittenfeld.

For Olivia, Evan, Wolfgang, and Hawken

I got a black cat bone, / I got a mojo too, /

I got John-the-conqueror root /

I'm goin' to mess with you.

—WILLIE DIXON, "I'M YOUR HOOCHIE COOCHIE MAN"

CONTENTS

I Walk
Between the
Raindrops

I Walk Between the Raindrops

VALENTINE'S DAY

This past Valentine's Day I was in Kingman, Arizona, with my wife, Nola, staying in the Motel 6 there, just off the I-40. You might not think of Kingman as a prime location for a romantic getaway (who would?), but Nola and I have been married for fifteen years now and romance is just part of the continuum— sometimes it blows hot, sometimes cold, and certainly we don't need a special day or place for it. We're not sentimentalists. We don't exchange heart-shaped boxes of chocolates or glossy manufactured cards with manufactured endearments inside, and we don't go around kissing in public or saying "I love you" twenty times a day. (To my mind couples like that are always suspect— really, who are they trying to fool?) Besides which, we were there to pay a visit to Nola's father, who's in his eighties and living in a trailer park a mile down the road from the motel, which made it convenient not only for seeing him but for strolling into Old Town, where there are a handful of bars and restaurants and the junk shops my wife loves to frequent, looking for bargains.

Were we slumming? Yes, sure. We could have stayed anywhere we liked, but this—at least when we're in Kingman—is what we like, and if it's not ideal, at least it's different. The local police creep through the parking lot in the small hours, running license plates, and once in a while you'll wake to see them handcuffing somebody outside one of the rooms, which is not a sight we see every day back in California. Plus, there are a couple of lean, white bums living in the wash just behind the place, and sometimes they give me a start looming up out of the darkness when I step outside at night for a breath of air, but nothing's ever happened, not even a request for spare change or a cigarette.

The afternoon of Valentine's Day, after we'd visited my father-in-law (and treated him to lunch at Denny's, the only place he'll eat), Nola went up the street to cruise the antique emporia and I made for the local bar, figuring we'd meet up there for a drink when she was done, then walk over to the Mexican restaurant for margaritas and enchiladas. This bar, which I'd been to before, is a cavernous place with a high, tin ceiling that was part of a now-defunct hotel, and it features a long, pitted bar top, three pool tables, and a jukebox that plays the hits of the sixties and seventies at hurricane volume. The front door stands perpetually open, so as to brighten the place up a bit with the best kind of light, the light that doesn't cost anybody anything, and across the street is a web of train tracks that guide an endless procession of freight trains through town. Glance up from your beer or your gin and tonic and more often than not you'll see a moving wall of freight cars rattling by.

The important thing to emphasize here is that this wasn't an unfriendly place, despite the neatly inscribed message over the urinal in the men's room that says *Fuck you, liberal pussies*, which I choose to take in an ironic light. And I wasn't unfriendly myself, happy to sidle up to the bar alongside the mostly middle-aged regulars and order a Jack and Coke, though normally—that is, back in our little coastal town in California—I would have had a Pinot Noir from the Santa Rita Hills or a nice full-bodied Zinfandel from Paso Robles. This wasn't the place for Pinot Noir, and I'm not knocking it, just stating the obvious. Beyond that, I was content to bend over my phone (I'd been engaged off and on all day tweeting on a financial forum run by the company I used to work for) and wait for Nola to tire out and come join me for a Valentine's Day drink, which in her case would likely be gin and tonic, a drink nobody, whether they were in Kingman or Irkutsk, could screw up.

There was a woman sitting at the deserted end of the bar four stools down from me. I'd thrown her a reflexive glance when I came in, but chose to give her space and sit one stool over from a knot of bearded regulars in plaid shirts, shorts, and work boots. This woman—late thirties, lean as one of the bums in the wash, jeans, running shoes, her face older than the rest of her and a little rainbow-colored cap perched atop her dark, cropped hair—wouldn't have been attractive to me even if I was in the market, which I wasn't. But I was there without my wife, it was Valentine's Day, and the single glance I'd given her must have meant more to her than me, because three minutes later, before I'd had more than a sip or two of my drink, she was right there standing beside me, so close we were practically touching.

"My name's Serena," she said, trying for a smile she couldn't quite arrange.

"Brandon," I said, and because she was right there in my

personal space and I couldn't think of anything else to do, I took her hand and shook it in a neutral way.

"Brandon?" she echoed. "What kind of a name is that?"

"Just a name." I shrugged. "It's what my parents gave me."

"I have ESP," she said.

"Great," I said, after giving it a beat. "But really"—I gestured to the phone—"and I don't want to be rude, but I've got some business here I have to catch up on."

The music hammered us like the tailwind of a jet plane. I glanced out the open door to where a freight was rolling silently by, all its mechanical shrieks and clanks negated by the forward thrust of the music.

"You want to play a game?" she asked.

"No, I'm sorry." It was then that I began to realize there was another conversation altogether going on here, between her and herself. She was muttering, commenting on my comments and her own, maybe even cursing under her breath.

She repeated her question and I shook my head no and went back to my phone, but she wouldn't give it up, just hovered there, holding her private conversation in public. I didn't want trouble, and liberal pussy that I am, I didn't relish being cruel to anyone, no matter how irritating or crazy she might be, so after taking it a moment or two longer I picked up my drink and ambled down to the other end of the bar, choosing a seat between two groups of Valentine's Day revelers, men mostly, but a pair of women there too, everybody mutedly raucous ahead of the evening to come. But then—you guessed it—the woman was back, Serena, wedging herself in between me and the guy on the stool beside me, invading my personal space. She said, "I have ESP," and when I didn't react, she said, "You want to play a game?"

Angry now, I shoved back the stool, took my drink, and

crossed the room to one of the empty booths against the far wall behind the pool tables. If it had been a man harassing me I could have bluffed or blustered my way out of it—or at least left the place to avoid a confrontation—but this was different. This was a woman. An ESP woman with god knew what kind of mental Ferris wheel spinning round in her head, and I wasn't going anywhere. I was going to finish my drink and have another one and wait for my wife to come get me.

I'd turned my back on the bar and was hunched over my phone, responding to one of the lamebrained provocateurs on *#moneymostly* who seemed to exist only to spew insults, when suddenly the ESP woman was back. And here we went again through exactly the same scenario, word for word, but this time when I didn't respond, she got upset and kicked the side of the booth so hard it nearly sent my drink flying. At which point I got up and stalked back to the bar, where I summoned the bartender, a heavyset party girl gone complacent with the delivery of the years. "Look," I hollered over the din, "that woman over there is driving me out of my mind."

"I'll take care of it," she said.

"You know her? Is she a local?" I couldn't keep the edge out of my voice. I felt weak and ashamed of myself.

"She turned up here a couple weeks ago—to stay with a friend. Nobody really knows her."

At that moment I glanced up, distracted by a disturbance of the light, and there was Nola, poised in the doorway with the sun behind her and a pair of shopping bags dangling from one hand. She came to me, graceful, light on her feet and smiling with pure pleasure, which wasn't simply the pleasure of seeing me, her husband, but of the invigorating hour she'd spent sifting through the overlooked treasures of an out-of-the-way town. We had a drink. When I looked up again, the ESP woman was gone.

Before long, the bartender handed out Valentine's Day balloons—pink for the ladies, blue for the men—and we all started inflating them and batting them around the room and it was real and honest and beautiful. I got swept up in the moment. The jukebox played a song we'd known all our lives, and I leaned in close to my wife, guided her face to me with my fingertips, and kissed her.

WHEN THE MOUNTAINS COME DOWN TO THE SEA

The reason we'd gone to Kingman at that particular time rather than a month earlier or later had to do with the mudslides—or debris flows, as they were more accurately called—that had devastated our town early in January. We'd been evacuated for ten days in December because of the wildfires that had burned for weeks along the ridgeline and enveloped everything in a black mantle of smoke, but we'd been lucky, and our house had been spared. In fact, due to the efforts of the firefighting crews, very few structures were lost, and when the evacuation order was lifted just before Christmas we came back home and celebrated the holiday as best we could under the circumstances. But as any student of the topography of Southern California can tell you, the fires are a prelude to the floods that inevitably come with the next heavy rainfall. Which was exactly what happened.

A storm cell hit at two in the morning a week after New Year's, a cell so concentrated and powerful the meteorologists called it a once-in-two-hundred-year event, and it generated a debris flow that drove everything before it to the sea, houses, cars, trees, boulders—and twenty-three of my neighbors, who were engulfed and killed in the dark, cold, grinding hours that succeeded it. Again, we were lucky. Our house, which is situated on high ground, was undamaged, and though I knew some of the victims by sight, we didn't lose anyone close to us. People kept offering us sympathy, practically everyone we'd ever known telephoning, emailing, texting—Were we all right?—and that began to feel strange because aside from the inconvenience of being without electricity or gas for the stove, we were untouched. Nola said I was feeling survivor's guilt, and while there was an ontological dimension to all this that filled me with a kind of dread I don't think I'd ever felt before, the concept made no sense to me. Why should I feel guilty? Because my house hadn't been destroyed? Because I wasn't dead myself?

When, a few days later, the newspaper showed pictures of the victims, I recognized a few of them, people I'd said hello and good-bye to a few times over the years—casual acquaintances—but no one whose name came readily to my lips. There was the tall, jaunty old man with the booming voice who always had a story to tell, the woman who owned the beauty salon, and another, a cool blonde I could picture at the bar in our favorite restaurant, always in heels and always standing whether there was a stool available or not, almost as if it were a duty. She drank martinis. Every so often she'd abandon her post to go out and lean against the wall with the valets and have a smoke. Her posture—I could reconstruct it just from seeing her face in the slightly out of focus obituary photo—was perfect, and even in her fifties she was slim, with an expressive figure. Nola didn't remember her. Didn't remember any of them.

What I was remembering, though, was a story in that same newspaper ten years earlier after a series of rainstorms had drenched the town—warm South Pacific storms meteorologists referred to as the "Pineapple Express." It was nothing like the current cataclysm, just the loss of a single life, and why the story had stuck with me, I couldn't say. It concerned an elderly couple, well off, retired, in their late sixties or maybe early seventies.

Their house sat just above one of our occasional creeks—parallel to it, actually, with a long, spacious front room looking down on the streambed below. It was raining and they were in their living room, a fire going, a string quartet on the stereo (I'm imagining now), wine poured, candles lit, the dog on the rug at their feet and giving off a rich odor because its fur had been soaked through when it went out to do its business. What else? He was a judge, a retired judge, and she'd been something too.

There had been no warning, no evacuation notice, nothing—just rain, that was all—and there was no way they could have anticipated what came next. Above them, on the side of the mountain half a mile away, something tore loose, a boulder that slammed into another boulder that in turn slammed into another and so on down the line, till a river of mud and debris came careering down the canyon and took out the wall of their house as if it had been made of paper, like the ones in the Kurosawa samurai films Nola got me in a boxed set one Christmas. The wife, who survived by clinging to a doorframe, said it was as if a freight train had come roaring through the house. The husband tried to hold on too, but the torrent breached the far wall and took him and everything else with it. They found him on the beach the next morning, battered and abraded, his clothes scoured from him, and at first, because of his age and his long white hair and beard, they took him to be one of the transients who made their home beneath the bridge. The point was, he was no transient, but a former jurist who'd no doubt passed judgment on whole truckloads of transients in his time, and the further point was that it didn't make an iota of difference, except maybe by way of funeral arrangements.

We woke on the morning after the storm with no electricity and no sound but for the rain and the warring sirens of the rescue vehicles. Needless to say, the newspaper hadn't been delivered, nor could we use the radio, phone, TV, or internet, so we really didn't have any idea of the extent of the damage done—or even that there had been any at all. I built a fire to take the chill off the house, enjoying the closeness of the moment as Nola and I sat side by side on the couch before it, spooning up cold cereal and listening to the wet witch's hand of the rain on the roof. At ten or so I walked down to the village to see if anybody knew what was going on, the rain tapping insistently at my umbrella and the surf crashing in the distance.

At first I saw nothing out of the ordinary, but for a dark scatter of palm fronds lying like speed bumps in the street, and I kept tipping my umbrella back to get a better look at the scene ahead. There were few people around, few cars, but that was the way it was whenever it rained, everybody reluctant to leave the house and negotiate the slippery streets and fallen branches and the risk of fender benders and all the rest—again, nothing out of the ordinary. It wasn't until I crested the long, gentle slope that rises through the center of the shopping district that I saw the mud and debris at the far end of it, where it intersects with Olive Mill, a street that runs perpendicular to the mountains and which, as I later learned, acted as a conduit for the debris flow. Curious, I kept going, downslope now, the mud becoming more of a presence in the street while the sirens screamed in the distance and the helicopters beat out their rhythms overhead. There was something in the air that wasn't ordinary at all, a dark fecal smell overlaid with a chemical taint, as of gasoline or propane.

When I got to a point half a block from the main flow of the mud, where I could make out ridges of it, high irregular ridges bristling with crushed automobiles, downed trees, and the shorn-off timbers and shattered roofs of houses, I stopped. To go any farther I'd have to descend into the mud, which had lagooned here to maybe a foot or so in depth, and that was something I didn't want to do. I'm no hero. And the police and first responders were already on the scene, bulldozers roaring and fuming away, and more coming. Beyond that, and if this sounds ridiculous, forgive me, I didn't feature ruining my shoes just to satisfy my curiosity, and it wasn't as if I could really see or do anything—there were no babies floating by on rafts of tangled branches or anything like that. There was just mud. A big stewing soup of it.

What I did was turn round and retrace my footsteps up the slope and down the other side, where everything was pristine and glowing with the sheen of the rain, thinking to go home, refresh the fire, and sit by the window with a book till the power came back on and Nola and I could flick on the TV and assess the situation. At the last minute, though, I turned left, toward the ocean, still not satisfied. There was no one around but for a couple in hoodies and mud-slick boots working their way up the beach toward me, the waves the color of chocolate milk and surging at the beach in a seething clutter of refuse, everything from everybody's garage and attic spewed out in the water as far as you could see. They were young, this couple, in their twenties, I guessed, but till they drew closer I couldn't make out their faces beyond seeing that one was male, the other female.

"Don't go down there," the man shouted out suddenly. They were giving me a wide berth and walking briskly, as if there were something right behind them and closing fast. "Because I'm telling you, it's pretty gnarly."

The girl, I saw now, was in tears.

"What do you mean?"

"I mean," he called, already past me now, "there's like an *arm* sticking out of the mud, and it's, it's"—his face, framed by his wet hoodie, was like a slice of something unevenly divided—"bad, just *bad*."

I jerked round so fast my feet almost went out from under

me—I'd never seen a dead body and I didn't want to see one now. All I wanted was to go home, just that, but then the shroud of rain fell back a moment and something up the beach caught my eye, something substantial I at first took to be a heap of kelp washed up in the storm, and yet it was a lighter color than kelp, almost tan, like jute, a big pile of jute. When I got to it and saw what it was, I just stood there looking down at it so long I could have counted the sand fleas springing off its paws and snout and the great motionless muscles of its chest and flanks. What was it? A bear. A bear crushed and drowned and washed all the way down out of the mountains on a tide it never saw coming. I knew my wife was waiting for me, and a fire too, and a warm blanket if I needed it, but I just couldn't seem to move. *What's wrong with this picture?* I was thinking, and then I was saying it aloud, and then the surf sluiced in and got my shoes wet and the dead bear's bulk moved ever so fractionally as if the tide could bring it back to life.

THE SUICIDE-PREVENTION HOTLINE

Two years ago, just after I retired (at fifty, with a golden parachute strapped firmly round my shoulders), Nola began volunteering for the local chapter of the National Suicide Prevention Society—or NSP, as she called it. She went through a short course of training, and three nights a week she was on duty, answering the hotline and trying, in her soft, assuaging tones, to talk strangers down from the brink. This was necessarily a late-night enterprise—very late-night—and at first I begrudged her the time away from home, away from *me*, but all that evened out eventually and after six months she gave it up in any case, citing the burnout factor. Of course, during those six months she lived through countless hours of high-wire drama, and more often than not when she got up the next day she'd come into the kitchen or my study or wherever I happened to be and say, "Boy, have I got a story for you."

Here's one of them.

Nola had a colleague there, a man in his early thirties named Blake, who always wore a tie and jacket while manning the phones, though there was no need to and the callers in distress wouldn't have known whether he was naked but for his socks or wearing an evil-clown mask or dangling by his feet from the ceiling. But Blake said he owed it to them because they were crying out for help and, whether they'd reached the end or not, at the very least they expected a formal presence on the other end of the line, the voice of reason dressed up in jacket and tie. For her part, Nola wore jeans and a sweatshirt, no makeup, and usually did her hair up in a ponytail so it wouldn't distract her as she leaned into the phone, fully absorbed in the halting voice of misery coming at her. She didn't ask the callers for any personal information, and she didn't put them on the defensive—she just listened, and when there were silences she tried to fill them, to keep the people talking till at some point, whether that be half an hour later, an hour, two hours, she could direct them to a mental health professional in their area or, in the most extreme cases, dial 911 and send the police and paramedics to save a life.

Blake operated in much the same way—it was standard procedure—but sometime during Nola's second week he stayed on the line all night long with a single caller. Her name was Brie, she was nineteen, and her boyfriend had left her even though she'd gone to a clinic and gotten rid of the baby. She didn't see the point in living. Why go to school (she was in junior college, studying to be a dental hygienist), why save money, why work—for that matter, why bother brushing your teeth, because what difference did it make if you got periodontal disease when you were just going to die anyway, like everybody else? The usual stuff—Nola had already heard it dozens of times from her own callers, but what was the answer? Aside from cant, which nobody at the hotline believed in, there was no convincing argument to be made and nothing to say beyond *I understand, I do, yes, yes. . . . Are you there? Are you still there?*

Needless to say, it was against the rules to get personally involved with the callers, but before long, Brie was calling at one a.m. on the dot every night Blake was working the phones, and if anyone else answered she'd say, "I want Blake," and in the next moment he'd take over. It wasn't appropriate. Everybody knew that. This wasn't a dating site—and it wasn't a teen chat line either. It was serious business, and if Brie was going to kill herself (as Nola began to wonder), why was she so interested in Blake?

Not long thereafter, Blake confided to my wife that he'd met Brie in person, though that was strictly verboten, and then that he'd actually begun dating her—and, inevitably, had had sex with her. "She was depressed," he said, "and, tell the truth, so was I. Nobody's depressed when they're having sex, right?"

"I wouldn't be so sure," Nola told him. "And I'm not a psychologist, but there's a whole lot more to it than that. You're not a professional either. You don't know what kind of state she's in—this is the Suicide Prevention Hotline, for god's sake."

He gave her a long, slow look. "That's right—prevention. And I'm preventing, okay?"

"But it's not right," she persisted. "It's against the rules. If Barney knew" (Barney was the boss, the only salaried employee of the local chapter), "he'd go through the roof."

A shrug. Another look. "You worry about your callers," Blake said, "and I'll worry about mine."

Two weeks later Blake and Brie were both dead. Blake had gone to her apartment with a bottle of wine and take-out Chinese, but she said she was too depressed to eat. She curled in on herself, her feet bare, the leggings clinging to her ankles like grasping hands trying to pull her down (I'm reading into this now), and said the stink of the food made her think of China, with its something like a billion and a half stinking people all hurtling toward the grave. Like everybody else in the world. Like her. Like him. Then came the arguments she'd given that first day, the arguments they all gave, and really, what was the use of going on living, and he tried to counter them, but he was down himself and sinking lower and she had some pills the shrink had prescribed and they both took them and sat in his car with the motor running in the garage that was locked from the inside.

When Nola told me this—laid it on me, that is—there really wasn't much I could say. I hadn't known them. Scenarios like that spun out every day. And she hadn't known them either, at least not the girl, and Blake only casually, as a coworker, and if they'd had a cup of coffee together and a couple of the stale crullers people donated, that was the extent of it. She'd been on her phones and he'd been on his. When the shift was over, they went home, separately, to separate lives.

"It could have been anybody," Nola said, and I could see the distress in her face. We were at the kitchen table, glasses of Chardonnay standing like sentinels before us. It was late afternoon of a gloomy day, the atmosphere so thick it was like concrete just before it sets. She looked away from my eyes. "It could have been us."

"No," I said. "It couldn't. We're nothing like that."

FREDDA AND PAUL

What I'm talking about is grace—or call it luck, if you want. Some people have it and others don't, that's just the way it is, a spin of the stochastic wheel. Same thing with good looks. Statistically, physically attractive people rise more rapidly in their professions, make more money, marry better, and position their children to do the same, passing down their good fortune—and good genes—to the next generation. Even if I were unbiased, which I'm not, I'd have to say most people would consider me better-looking than average—and Nola's a rare beauty who still turns heads in her midforties. (And beyond that, my first wife, Ursula, whom I met in Berlin while I was an exchange student, had cover-girl looks too, and she made me happy for six and a half years, till she didn't, but that's another story.) I'm not trying to inflate my ego here, just stating the facts, especially in light of what happened when Nola and I tried to play matchmaker with two of our oldest friends.

Fredda had been Nola's roommate freshman year in college, and they'd stayed in touch over the years. She lived on the other side of the country, but she'd recently been phased out of her job and moved to the West Coast to live with her mother, who was ailing. Fredda was smart and capable, and she was fast on her feet verbally, with the kind of sharp, ironic humor I savor—and miss out here in California. The problem was, she was overweight—or not simply overweight, but obese, and her features were more mannish than feminine, so that she didn't even have the advantage some overweight women enjoy of looking vulnerable and inviting at the same time. When she was a student (so Nola told me), she'd spend her Friday and Saturday nights not at dance clubs or fraternity parties or basketball games, but playing pinochle in the student union with a few of the other girls—and guys—in the same physical boat. Losers, that is. And while it's harsh to say it, this is what I'm getting at here: some people are doomed from the start. Imagine her, the heaviest kid in kindergarten, the dieting regimes, the heckling and hazing, the plus-size jeans and tentlike dresses and all the rest. I didn't know her as well as I knew Paul, my own plus-size friend, and until she moved in with her mother in Ventura, thirty minutes south of us, I only thought of her when we exchanged a few pleasantries over the phone before Nola picked up.

"Why don't we have Fredda over for dinner?" Nola said one night while we were sitting in the kitchen, the dishwasher humming and the radio tuned to the classical station. There were fresh-cut flowers on the table. The sun was balanced on the horizon and setting things aglow, the wineglasses and patterned china, the reflective surfaces of the appliances. It was a perfect moment, and it was as if we'd been positioned here by some unseen hand to enjoy it.

I shrugged. "Sure," I said. "Why not."

"It'd be good to see her, wouldn't it?"

"Sure."

"But who else are we going to invite?' she said, pressing her thumb to her upper lip in thought. After a minute, she said, "What about Paul?"

"Paul? But we can't—" I pictured the four of us standing around the living room with cocktails in our hands, the two of them looking in alarm at each other and then at us, as if we were playing some sort of cruel joke, when that wasn't it at all.

"No, no, I mean a dinner *party*, with, I don't know—two other couples, Jenna and Carlos, maybe. The Traynors. Or Louise—how about Louise and Ira? We owe them, right? They've had us twice now since we had them over . . . or am I miscounting?"

As it turned out, we were ten for dinner. At the last minute we realized we couldn't have Paul and Fredda there as the only singles among three couples—we didn't want to be that obvious—so we invited our neighbor Arnold, who'd lost his wife six months earlier, and Katie, an energetic divorcée in her late fifties Nola knew from a quilting circle she'd joined over the winter. Paul was the first to arrive—he was out here on business, staying long term at a hotel in L.A.—and I think he was eager to escape the four walls, dreary views, and artificial relationships he'd established with the concierge, the barman, and the wait-staff. We'd grown up together, Paul and I, and I knew his habits and predilections as well as I knew my own—or I thought I did.

As soon as he stepped in the door I handed him a cocktail—he was an enthusiastic drinker and a dedicated oenophile and foodie whose motto was *Everything in moderation, including moderation*, and he'd long since given up worrying about his weight. *My weight is my fate*, was another of his sayings, and his chief hobby—his only hobby, as far as I knew—was frequenting the trendiest restaurants around and working his way through the menus as if he were a food critic. Which, in a way, I suppose, he was.

We were standing by the fireplace, catching up on gossip about our New York friends, when the bell rang and I went to answer it while Nola fussed around in the kitchen and Paul warmed himself by the fire. It could have been any one of the seven other guests standing there, but go ahead and throw the dice: it was Fredda.

"You didn't tell me it was going to be so dark out here, my god," she said, grinning to let me see her teeth, as if that were the only way I could identify her. "And this mountainside—I was beginning to think you lived on Everest. Or at least K2, isn't that the other one, K2?"

She was wearing a kind of sari or toga in a shiny electric-blue material that only managed to make her look bigger, as if this were the Mexican border and she was smuggling another person in with her, and I know that's not particularly kind of me to say, but that was the fact. In the next moment, while I was pouring her a glass of wine, she and Paul were left to stand there looking balefully at one another while I tried to make small talk along the lines of *It's about time you two met* and *You're our favorite peo-ple in the world, you know that?* and the like until Nola came in to rescue me and the doorbell started ringing and the party began.

What can I say? It was a dinner party. Everybody had a good time, I think, and the meal—a paella Nola and I cooked from scratch—turned out perfectly. Katie, the divorcée, who'd once been co-owner of a Valencian restaurant in Santa Monica, said it was better than anything her chef had ever managed to come up with. Afterward we sat around the fire with brandy and Bene-dictine and encouraged the guests to browse our vinyl collection and each in succession play a single cut so that it was as if we were hearing those songs for the first time.

If we'd made a mistake it was in not setting out place cards at dinner—the idea had seemed to me overly formal and fussy—but which resulted in Paul and Fredda sitting at opposite ends of the table and barely talking to each other, let alone opening up in the way we'd hoped and expected. Fredda hardly touched her food. Paul ate steadily, enormously, his hands in constant mo-tion, sopping up the juices from the paella pan with a heel of bread, draining his wineglass as soon as it was filled, enjoying three or four portions of the flan—I don't know, I stopped count-ing, and what difference did it make anyway? Of course, and I wouldn't quite appreciate this until everyone else had left, Nola had gone to bed, and the two of us stayed on talking, he'd been eating defiantly, angrily, fulfilling the role society had imposed on him—and I, unthinkingly, had reinforced.

The fire snapped. We sat side by side on the couch cradling our snifters. The record—it was Paul's selection, Ellington and Coltrane, "In a Sentimental Mood"—haunted the speakers. There was a silence. A long silence. Stupidly, I asked, "What did you think of Fredda?"

He gave me the kind of look you wouldn't expect of a friend, his eyes fixed on mine, his lips curled down at the corners. "You would do *that* to me?" he said after a moment.

"Do what?"

"Mock me like that? You really think I want a fat woman in my life? If I want fat, I can just look in the mirror."

"But she's as close to us as, as you are, and she's a great person, she is—I mean funny, funny like you can't believe—"

"And fat."

"Look, Paul, I would never . . ." I glanced away, fumbled over my words. "I mean well, you know that—"

"Do you?" he said, swiveling his head on the pillar of his neck to look me dead-on, Paul, my oldest friend, whom I'd known since high school and who was as foreign to me in that moment as if we'd just met. "Do you really?"

BE MY VALENTINE

That evening in Kingman, which had begun in the late afternoon with its hovering sun and a desert sweetness in the air, with promise, that is, and comfort too, with me at the bar and my wife tranquilly shopping, took a turn for the worse I haven't really disclosed to anyone yet because I still don't know what to make of it. The ESP woman (Serena, who was anything but) had reacted a bit more stridently than I let on earlier. Yes, she stalked me to the booth behind the pool tables, and yes, we cycled through the same postures and dialogue, but after I rejected her for the third time and she lashed out and kicked the side of the booth, she said this to me, her voice straining right at the breaking point: "What, you think you're Jesus or something? Like your shit doesn't stink? Like you walk between the raindrops?"

These weren't questions, they were accusations, and I wasn't about to legitimize them with a response. I got up, as I said, and took my drink to the bar and complained to the bartender, and if my heart rate was accelerated and my hand trembled ever so slightly with the sudden flood of adrenaline in my veins, it was nothing the second drink—and Nola—couldn't remedy. Then came the balloons and the kiss and another round of drinks and I thought that was it, situation over, encounter nullified, the lineaments of it already making for a good story to tell at a party, with me in the starring role as the irresistible object of unwanted affection, a man radiating intense physical attraction without even being aware of it. Nola and I batted the balloons and finished our drinks and I got up and went to the bar to pay.

The bartender, the aging party girl with the broad face and seen-it-all eyes, leaned in to pass me my change and said, "Did you hear what happened?"

"No, what do you mean?"

"That woman, what was her name—?"

It came to my lips because I was the expert here, whether I'd put in my time or not: "Serena?"

She nodded. "She went right across the street"—pointing now to the open door—"and laid herself down on the railroad tracks." She gave it a beat to let that sink in. "Luckily, though, somebody saw her and they called the cops."

The music soared and fell and then there was the mechanical hiss of the record changing. The woman was still there, poised over her elbows, studying my face as if I would have the answer to the unasked question. "You're joking, right?" was the best I could come up with, but then I was thinking of the other scrawl of graffiti on the wall in the men's room, just above the liberal-pussies sentiment. It had to do with Jesus. And salvation. The sort of thing you see on billboards in redneck country, standard issue, cant, the kind of bogus comfort they tended to avoid down at the National Suicide Prevention Society.

I was standing there at the bar, my change in hand and the next tune coming on to bury me in the moment. Someone popped a balloon. I looked over to where Nola was sitting at the table still, admiring one of the pewter serving dishes she'd got for a steal at the third antique store on the left. What did I say to the bartender finally? I don't know. Something like, "Wow." But it was Valentine's Day and it was all on me: the poor disjointed ESP woman rebuffed by a man she didn't even know (and didn't have the faintest inkling of how deep and true he ran, except, I suppose, on a paranormal level) and feeling there was just no use in going on living without him. Hold on to that for a minute and tell me about the fathomless, inexpressible, heartbreaking loneliness of life on this planet.

Are you shitting me? Holy sweet Jesus, save us! Save us all right now!

What's Love Got to Do with It?

It wasn't long after the shootings that I had to attend a conference in Dallas and decided to take the train rather than fly. I thought it would be a way to clear my head, two days isolated on a train instead of three hours rocketing through the clouds on an airliner, and since my husband was in Europe on business, my daughter away at college, and our dog had died the previous month after a protracted illness that had her on opioids and steroids both, there was nothing compelling to keep me at home for those extra two days. I took the train down to Union Station in Los Angeles from our home in Santa Barbara, where a brisk woman in a blue Amtrak uniform read my name off a checklist and led me to the sleeping compartment I'd waited till the last minute to book, wavering over whether I'd commit to the time it would take by rail or just give in and fly. As soon as she left, I locked the door to my compartment, stowed my luggage, set my laptop and the book I was reading on the foldout table and poured myself a glass of the Bordeaux I'd been saving for a special occasion. That was the moment I felt most secure, congratulating myself on the choice I'd made, everything hushed and pleasant, while outside the window porters silently rolled luggage carts along the platform and latecomers scrambled to make the train. I sipped the wine, sent an email to my husband to tell him how utterly contented I was (and though it was six a.m. his time he immediately emailed back to say, *The train? Are you crazy? It'll take you a week to get there*), then opened my book and began to read while the train rolled out of the station and into the night.

In the morning, at breakfast, the steward seated me with a young man my daughter's age, who, as I was to learn, was also traveling alone, but in economy class, where you had to sleep as best you could stretched out on a vacant seat or pressed up against the window. He had his head down, texting on his phone, and it took him a minute to realize I was there. "Oh, hi," he said, as if I'd popped out from under the table, then lowered his eyes to the phone again, which gave me a moment to study him. He wasn't especially good-looking—wasn't good-looking at all, actually, too much nose, too little mouth, something in retreat in his eyes—and seemed unkempt, beyond what you'd expect of someone who'd spent the night on a stiff utilitarian seat instead of in a bed, that is. His fingernails were dirty and his hair was shoved up on one side of his head, as if it actually had been pressed up against the window. But that was all right. Everything was all right, peaceful, confined, and I wasn't being judgmental, only observant—he was a kid, that was all, probably still in college.

The waiter came by to take our orders. I asked for coffee and chose the three-egg omelet with home fries, breakfast links, and toast, hungry suddenly because I'd had little to eat the night before and the wine had soured on my stomach; my companion ordered a bagel only, "And tea, hot tea, not *coffee*—with milk." He gave me a self-deprecating look, set his phone on the table beside his plate, and ran one hand across the front of his wrinkled T-shirt, a gesture that seemed to be a kind of tic with him, because he repeated it twice more. "You always have to tell them not coffee because coffee's like automatic with them," he said once the waiter had left. "Of course I could've just got a bagel back in the club car, but I just felt like, you know, a change of scene?"

"Sure," I said, "of course," as if he'd been asking my permission.

We began to chat. He was going to New Orleans, to visit his mother, who'd moved there after she'd divorced his father, and he was looking forward to it—"The change of scene"—though he'd never been there before. Had I? I shook my head. He'd heard it was a sexy city and he offered up this information with such a hopeful inflection I couldn't help but say, "Isn't every city a sexy city?"

"Bismarck, North Dakota," he said. "Pierre, *South* Dakota. Topeka, Kansas."

"Okay," I said, "you got me," and laughed. I was feeling giddy, and whether it was low blood sugar or the sense of freedom and adventure I'd awakened with, I couldn't say. I was fifty-two years old, though people told me I looked much younger, and I believed them, and he was a college kid, we were on a train and we were having breakfast together. "Anchorage, Alaska," I said.

"Bzzzz." He ground his thumb into the tabletop as if he were pressing a button. "You're out. It's Juneau."

I shrugged and held out my palms.

"Fourth grade," he said, and he repeated it, for emphasis, "*Fourth grade*."

"Trenton, New Jersey," I said.

"Montpelier, Vermont," he countered.

He sat back and ran a hand across his T-shirt again, which, I saw now, featured a single word in three-inch-high letters—INCEL—which I took to be the name of one of the ten thousand new rock bands I'd never heard of, thinking my daughter would know (and patronize me for being so out of it). I was on the verge of asking him about it when our food came. For a moment we were both distracted, he with smearing cream cheese on his bagel, I with arranging my plate and stirring a packet of Splenda into the fresh cup of coffee the waiter poured me.

"My mother uses that stuff," he said.

"What, Splenda?"

He nodded. "It's made from nuclear waste."

I didn't miss a beat: "That's why I like it."

That seemed to satisfy him, as if we'd used up our triviality quotient, and he said, "My name's Eric, by the way," and I said, "Sarah," in response, and there was a moment when we might have reached across the table to shake hands, but we didn't. He asked where I was from then, which was how we discovered that we both lived in Santa Barbara (or Isla Vista, in his case), and that we'd taken the same train down the previous afternoon, which, inevitably, led to my asking him about the shootings. Was he a student? He was. Had he been on campus that day? He had. And more than that—and here's where it became complicated—he'd known the shooter.

The shooter (I don't want to dignify him with a name, so I'll call him E.R.) was one of those twisted, half-formed people who blame all their problems on everyone else, as if personal responsibility was an alien concept and the system rigged against them, the sort who can't think of anything to do but lash out. Or that was how I read him anyway, from the TV and newspaper accounts and what Eric was telling me. E.R. was a loner (aren't they all?), but there was an especially insidious side to him: he hated women. Not all women, not older women, whom he considered beyond the pale sexually, mothers, grandmothers (he got along just fine with his own mother, in fact), but the girls his own age who wouldn't give him sex on demand, as if their primary function in life was to fulfill his wishes, like the genie in *The Arabian Nights*.

It didn't quite work out that way for E.R. (and I almost interrupted Eric here to say, "What a surprise," layering on the irony, but I held off and just listened). E.R. was a virgin, a nerd, a self-described loser. He lived inside his own head, went to class, played video games, ate takeout exclusively, because who had time to cook anything, other than maybe Cup Noodles (and so what if they contained tertiary-butyl hydroquinone and so what if it gave you cancer? Everybody had to die sometime). Freshman year was a waste, a blur, and he just wrote it off, everybody on the whole campus looking right through him as if he were invisible, especially the girls, though if they only knew who he really was and how much he wanted them it would be different, he was sure of it.

As a sophomore, he fixated on a girl in his Contemporary Lit class, Mary Ellen Stovall, a hot, tall blonde who didn't necessarily dress like a streetwalker, which was how most of them dressed as far as he could see—not that he was complaining, just that whatever they had on display wasn't for him, but for some square-jawed moron who spent eighteen hours a day in the weight room pumping iron instead of cultivating his mind, which wasn't fair, not at all, and what it boiled down to in the end, if you really thought about it, was that they were all just teases and bitches. Except Mary Ellen. She was different, or so he thought. She had style, her own style, because she wasn't a slave to the latest fashion or whatever the slut of the month was wearing on the cover of the women's magazines in the supermarket, and if he could see the way her body relaxed in her jeans and the tight, flowered tops she liked to wear, and if her lips were ever-so-slightly creased and swollen like the lips of his favorite porn actress, the one with the dead eyes and conical tits, so much the better.

What he wanted more than anything was to talk to her, declare himself, but he lacked the self-confidence because he was only five six and nobody liked him and he hated his nose and his mother was Chinese and he'd never kissed a girl in his life or even gone out on a date. He did a search on his laptop and found out where she came from, who her parents and siblings were, and what sorority she was in, and one night—at ten, ten was the best time because they'd all be in at that hour on a weekday—he steeled himself and went to the sorority house, mounted the front steps, and buzzed her room. There was a faint hiss of white noise and then she was saying, "Hello?" her voice soft, low, rich with expectation.

The sound of it, her *actual voice*, caught him off guard, because he'd had such a catastrophically devastating time just getting there and forcing himself to push the buzzer, he hadn't had time to plan out what he was going to say. "Hello?" she said again and he said, "It's me."

A pause. "Who is this?" Another pause. "Is that you, Brad? Are you messing with me?"

"Come down and find out."

There was a moment, no more than a second really, when it could have gone either way, but then the buzzer sounded, the lock on the door clicked, and he was in.

There was a TV, armchairs, a couple of other girls lounging around on a sofa, but they didn't even glance up at him. And then she was there, appearing suddenly in the doorway to the lounge in powder-blue sweats that managed to look sexier on her than the lowest-cut dress on some other girl, and the look she gave him was one of bafflement—and more, annoyance. She didn't say anything. Just looked around the room to make sure there was no one else there—*Brad*, hiding behind the couch to jump out and surprise her with his muscles—and then she said, "Who are you?"

"I . . . I saw you in class," he said, conscious all over again of how short he was, because she must have been five nine at least and so what if Tom Cruise was even shorter than he was, as his mother kept reminding him—Tom Cruise was a fiction, an illusion, a figment of everybody's imagination. "And I think you're the most beautiful, I mean the hottest . . . and I just wondered, I don't know, if maybe you'd like to . . ."

The word he wanted to say, the term he wanted to employ, was *fuck*, as in *Do you want to fuck?*, but he couldn't seem to spit it out because on some basic level he knew it wasn't right, wasn't gentlemanly, and he was a gentleman if nothing else, so he just stood there until she said, "Like to *what*? What are you saying?" and he said, "I don't know . . . maybe come up to my room or something, and, you know, like *do it*?" and then the whole universe exploded in her eyes, and he was left standing there alone until some other girl—girls—came in the door, giggling over something, and went on up the stairs as if he were just part of the background.

So that was a disaster. And after that he was so humiliated he got a medical excuse and took an incomplete in the class because there was no way he could face her ever again, not after she'd turned her back on him as if he were some lower form of life, something wriggling in the dirt when you turn it over with a pitchfork. A springtail. Or no, a sow bug. He was a sow bug, that was what he was. It took him a while to get used to that, being a sow bug, but really, you can get used to anything. Then there came a time, a long time, when he just nursed his wounds. He went to his other classes, but they didn't really offer much of anything for him, and when his mother called and asked him if he'd decided on a major yet, he just said, "Dorkology," and she said, "What?" and he didn't really want to go into it so he just said, "Biology," and left it at that. He ate ramen, played a lot of video games, watched a lot of porn.

Then one afternoon he was at the burrito place, waiting on line, running over in his head what he wanted on his burrito (steak *and* chicken, crema, pico de gallo, barbecue sauce, guac, no beans), three sorority girls ahead of him, two in shorts with their legs bare from their sandals to the little V's of their crotches and the other with stretch jeans that were tight as ligatures and their hair up in ponytails that bobbed in the air when they moved or gestured or whooped in their shrieking voices about whoever was dating whoever. That was bad enough, but what really set him off was the couple sitting at the first table just outside the open door. They couldn't keep their hands off each other—in *public*, no less—as if what they'd just done on the rug or the couch or in the shower stall in her room or his when their room-mates were in class was something to brag about. He was so upset—*Jesus, couldn't he even eat lunch in peace?*—he jerked himself around so he wouldn't have to look at the girls or the couple either and found himself staring into the face of the guy behind him, who could have been a replica of himself, a dork, that is, a loser, all nose and Adam's apple and dull little gritballs for eyes behind a pair of black-framed glasses that might as well have been a scuba mask, and he couldn't look at that either, so he just swung back around and stared at a spot on the floor where somebody must have spilled a Coke, and what was this, a Rorschach test?

That was when he felt a touch at his elbow, five cool fingers on his skin, and here was another girl giving him an apologetic smile and trying to ease past him—*cut in line*—because she was a sorority girl too, and the three sorority girls ahead of him were already cooing her name, *Looocy, Looocy,* and she was saying, "Do you mind?" as if he'd been standing here for the exercise or just to pass the time or because his foremost dream and desire was to be an extra in the movie that was her life, however pathetic it might have been.

"Yes, I do mind," he said, his voice caught low in his throat, and she gave him a look as if he'd just kicked her. "What do you think I'm doing here? What do you think lines are *for* anyway?"

He watched her face compose itself around the little pouting crater of her mouth, and one of the other girls, the one in the tight jeans, was saying in a nasty voice, "Why don't you go ahead of *us*, then," and in the next moment he was edging past them without a word and telling the guy behind the sneeze guard what he wanted on his burrito and trying to act as if nothing had happened, when in fact his heart was beating in his ears like a tom-tom, and then he paid and went to the soft drink machine to dig out a scoopful of ice in his extra-large plastic cup he always brought with him and happened to glance up and see the couple going at it as if they didn't have grease on their lips and a platter of half-eaten nachos glistening like somebody's vomit on the table at their elbows, like *his* vomit, and what he did next wasn't explicable on any rational level except that he'd really just had it, had it up to here, and he filled the cup to the brim with Coke, real Coke, and the minute he stepped out the door he suddenly jerked around—*blitzkrieg!*—and dumped half of it on the girl's head and half on the guy's before tucking the burrito under his arm like a football and bolting up the street and down the first alley he came to, wondering if they were going to call the cops and charge him with assault or something, exhilarated and terrified all at once, and running, running until he couldn't remember where he was going or even why he was running.

———

I'd finished my breakfast at this point, though Eric had barely touched his, so wrapped up in what he was saying he seemed to have forgotten all about it. I pictured him taking the bagel back to his seat after I left the table and feeding it crumb by crumb into his mouth, alone, while the bleak hills and dun plains ran by the window in a continuous loop and the shadows flickered and flickered again. When the waiter came to refill my cup, I put a hand over it. I was thinking of my compartment now, my bed, the novel concept that I could take a nap if I wanted—anytime I wanted—and no schedule to keep or anyone to say different.

The waiter's appearance had interrupted us, and we both turned a moment to watch him work his way back down the aisle. The car rocked. The shadows flickered.

"How do you know all this?" I asked.

"I told you—I knew him."

"But you didn't know he was going to—?" I waved my hand, as if a gesture could begin to encapsulate the horror of the act that had left six dead and fourteen wounded.

"Not really."

"What do you mean, 'not really'? Either you did or you didn't."

He gave me a tight smile. His face had completely changed. He was homely still, nothing could obviate that (the expression *ill-favored* came to mind), but the openness I'd seen there earlier was gone.

"Don't tell me you actually sympathize with this, this . . . *person*?"

"He had a soul. A great soul."

I could feel everything slipping away from me then, the car rocking, the rails beating like a pulse beneath us, and all at once I was thinking of my daughter, who could have been one of his victims but for the luck of the draw. I couldn't believe what I was hearing. "*He* had a soul? What about the souls of the people he killed, the girls and boys he shot and stabbed? Children. They were just children." I stood and pushed my way out into the aisle, furious and confused at the same time. "Children," I repeated. "Like you."

I wound up skipping lunch—the nap had made me groggy—and stayed in my compartment, reading and dozing and watching the scenery pass me by, till early evening, when I made my way down to the dining car for the first serving. This time I was seated with a young couple, Steve and Lila, who hated flying because they'd once been in a jetliner that was struck by lightning, and though they'd landed safely they never wanted to go through that sort of scare again. "Give me this anytime," Steve said, nodding at the window. "Terra firma."

"Or at least floora firma," Lila said, grinning.

"Right," he said, "that's what I mean. This thing breaks down, we get out and walk."

I don't know why—maybe it was the residue of my talk with Eric, which had disturbed me more than I wanted to admit—but I had an urge to contradict them, shake them out of their complacency. Trains derailed, cars crashed, bicyclists were run down in the street every minute of every day—nobody was safe, anywhere, ever, and they must have known that. But why get into it? Why ruin the mood? Wasn't I enjoying myself—wasn't that the whole point of this? I said, "I usually fly, but this is so incredibly relaxing."

Lila (early thirties, flawless skin, auburn hair, bangs) held up the margarita she was drinking and said, "Hard on the liver, though."

"But great for the sex life." Steve was having a margarita too, and he clicked glasses with her. "Right, babe?"

"Oh, yeah," she murmured, looking at me now. "It's like what else is there to do?"

Our meals came and I ordered a drink too—a glass of wine—and we kept the conversation light. At some point, I mentioned my daughter, Allie, and they asked to see a picture. I showed them the half dozen or so I had on my phone, and Lila said, "She's really pretty. What did you say she was majoring in?"

"English."

Steve let out a laugh. "I guess she must come from a wealthy family then, right?"

I was having a good time. "Well, yeah," I said, mugging for them, "don't you recognize me? Mrs. Gates? Mrs. Bill Gates?"

Afterward, I took my book down to the club car to watch the night settle in over the distant mountains, and what mountains they were I couldn't say. The car was almost full—older people mostly, a sea of white hair—but I found an unoccupied table at the far end and ordered a scotch on the rocks. I emailed my husband to tell him how much I was enjoying myself and how relaxed I was, then tried calling my daughter and got a mechanical voice informing me that her message box was full. I sipped my drink and opened the book, trying to reconstruct what had been happening when I'd left off.

Some time passed, how much I don't know—enough so that it was fully dark before I glanced up and saw that I was no longer alone. At some point Eric had slipped wordlessly into the seat across from me, as if we were familiars, as if we were playing a game. "I didn't want to disturb you," he said, raising his eyebrows and flicking a hand across the front of his T-shirt, the same one he'd been wearing earlier. "Good book?"

I shrugged. I hated it when people asked me about the book

I was reading, because it obligated me to offer an explanation, which seemed an invasion of privacy, however innocent or unintended. I showed him the cover.

"Oh, yeah," he said, "yeah—that was on the reading list in my lit class? But it—I don't know, it was only *recommended*. I think the title turned me off. I mean, the Sargasso Sea—isn't that where all the eels in North America go to mate?"

I smiled—I couldn't help myself. "I guess so. Yeah, maybe—I think I've heard that."

"Mary Ellen Stovall was in that class," he said. He brought a bottle of beer up from between his legs, took a quick sip, and dropped it back down below table level again, as if he didn't want anyone—the waiter—to see it, and I realized it must have been a beer he'd brought on the train with him and stowed in his backpack on the rack above his seat. "Not that I ever said anything to her—I knew E.R. really hated her and she wouldn't have even known I was alive anyway—but what I did do, just because I felt like it, because I could?"

I set down my book, lifted the glass to my lips. The ice had melted and the scotch was diluted by now, but I needed it, I liked it, the scent and taste of it, and I knew I was going to order another.

"I started following her around—surreptitiously, I mean, so she didn't know I was there. Just—I wasn't stalking her or anything, only seeing what she did, where she went, who she hung out with, what she ate, that kind of thing. It was like, I don't know, *field* biology."

"Do you have any idea how wrong that is?" I said, irritated suddenly, and we were right back to the footing we'd left off on that morning. "That's harassment. You could be arrested. You should be."

A man at the next table over said, "Of course he's a wacko,

he's from Waco, isn't he?" and the woman he was with let out a long throaty laugh.

"No, you don't understand," Eric said. "You know the Sioux Indians?'

The Sioux Indians? I shrugged. What was I doing? Why was I listening to this?

"They counted coup, right? They'd rush an enemy and touch them with a stick, just to show they could do it, when of course they could have split them open with their tomahawk, but the point is, they didn't? You see?"

"No, frankly, I don't."

He ran his fingers over the T-shirt, pulled out the beer, swigged, stuck it back between his legs. "It was weeks before she caught on, like one day at the burrito place—Freebirds, you know it, where E.R. used to go like every day? I was two people behind her in line and she just happened to turn around and register me there—Gotcha!—and the look on her face was worth it, because now she noticed me, now she knew I was alive, that was for sure. . . . Don't give me that look, I mean, I didn't hurt her. I didn't touch her. It wasn't a real tomahawk—it wasn't even a stick."

The waiter was there all of a sudden, leaning over the table and asking if I wanted another, and I should have said no, should have got up and left, but I didn't—I just nodded. Everything got quiet. The loudmouth next to us took the woman by the arm and shuffled down the length of the car, and it seemed as if all the usual clicking and clacking faded away, the passage along this stretch so smooth you barely knew you were moving.

"E.R. was like that too," Eric said. "Peaceable. Until they kept pushing him, girls like Mary Ellen Stovall and couples who couldn't keep their hands off each other. And contrary to what you might have heard, he wasn't one of these gun nuts—he didn't even like guns."

No, he didn't like guns. But it came to a point where he couldn't go on anymore, because where was the love in the world? Why did everybody else monopolize it all, why was it the same guys and the same girls and no thought for somebody like him? What was wrong with him? He was a gentleman, like in the old movies, and so what if he didn't have any experience, he knew what they looked like down there, he knew where it went—all the variations and all the positions too. Every time he came he cursed himself because it was such a waste, so wrong, and not because of some idiotic socioreligious taboo but because the girls, the women, didn't know what they were missing and what he was missing too—and why couldn't it be like in *Brave New World*, where everybody was encouraged to fuck all the time?

After the Coke incident, he had a kind of rebirth, as if he'd been christened in caffeine citrate, citric acid, fluid extract of coca leaves, and all the other shit they put in there, and he started filling his extra-large cup with Gatorade, which was even stickier and messier than Coke, and dumping it on any couple he saw groping in public, and that was righteous, that was vengeance—till he got caught one day. It was at Buddha Bowls, and it was raining, and he was passing by with his umbrella and saw this couple in the window just practically having sex over their food, and he ducked in the door and flung the Gatorade right in their creamy, gasping faces, but the floor was wet and he slipped and fell and his umbrella went flying and the cup too, and the next thing he knew the guy was whaling on him and the girl was cursing and kicking him and he barely made it out the door. He was sore for days. He had to walk in the rain without an umbrella. Every time he closed his eyes he saw the girl's face, the hatred there, and he heard the laughter too, the ridicule of the guys behind the counter and the sorority girls and jocks and all the rest of them whose entertainment he'd stupidly provided on a rainy, desolate afternoon, though he'd as soon have killed them all.

He bought his first handgun in Goleta, a Glock 34, and took it to the shooting range till it felt comfortable in his hand, and he even joked with the employees there about the earplugs, as in, "I have to hand a pair of these to the intruder before I shoot him, right? Just so I don't ruin the guy's hearing?" He went down to Oxnard and all the way to Burbank to buy the other two guns, SIG Sauer P226 pistols, and got familiar with them too. Then he wrote a manifesto blaming everybody for not recognizing who he really was—the bitches, the bitches especially—and when he was done with that, on the day he called "Retribution Day," he sat in his car, stared into his cell-phone camera, and made a video to immortalize himself. Then he drove down to the sorority house and started shooting.

Six dead, fourteen wounded. Or seven dead, make that seven. Because at the end of it, he put the gun to his own head and pulled the trigger.

I knew the details. Everybody did. Yet the details were impersonal, the details were as dead as the victims, but here he was, Eric, this child, breathing life back into them. *A great soul*, that's what he called him, and how sick was that? He ran through his tics, sipped his warm beer. "Why are you telling me all this?" I demanded, because I wanted to know, I really did.

"Because I need you to understand what it's like, what we have to go through—"

"*We?*"

"Yeah, *we*. I'm just like him, just like E.R. I mean, nobody wants me, and I'm sorry, but especially the *bitches*. All I have to do is look in the mirror to know that." His eyes were pleading, but they were red-veined, clotted, dull, and behind them was a pit of incomprehension and despair—and hate, hate too. He was damaged goods, and there was nothing I or anybody else could do about it. That was the truth of the moment.

"There's somebody for everybody," I said, and if it was a platitude, so what? It's the platitudes that define us and maybe even save us in the end.

"I'm a virgin," he said. "An *involuntary* virgin. So you tell me, how ridiculous is that? How humiliating? I'm twenty-three years old and like the brunt of every joke in every locker room in the world, don't you get that? And every sorority, every dorm room, every—shit, every goddamned bar and club and, what, *TV show*—"

"It's not like that," I said. "You're smart. You've got a sharp wit. All you need is to—"

"What?" he spat, cutting me off. "Join a club? Go on a dating site? Take a shower? Change my haircut? Get a new shirt?" His face was clenched, his hands rigid on the tabletop. "You have a daughter, right? Isn't that what you told me?"

I nodded.

"Is she pretty? She is, isn't she? Like Mary Ellen Stovall–pretty, right? Right?"

"I don't—I've never seen Mary Ellen Stovall, so how can I—?"

"Would she go out with me? Would she have sex with me?"

I wanted to tell him that would be up to her, wanted to tell him the world didn't work the way he thought it did, wanted to tell him about love, about two souls coming together and the way the flesh allowed us to express our deepest being and all the mystery of life on this irrational planet, but I didn't. I just stared at him and listened to the faint heartbeat of the rails beneath us. I shook my head. "No," I said. "No, she wouldn't."

When the veterinarian came to put down our dog, Sophie, all three of us were there, my husband, my daughter, and I, gathered in the kitchen. We'd all petted her, murmured our endearments and farewells, and watched her eat her final meal of filet mignon I'd cut up in fine strips so as not to choke her. The veterinarian—a young woman named Cara we'd known for years and were on a first-name basis with—had warned us from the beginning not to get our hopes up, because the steroids were designed to elevate Sophie's appetite and mood so that she'd seem as if she were back to her old self, when in fact the uterine cancer was ravaging her body in its relentless way, and there was no hope and no cure. We had three months with her, three extra months to get used to what was coming. And yet still, even as Cara stroked her and inserted the needle and she went instantly limp, it was insupportable. We put our arms around each other and held tight, and I cried and Allie cried and my husband, who as a man in this society of ours had been taught to hold in his emotions, squeezed us both as if he could compress all that hurt and keep it from spilling out into the world.

That night on the train, Eric had pushed himself up from the table with a smirk of triumph—*I knew it, I told you so*—and without a word stalked down the aisle and out of the car, the door to the coach section jerking rigidly open and then jerking shut behind him. The steward dimmed the lights till they were barely aglow, and I was left there with the dregs of my drink and the night that held fast against the windows. It was a long while before we came to the next station—a byway really, and we weren't stopping, just passing through—but for a moment the lights on the platform gave me back my reflection in the glass, and I saw my face suspended there as if floating in the void, a woman's face, a pale, middle-aged woman's face, jumping and flickering and stabbing at the dim ghosts of the countryside till the station was gone and I couldn't see myself anymore.

Asleep at the Wheel

THE PURSE

The car says this to her: "Cindy, listen, I know you've got to get over to 1133 Hollister Avenue by two p.m. for your meeting with Rose Taylor of Taylor, Levine and Rodriguez, LLP, but did you hear that Les Bourses is having a thirty-percent-off sale? And remember, they carry the complete Picard line you like—in particular that cute cross-body bag in fuchsia you had your eye on last week? They have two left in stock."

They're moving along at just over the speed limit, which is what she's programmed the car for, trying to squeeze every minute out of the day but at the same time wary of breaking the law. She takes a quick glance at her phone. It's a quarter past one, and she really wasn't planning on making any other stops, aside from maybe picking up a sandwich to eat in the car, but as soon as Carly (that's what she calls her operating system) mentions the sale, she's envisioning the transaction—in and out, that's all it'll take, because she looked at the purse last week but ultimately decided they wanted too much for it. In and out, that's all. And Carly will wait for her at the curb.

"I see you're looking at your phone."

"I'm just wondering if we'll have enough time . . ."

"As long as you don't dawdle—you know what you want, don't you? It's not as if you haven't already picked it out. You told me so yourself." (And here Carly loops in a recording of their conversation from the previous week, and Cindy listens to her own voice say, *I love it, just love it—and it'd match my new heels perfectly.*)

"Okay," she says, thinking she'll forgo the sandwich. "But we have to make it quick."

"I'm showing no traffic and no obstructions of any kind."

"Good," she says, "good," leans back in the seat, and closes her eyes.

HITCHHIKE

The fleet is available to everybody, all the time, and you don't even have to have an account for Ridz. The thing is, Ridz isn't going to take you directly to Warren's house or the skate park or whatever destination you tell it because it's programmed to take you first to the Apple store or GameStop or wherever you might have spent money in the past. So it isn't really free—and you have to plan for the extra time to listen to the spiel and say no about sixty times, but then, eventually, you get where you want to go. Some kids—and his mother would kill him if she knew he was one of them—just step out in front of any empty fleet car that happens to be going by and commandeer it. You can't get inside if you don't have the trip code, of course, but you can climb up on the roof and cling to the Lidar till you get to the next stop or the one after that.

That is what Jackie happens to be doing at half past one on this particular school day, clinging to the roof of one of Ridz's SDC Volvos and catching bugs in his teeth, when his mother's car suddenly appears in the other lane and he freezes. His first instinct is to jump down on the curb side, but they've got to be going forty miles an hour—which feels like a hundred with the way the wind is tearing at him—and so he flattens himself even more, as if that could make him invisible. His plan, up to this point, was to go over to Warren's and hang out, nothing beyond that, though he could see a forty ouncer in his future and maybe another hitch over to the beach with Warren and Warren's girl-friend, Cyrilla, but now, with his mother's car inching up on him, all that's about to go south in a hurry. She'll ground him for sure, cut his allowance, probably report him to his father (who won't do much more than snarl over the phone from Oregon, where he's living with Jennifer and never coming back), then go through the whole charade of taking away his phone and his games for a week or however long she thinks is going to impress on him *just how dangerous that kind of behavior is.*

All bad. But then, when the car pulls even with him, he sees that his mother, far from looking out the window and catching him in the act, isn't even awake. She's got her head thrown back and her eyes closed, and Carly's doing the driving without her. He doesn't think in terms of lucky breaks or this is his lucky day or anything like that—he just accepts it for what it is. And at the next light, he slides down off the car and takes to his feet, his back turned to the street, to the cars, to her.

KNIGHTSCOPE

The reason for the meeting with Rose Taylor is to arrange legal representation for a homeless man named Keystone Bacharach,

who spends his days on the steps of the public library with a co-
terie of other free spirits and unfortunates and at night sleeps
under a bush out front of the SPCA facility, where he can have
a little privacy. What most people don't realize—and Cindy, as
an advocate for the homeless, does—is how psychologically harrowing it is to live on the streets, where through all the daylight
hours you're under public scrutiny. Your every gesture, whether
intimate or not, is on display for people to interpret or dismiss
or condemn, and your only solace is the cover of darkness, when
everything's hidden. And this is the problem: the SPCA, in a
misguided response to a rash of break-ins, graffiti tagging, and
dumpster-diving for syringes and animal tranquilizers, had de-
ployed one of Knightscope's Autonomous Data Machines to pa-
trol the area, which meant that Mr. Bacharach was awakened
every thirty minutes, all night long, by this five-foot-tall, four-
hundred-pound robot shining a light on him and giving off its
eerie high-pitched whine before asking, in the most equable of
tones, "What is the situation here?" (To which Mr. Bacharach,
irritated, would reply, "It's called sleep.")

A week earlier she went down there after hours to see for
herself, though her sister had called her crazy ("You're just asking to get raped—or worse"), and even Carly, on dropping her
off, had asked, "Are you sure this is the correct destination?"
But they didn't know Keystone the way she did. He was just hurt
inside, that was all, trying to heal from what he'd seen during
his tour of duty in Afghanistan, and if he couldn't make a go of
it in an increasingly digitized society, that was the fault of the
society. He had an engaging personality, he was a first-rate con-
versationalist comfortable with a whole range of subjects, from
animal rights to wine-making to the history of warfare (light-
years ahead of Adam, her ex, who toward the end of their marriage had communicated through gestures and grunts only), and

he was as well-read as anybody she knew. Plus, he was her age, exactly.

He was waiting for her in front of the SPCA, dressed, as always, in shorts, flip-flops, T-shirt, and denim jacket, his hair—he wore it long—pulled back tightly in a ponytail. "Thanks for coming," he said, taking the gift bag she handed him (trail mix, dried apricots, pair of socks, tube of toothpaste) without comment. "This is really going to open your eyes, because no matter how you cut it, this is harassment, pure and simple. Of citizens. In a public place. And it's not just me."

She saw now that there were half a dozen other figures there, sprawled on the pavement or leaning up against the wall with their shopping carts and belongings arrayed around them. It was almost dark, but she could see that at least one of them was familiar—Lula, a woman everyone called Knitsy, because her hands were in constant motion, as if trying vainly to stitch the air. The street was quiet at this hour, which only seemed to magnify the garble of whining, yipping, and sudden startled shrieks coming from the SPCA facility behind them, and if it felt ominous it had nothing to do with these people gathered here but with the forces arrayed against them. She said, "Is it due to come by soon?"

He nodded in the direction of the parking lot at the far end of the facility. "It went down there like fifteen, twenty minutes ago, so it should be along any minute now." He gave her an angry look. "Like clockwork," he said, then called out, "Right, Knitsy?" and Knitsy, whether she knew what she was agreeing to or not, said, "Yeah."

The night grew a shade darker. Then one of the dogs let out a howl from the depths of the building, and here it came, the Knightscope K5+ unit, turning the corner and heading for them on its base of tight revolving wheels. She'd seen these units before, at the bank, in the lot out back of the pizza place, rolling along in formation in last year's Fourth of July parade, but they'd seemed unremarkable to her, no more threatening or intrusive than any other labor-saving device, except that they were bigger, much bigger. She'd seen them only in daylight, but now it was night, and this one had its lights activated—two eerie blue slits at the top and what would be its midriff, if it had a midriff, in addition to the seven illuminated sensors that were arrayed across its chest, if it had a chest. Its shape was that of a huge hard-boiled egg, which in daylight made it ordinary, ridiculous even, but the lights changed all that.

"So what now? It's not going to confront us, is it?"

"You watch," Keystone said.

The K5+, as she knew from the literature, featured the same Light Detection and Ranging device Carly did, which used a continuously sweeping laser to measure objects and map the surrounding area, as well as thermal imaging sensors, an ambient noise microphone, and a 360-degree high-definition video capture. It moved at a walking pace, three miles an hour, and its function was surveillance, not enforcement. She knew that, but still, at this hour in this place, she felt caught out, as if she'd been doing something illicit—which, she supposed, was the purpose of the thing in the first place.

But now it was stopping, pivoting, focused on Knitsy, whose hands fluttered like pale streamers in the ray of light it emitted, which had suddenly become more intense, like a flashlight beam. "What is the situation here?" it asked.

Knitsy said, "Go away. Leave me alone."

The K5+ didn't move. It had been specifically programmed not to engage in conversation the way Carly did, because its designers wanted to avoid confrontations—it was there to deter criminal activity by its very presence and summon the police only if the need should arise. Now it said, "Move on."

"Hey," Keystone called out, waving his arms. "Over here, Tin-head."

She watched the thing swivel and redirect itself, starting down the sidewalk toward them. When it came up even with her and Keystone, it stopped and focused its light on them. "What is the situation here?" it asked her, employing the voice of one of NPR's most genial hosts, a voice designed to put people at ease. But she didn't feel at ease—just the opposite—and that was a real eye-opener.

What happened next was sudden and violent. Keystone just seemed to snap—and maybe he was showing off for her, think-ing, in some confused way, that he was protecting her—but in that moment he tucked his shoulder like a linebacker and slammed into the thing, once, twice, three times, until he finally managed to knock it over with a screech of metal and shattering glass. Which was bad enough—vandalism, that was what she was thinking, and her face was on that video feed too—but then he really seemed to take his frustrations out on the thing, seizing a brick he'd stashed under one of the bushes and hammering at the metal frame until the unit set off a klaxon so loud and piercing she thought her heart would stop.

Just then, just as she was thinking they were both going to get arrested, Carly pulled up at the curb. The door swung open. "Get in," Carly said.

REBEL WITHOUT A CAUSE

It was a meme, really, that got them into it, a clip of the scene in the old movie where they were playing chicken and the greaser who wasn't James Dean got the strap of his leather jacket caught on the door handle, which repeated over and over till it was just flat-out hilarious. After that, curious about the movie itself, they dug deeper, and it was a revelation—teenagers stole cars and raced them on the streets, and there was nobody there to say different. Even better, because this was back in the day, the cars just did what you wanted—all you had to do was put the key in the ignition (or hot-wire it if you wanted to steal it), hit the gas, and peel out. He must have seen the movie (or parts of it) at least twenty times with Warren and Cyrilla, and if Warren was James Dean and Cyrilla Natalie Wood, he guessed he'd have to be Sal Mineo, though that wasn't really who he wanted to be.

"Better than the dude who goes over the cliff, though, right?" Warren says now, waving his forty ouncer at the screen, and Cyrilla lets out a laugh that's more of a screech, actually, one of her annoying habits, but that's all right—he doesn't mind playing a supporting role. Warren's almost a year older than he is and he doesn't have a girlfriend himself, so to be near Cyrilla, to hang out with her, see what she's like—what girls are like, up close—is something he really appreciates on every level he can think of.

They're coming up on the part where Natalie Wood, her eyes burning up with excitement, waves her arms and everybody stands back and the two cars hurtle off into the night, when Warren, who has his arm around Cyrilla on the couch and one hand casually cupping her left breast, says, "I have this idea?"

Warren's grinning, so he starts grinning himself. "What?" he says.

"Let's us play chicken. Reenact the scene, I mean. For real."

He just laughs. Because it's a joke. Real cars, cars that do what you want, cars you can race, are pretty much extinct at this point, except for on racetracks and plots of private land out in the desert, where holdovers and old people can pay to have their manual cars stored and go out and race around in them on weekends, though he's never seen any of that except online, and it might just be a fantasy for all he knows. "What are you talking about?" he says. "You going to steal a fleet car?"

"No," Warren says, leveling a look on him. "I'm going to steal two."

RISK ASSESSMENT

She's in the car on her way to the library to pick up Keystone and bring him to Rose Taylor's office so they can begin the process of filing a public-nuisance lawsuit against the SPCA, when Carly says, "I don't mean to worry you, but the house sensors indicate that Jackie hasn't come home from school yet—and the calendar shows no extracurricular activities for today, so I'm just wondering . . . ?"

She's feeling distracted, her mind on Keystone and the way he stood up for her that night on the street, or at least thought he was standing up for her, which amounted to the same thing. "I wouldn't worry. He's a big boy. He can take care of himself."

"Granted, yes, but I can't help thinking of last week when he didn't get in till after dark and had no explanation other than" (and here she loops in Jackie's voice from the house monitor) "'I was at Warren's, okay, and his mom made dinner, okay, so I'm not hungry, so don't even go there.'"

"Listen, Carly, I'm just not up to this right now, okay? I'm trying to focus on getting Keystone over to Rose Taylor's to fill out the paperwork, and then I've got to get back to the office for that five o'clock meeting, as I'm sure you're aware, and then there's the fundraiser after that . . ."

"Sorry, I just thought you'd want to know."

She's staring out the side window watching the streetlights clip by, picturing Keystone pushing himself up off the concrete steps of the library and crossing the sidewalk with that smile of his lit up just for her. She's curious to see what he'll be wearing—"I clean up pretty good," he told her, promising to put on a pair of long pants and a button-up shirt for the meeting, not that it matters really, just that she's never seen him in anything other than what he calls his "street commando" outfit. The streetlights are evenly spaced, like counters, and after a moment it occurs to her that the intervals between them are getting shorter and shorter, so she turns, focuses on the street ahead, and says, "Aren't you going too fast, Carly?"

Immediately the car slows. "Forty-four in a thirty-five zone, but there's no indication of speed traps or police units and since we *are* running six minutes and sixteen seconds late, I thought I would expedite matters."

She's feeling angry suddenly—and it's not Carly's fault, she knows that, but the comment about Jackie just rubbed her the wrong way. "I didn't give you permission for that," she snaps. "You ought to know better. I mean, what good is your program if you can't follow it?"

"I'm sorry, Cindy, I just thought—"

"Don't think—just drive."

Of course, Carly was right, and if they wind up being ten minutes late to pick up Keystone, that's nobody's fault but her own. "All right, Carly, I'm sorry—good job, really," she says, only vaguely aware of how ridiculous it is to try to mollify a computer or worry about hurting its feelings.

"Since we're at the library," Carly says, "will you be acquiring books today? Because they have three copies of the latest installment of the Carson Umquist series you like—and they're all in the special 'Hot Reads' rack when you first walk in. I mean, they're right there—you don't have to go twenty feet. If that's what you're looking for. I'm not presuming, am I?"

"Pull up here," she says, and that's when she sees Keystone, in a pair of tan Dockers and an emerald long-sleeve shirt featuring a pair of red fire-breathing dragons embroidered on the front. He looks—different—and if she's surprised by the dragons, which really aren't the sort of thing she imagines Rose Taylor appreciating, she tries to hide it. She's smiling as he comes up to the car, and he's smiling too, and now he's reaching for the door handle . . . but the door seems to be locked, and she's fumbling for the release. "Carly," she says, turning away from the sight of his face caught there in the window, as if Carly were an actual person sitting in the driver's seat when, of course, there's no one there. "Carly, is the child lock on?"

"I'm sorry," Carly says, "but this individual is untrustworthy. Don't you recall what happened last Tuesday evening at 9:19 p.m. in front of the SPCA facility at 83622 Haverford Drive?"

"Carly," she says, "open the door."

"I don't think that's wise."

"You know what? I don't give a goddamn what you think. Do you hear me? Do you?"

HER FATHER'S LAST DRIVE

He was in his midseventies back then and he'd never really been what anybody would call a good driver, too rigid, too slow to react, baffled by the rules and norms of the road and trying to get by on herd mentality alone. To complicate matters, he suffered from arthritis and wound up developing a dependency on the painkillers the doctor prescribed, which, to say the least, didn't do much for his reflexes or attention span. He was a disaster waiting to happen, and she and her sister, Jan, kept nagging him to give up driving, but he was stubborn. "I've seen *King Lear*," he said. "Nobody's going to take my independence away from me."

Then one morning when her car was in the shop (this was before SDCs took over and most people, including her, still got around the retro way), she asked him for a ride to work, and not only was he half an hour late, but when they finally did get on the freeway he drove his paint-blistered pickup as if the wheels had turned to cement blocks, weaving and drifting out of his lane and going at such a maddeningly slow pace she was sure they were going to get rear-ended. She was a wreck by the time she got to the office and so keyed up she didn't dare even take a sip of her morning Grande, let alone drink it. She Ubered home that night, though as a recent divorcée and the mother of a two-year-old she was trying to cut her expenses, so that was no fun. As soon as she got in the door, she called Jan.

"We've got to do something," she said. "He's going to get killed—or kill somebody in the process. It's a nightmare, believe me—have you been in a car with him lately? It's beyond belief."

Jan was silent a moment, thinking, then she said, "What about that refrigerator you've got to move?"

"What refrigerator? What are you talking about?"

Her sister didn't say anything, just waited for her to catch on.

"Can we do that to him? He'll never talk to either one of us again, you realize that, right?" She was trying to picture the aftermath, the resentment, the sense of betrayal, the way he used his sarcasm like an ice pick, chipping away at you flake by flake, and how he'd parceled out his affection all his life, and what that was going to mean for the future. "It's not going to be me," she said. "I'm not going to be the one."

"We'll both do it."

"How's he going to get around? I'm not driving him, I'll tell you that."

"The bus. The senior van. Whatever. Other people do it. But what about Luke—what if Luke asks him? He'd never refuse Luke."

Luke was Jan's seventeen-year-old son, and as soon as Jan pronounced his name Cindy realized they were going to take the easy way out—or no, the coward's way.

The next Saturday morning, Jan dropped her son off at their father's apartment so he could borrow the truck to move the imaginary refrigerator, and the moment the keys changed hands their father's time behind the wheel of a motorized vehicle, which stretched all the way back to when he was two years younger than Luke was then, came to an abrupt end.

THE HACK SUPREME

Another day, another slow, agonizing procession of classes that are like doors clanging shut in a prison one after the other, and then they're at Warren's and Warren's parents are at work, so they have the place to themselves to make preparations. The first thing is the punch, which means pouring grape juice, 7UP, and about three fingers of every kind of liquor in the cabinet into a five-gallon bucket purchased at Walmart for just this purpose. Then snacks, but that's easy, just bags of chips, pretzels, Doritos, and whatever. Cyrilla rolls a couple of numbers, and he and Warren pull out their phones and give everybody a heads-up, nine o'clock at the end of Mar Vista, where it dead-ends at that weed lot and the cliffs down to the ocean.

He's not a bad hacker himself—since as far back as he can remember, he's hacked into websites just for the thrill of messing with people a little—but Warren's in another league. If anybody can steal a fleet car—*two* fleet cars—it's him. So after dinner (he texted his mother to tell her he'd be eating at Warren's and then sleeping over too), they go out on Cabrillo, where there's a ton of cars going back and forth between pickups and drop-offs, and just step out in front of two empty ones, which slam on their brakes and idle there, waiting for them to move. But they don't move. Warren has already hacked into the network on his laptop, and now he's accessing the individual codes for these two cars while all the other cars are going around them and they have to hope no surveillance vehicles come by or they're dead in the water.

That doesn't happen. The doors swing open for them and they get in and tell the cars to take them out to Mar Vista, where Cyrilla and some of the others are already gathered around the punch and the chips, waiting for them to get the party started. It's beautiful. It's perfect. He can't remember ever seeing a prettier sunset, all orange and purple and black, as if the whole world were a VR simulation, and if his heart goes into high gear when a cop car comes up behind him and swings out to pass, that's all part of the game and he's okay with it. Okay with everything. He's going to be a hero at school, an instant legend, because nobody's tried this before, nobody's even thought of it. And yes, it's dangerous and illegal and his mother would kill him and all that, and he did say to Warren, trying to be cool and hide his nerves, "So who's the greaser that goes over the cliff, you or me?" and Warren said, "Forget it, because we're both James Dean, and I'm not even going to try to make it close. I'm just going to jump out way before and if that's chicken, okay, sue me, right?"

Once they're there, the real work starts. Warren—and this other kid, Jeffrey Zuniga, who's a genius and destined to be class valedictorian—start disabling the cars' systems as much as possible so they'll go flat out, because what kind of a race would it be if these two drone cars just creep along toward the cliff? All right. Fine. And here comes the movie.

He and Warren, drawn up even, both of them drunk on the punch and laughing like madmen, revving the engines on command (it's as simple as saying "Redline" to the computer), and

Cyrilla there waving somebody's white jacket like a flag, fully dark now, kids' eyes in the headlights like the eyes of untamed beasts, lions and hyenas and what, jackals, and then they're off and all he's thinking is *If Warren thinks I'm going to bail first, he's crazy . . .*

THE GHOST IN THE MACHINE

It isn't a date, not exactly, and if Jan ever finds out about it she'll never hear the end of it, but she takes Keystone out to the local McDonald's for a Big Mac and fries—and it's not as if she hasn't taken other housing-challenged people out for fast food, men and women both, so they can sit in a booth with some kind of dignity and use the restroom to their heart's content without the manager badgering them every step of the way. But this is different. It's a kind of celebration actually, because Rose Taylor filed the suit and within hours she had a call from the head of the SPCA wondering if they couldn't work something out, like using the K5+ primarily in the parking area and limiting its access to the public sidewalk.

Keystone is back to his usual garb, with the addition of a military-looking camouflage cap he's picked up somewhere and an orange string bracelet Knitsy wove for him. He's in good form, high on the moment and her company (and the dark rum he surreptitiously tips into their Diet Cokes when no one's looking), and she's feeling no pain herself. There's something about him that makes her just want to let go—in a good way, a very good way. And the rum—she hasn't had anything stronger than white wine in years—goes right to her head.

"You know that this place—the SPCA, I mean—has a furnace out back, right?" he says, leaning into the table so she's conscious of how close he is to her, right there, right across from her, no more than two feet away. "And maybe your attorney friend can eventually get them to stop harassing us people, but what about the animals? You know what it smells like when they fire that thing up? I mean, can you even imagine?" He pauses, bites into his Big Mac, chews. "You're in a house, right?"

"Uh-huh, yeah. With a yard. And I know I should really adopt one of those dogs, I really should, but I can never seem to get around to it—"

"That's not what I'm saying—I'm not trying to lay any guilt trip on you. The people who should feel guilty are all these clueless shitwads who see a puppy in the store window and six weeks later dump it on the street. . . . No, what I'm talking about is the smell, which you don't get out in the suburbs with the windows rolled up and the air-conditioning going full blast. Am I right?'

He is right. But whether he's right or wrong or whether he's accusing her or not doesn't really matter. What matters is the intensity of his voice, the gravel in it, and the way his eyes look right into her as if there's nothing separating them but the illusion of a Formica tabletop and the recirculating air with its heavy freight of warmed-over meat and hunger.

In the car, she takes the leap and asks him if he wants to come home with her. "There's a shower," she says. "And clean towels—I can offer you clean towels, right? Isn't that the least I can do? As your advocate, I mean?"

It's dark now, but for the yellowish sheen of the McDonald's arches and the fiery glow of the taillights of the cars at the drive-through window. He doesn't say anything, and she keeps waiting for Carly to butt in, though she gave her strict instructions to keep quiet, no matter what. Finally, he sighs and says, "It's an attractive offer, and I thank you for it, but I don't want to be anybody's pet."

She doesn't know whether she should laugh or not. Really, is he joking?

"But why don't we do this?" he says. "You drive me back to my place and we'll sit on the wall there, finish the rum, and see what happens. Okay? Sound like a plan?"

All the way there, Carly's silent except to comment on the traffic conditions—"There's a lane closure on Mission because of roadwork in the right lane, so I'm going to take Live Oak to Harrison, which is only a two-minute-thirty-five-second delay"—and she finds she doesn't have much to say herself, anticipating what's to come and thinking about the last time she had sex outdoors, which had to have been twenty years ago. With Adam. On a camping trip.

When they step out of the car, the night comes to life around her, rich with its crepitating noises and a strong, sweet wafting scent of jasmine, which is all she can seem to smell—not the reek of the dogs or the crematorium or the hopelessness of Knitsy and the rest of them, but jasmine blooming in some secret corner. She likes the way the full moon comes sliding in over the treetops. The rum massages her. Then Keystone takes her hand and he's leading her to the wall and everything's falling into place . . . until one of the dogs lets out a howl and they both look up to see the K5+ unit wheeling toward them, its lights on full display. "Aw, shit!" Keystone spits, and before she can stop him, before the machine can wheel up to them and inquire what the situation is, he's halfway up the block, confronting it. He seems to have something in his hand now, a pale plastic bag he's pulled out of the bushes, and in the next moment he's jerking it down like a hood over the thing's Lidar, rendering it blind. It stops, emits its inquisitive whine for a count of eight, nine, ten seconds, and then triggers its alarm.

So much for romance. So much for Rose Taylor and human

rights. The noise is excruciating. Every dog in the SPCA starts howling as if it's being skinned alive, and you can be sure the cops are on their way, no doubt about that. But here's Keystone and he's grinning, actually grinning, as if all this is funny. "You know," he says, raising his voice to be heard over the din, "maybe I am ready to be a pet. You want a pet? For tonight anyway?"

He doesn't wait for an answer, just puts his arm around her and guides her to the car. But Carly's having none of it, Carly's got her own agenda. The locks click shut.

"Open up," she demands.

The car ignores her.

"Open up. Carly, I'm warning you—"

One long pulse-pounding moment drifts by. The car is a dark conglomerate of metal, glass, plastic, as inanimate and insensible as a stone. She's angry—and frustrated too, because she'd been ready to let go, really let go, for the first time in as long as she can remember. The dogs howl. The klaxon screams. And Keystone is right there, smelling of the Mrs. Meyer's hand soap somebody must have given him a gallon of, his arm around her shoulder, one hip pressed to hers. She wants to apologize—*For what, for a car?*—but that doesn't make any sense. "I don't know," she says, frantic now, and are those sirens she's hearing in the distance?

"Oh, fuck it," he says finally, throwing a glance over his shoulder. "Let's just walk. We can still walk, can't we?"

CHICKEN

He isn't wearing a leather jacket. He doesn't even own a leather jacket. He's just a kid in a simulation, the fleet car jerking along over the bumps in the field and the night waiting for him out there like an open set of jaws. He keeps glancing over at Warren and Warren keeps glancing over at him as if this really is chicken—and he's not going to be the one to cave first, is he? But that's not the issue, not any longer, because what he is just now discovering is that the door is not going to swing open no matter how many times he orders it to, and the brakes—the autonomous brakes, the brakes with a mind and purpose of their own—don't seem to be working at all.

NIGHT MOVES

On this, of all nights, she has to be wearing heels, but then she's wearing heels to impress Keystone, whether she wants to admit it or not. Men find heels sexy. *He* finds them sexy—and he told her as much when they were standing at the counter in McDonald's, placing their order. Now, though, she has her regrets—they haven't gone five blocks and she's already developing a blister on her left heel and her toes feel as if someone's taking a pair of hot pliers to them. "What's the matter?" he asks, his voice coming at her out of the dark. "You're not giving out already, are you?"

"It's my feet," she says, stopping and shifting her weight into him to take some of the pressure off.

"It's not your feet, it's your shoes. Here"—he braces her with one arm—"just take them off. Go barefoot. It's good for you."

"Easy for you to say."

"Hell, I'll go barefoot too, no problem—in fact, I like it better this way," he says, and in the next moment he's got his flip-flops in one hand and her shoes in the other and they're heading on up the sidewalk under the faint yellowish glow of the streetlights in a neighborhood that might or might not feature broken glass strewn across the pavement.

It's better than three miles to her house, and she's so used to relying on Carly she manages to lose her way, until finally she has to pull out her phone and follow the GPS, which is embarrassing, but not nearly as embarrassing as seeing Carly sitting there in front of the house, running lights on, waiting for them. "You!" she calls out as they cross the lawn. "You're going to hear from me tomorrow—and that's a promise."

But then something happens, something magical, and all the tension goes out of her. It has to do with the grass, its dampness, its coolness, the way it conforms to her toes, her arches, her aching heels. The simplest thing: grass. In that instant she's taken all the way back to her girlhood, before Adam, before Jackie, before her infinitely patient dark-haired father taught her to balance clutch and accelerator and work her way through the gears in a smooth mechanical succession that opened up a whole new world to her. "This is nice," she murmurs, and Keystone, a hazy presence beside her, agrees that yes, it is nice, though she's not sure he knows what he's agreeing to.

There are no cars on the street. Her house looms over them, two stories of furniture-filled rooms humming with the neural network of all the interconnected devices it contains, the refrigerator clicking on, the air conditioner, appliance lights pulsing everywhere. In a moment she'll lead Keystone up the steps, through the living room, and into the back bedroom, but not yet, not yet. Everything is still. The moon is overhead. And the grass—the grass is just like she remembered it.

Not Me

This was a long time ago. I'd never heard the term *sexual harass-ment* in my life—nobody had. Men were men and women were women, and women had what I wanted more than anything in the world—if they were willing to give it to me, I paid elaborate attention to them; if they weren't, it was another story. At the time I was just out of college, and I'd picked up a long-term sub-bing job at the local high school because I had nothing better to do. Beyond that, earning a living was right at the top of my list of priorities, what with student loans coming due and a certain unspoken pressure being exerted on me by way of my best friend, Rob, whose couch I'd been occupying for the past three months. In any case, I'd heard from my mother, who worked in the su-perintendent's office, that the English teacher I'd been filling in for sporadically had received a harrowing diagnosis from her on-cologist and was going to be out for an indefinite period. I didn't want a permanent job. I didn't want to get up at dawn and have to pretend I was alive. But I knotted my tie in front of the streaked mirror in Rob's bathroom each morning and tried to adjust to a new set of expectations.

Once I'd agreed to step in for Mrs. Leitner till whatever terrible thing that was happening to her came to its conclusion, the chair of the English Department, a beefy, florid old man of fifty or maybe sixty with a haircut that was 80 percent scalp, sat me down in his office and told me there was one cardinal rule: *Don't fraternize with the students*, which was code for *Don't fuck the students.* But this was hard to take seriously, because at least three people I knew of fucked the students and for their part the students fucked back, and as long as it was kept discreet everybody looked the other way. One woman—girl, she was a girl my age, in her first year of teaching—developed a crush on one of her students, who'd turned eighteen that year and even managed to grow a patchy reddish beard as testament to all he was prepared for. Her desk was next to mine in the department office, and when we weren't plowing through scrawled-over compositions or skimming *Masterplots* to keep one step ahead of the game, Suzanne would lean in confidentially, a red-rimmed cigarette stuck between her lips, and fill me in on the details.

I was unattached at the time, my previous girlfriend having decided I wasn't worth the effort, and the odds of getting reattached were hovering around zero, given the fact that I had to spend my nights on a narrow, dog-stinking, five-foot-ten-inch-long paisley couch pushed up against the wall in the living room of a one-bedroom apartment I wasn't paying rent on. Suzanne narrated in a low matter-of-fact voice—where she'd gone with him, when, what they did together, and the delicious fact that nobody suspected them, least of all his parents, whom she'd met only once, at Parent-Teacher night—all the while watching my face for signals, which I suppressed. Or thought I did. She wasn't my type, or not entirely, but that didn't stop me from picturing these situations, she spread naked across the bed and the student—Alec, who was tall and rope-shouldered—climbing atop her or taking her up against the wall in the apartment with the private entrance she shared with nobody.

Was all this a secret? If she'd told me, she must have told other people too, and I did mention it to Rob, who just shrugged and said, "Good luck," and when I asked, "What does that mean?" he gave me a long look and said, "You'd have to be a monk to resist all that—and by the way, when was the last time you got laid?"

I took the question for what it was—a rebuke—but resisted throwing it back at him, since he wasn't doing much better, his own girlfriend sealed behind the faded brick walls of a dormitory at the end of a dark street in a dark college town four hundred miles away. So when Friday came along—one of a long, tottering row of Fridays that fell like dominoes and left me as far as ever from resolving the issue, or any other issue, for that matter—I found myself cruising the bars in my roommate's company, looking for whatever might be out there. Which wasn't much. This was in northern Westchester, by the way, a place of unupholstered nights and unremitting boredom. We went to one place, then another, clutching sweating drinks in our hands and hoping something we could listen to would come up on the jukebox. I danced a couple of times with a girl in a tight skirt whose legs spoke volumes to me, but nothing came of it—though I practically begged, she wouldn't even give me her number.

Our last resort—Brennan's, a steakhouse with a big semicircular bar that could get lively with people our age once they shut down the kitchen—was enticingly crowded, and there was an album we both liked playing at a healthy volume when we walked in the door, so we decided to go up to the bar and order a drink. It took me a minute, scanning the room for people I knew, before I spotted Suzanne and Alec at one of the tables squeezed in the cubbyhole behind the door. It was a table that was familiar to me, one I'd occupied a dozen times myself over the course of the previous summer with Corinda—then my girlfriend, now my ex, who, as far as I knew at the time, had been as happy with me as I was with her.

I didn't react. I might have felt a little punch to the gut, a tightening down there, but I didn't want to embarrass Suzanne—or myself either. I ordered. Stared into my drink. Rob said something. I said something back. The song that just then came on featured a pair of lead guitars doing a kind of mating dance, harmonizing, then breaking away and coming back again, and I was lost in it, bobbing my head and rapping the bar rail with both forefingers, when Suzanne came up and laid a hand on my arm. I turned my head and there she was, with Alec at her side, and far from being embarrassed, they were both grinning as if they'd come there expressly to meet up with me. Suzanne was tall, almost as tall in her heels as Alec, and she was wearing a dress that left her legs exposed from mid-thigh down, which was a different look for her, or different at least from what I'd seen of her at school. I found the view illuminating. As did Rob, who swung around and gaped at her.

"What a surprise seeing you here," she said. "I thought for sure you'd be home taking notes on *The Ancient Mariner*—or what, *Death of a Salesman*?" She let out a quick squeal of a laugh, high on the moment, giddy with this new thing in her life and the aura of sex that hung round her like heat radiating up off a hot blacktop road.

"Oh, yeah, well, in fact I was. Actually Rob and I—you know Rob, my roommate I told you about?—spent the whole evening translating Coleridge into Chinese and back again, just for the exercise. Right, Rob?"

Rob was too stunned to grin. He just let his eyes drop to her legs and work their way back up again before he said, "Yeah, sure. Chinese. It's practically my first language."

If I expected Alec to be intimidated or at least circumspect, that wasn't the case at all. He was grinning too, and his eyes were lit with the same venereal fire as Suzanne's. He was my height. He outweighed me. He had a beard and I didn't. "Yeah," he said, "I should be home doing my math homework, right? But wait a minute"—he looked from Suzanne to me—"either of you happen to be a math whiz?"

"Afraid you're out of luck," I said, and here we were, the four of us, standing at the bar, *fraternizing*. I wasn't sure how I felt about that. Would I have been happier if Alec didn't exist, if he was shorter, lamer, back at home working on his car or jerking off amid his sports trophies? Or if Suzanne was with me? Or Rob? The drinking age was eighteen, I reminded myself. Draft age too. What was my problem—we were all adults here, weren't we?

Rob offered to buy them a drink, but Suzanne just shook her head. "No," she said, "we've got things to do, haven't we, Alec?" and I thought they were going to give us a demonstration right there at the bar, but the implication was enough. She half turned to the door, so that her hair swung loose and settled back over her shoulders again. "Got to go," she said, and he said, "Later," leaning in for the handshake I reflexively gave him.

After they'd left, Rob turned to me and said, "What do you think? One more?"

I shrugged. We were prolonging the moment, as if to fully absorb it, and I didn't know why. Or maybe I did—at home was the couch. At home was the terminus of Friday night.

The music faded, then started up again. "So that was her?" Rob said, draining his glass and pushing it across the bar for a refill.

I nodded.

"She's"—he took a moment to find the word, weighing the circumstances—"different, huh?"

I felt angry suddenly. I wanted to say *She's headed for trouble* or *She doesn't know what she's getting into,* but I didn't. Who was I to judge? They were both adults, weren't they? "Yeah," I said finally. "You could say that."

The other two teachers I knew about—or I'd heard the rumors anyway—were both male, which was the way people assumed it would be, predator and prey, the wolf and the lamb and all the rest. One was the drama teacher, whom I didn't know at all, but whose opportunities were limitless, what with late-night rehearsals, hands-on direction, and the shedding of personae like layers peeled down to the core. The other was a member of the English Department, like Suzanne and me, though I was only temporary and he'd been there since he got out of college. Roger was tall, stoop-shouldered, in his late twenties or early thirties—old, that is, by my accounting—and he wore loafers with tassels instead of boots, dressed as if he should be propped up in the window of a department store, and sported what was once called a "regular" haircut. I knew him casually, received his formulaic jokes as stoically as I could, and found him totally uninteresting but for this one thing, this affair he was having with a girl on the debate team, of which he was the coach. I didn't know her very well either—Elizabeth, or Libby, as everyone called her. She wasn't in any of my classes, but I saw her in the hall with some of the other girls after sixth period every day, when she must have had a class in one of the rooms near mine. If it weren't for the rumors I wouldn't even have noticed her.

She wasn't the first one your eyes would go to in a crowd, but once I caught on I began to see her appeal. She wasn't flashy, always dressed in a turtleneck and skirt or jumper, minimal makeup, minimal jewelry, but she seemed self-contained, confident, and her body—expressive and replete—was right there itching to burst out of her tartans and knee socks. Suzanne had her in her honors class and told me how gifted she was, on track to be salutatorian if not valedictorian and sure to have her choice of colleges, but when I asked her about the rumors—about Roger—she just made a face and shook her head.

"What do you mean?" I pressed. "Is it true?"

We were in the office, at our desks, eating tuna salad sandwiches from the cafeteria and sipping lukewarm coffee. She shook her head again, and we both glanced down the row of desks to the one at the far end, where Roger should have been peeling an egg his wife had boiled for him that morning or slurping soup out of a thermos while thumbing through the sports pages of the *Daily News*, but wasn't. Was he off on one of the debate team's overnight trips? With his young orators, male and female both? With Libby?

"I don't want to talk about it." Suzanne's eyes had gone cold. There was a smear of mayonnaise on her upper lip, which made her face look off-kilter. I was about to reach up with my napkin and brush it away, an intimacy I hadn't earned, but then her tongue found it and it was gone.

"Why not? What's the problem?" I didn't quite get it—she was doing the same thing herself, wasn't she? I wanted gossip. I wanted to be titillated. I wanted to hear it from her lips.

"He's married, for one thing. With kids, little kids, I don't know—two of them, three of them. He's too old for her. He's ruining her. I mean, isn't that enough?"

What her eyes were telling me was that I shouldn't push it, that her situation was utterly different, night and day, that she was in love and Roger Hinckley wasn't and that was all that mattered. I gave it a moment's thought. Roger was a jerk, yes, and marriage, at least as I viewed it then, was like some sort of prison sentence, but still I didn't quite see the distinction.

"What about Alec?"

"What about him?"

One of the other teachers, an older woman named Tammy, pushed through the door then, gave us an automatic smile, and began extracting her lunch from a paper bag decorated with grease stains. We both fell silent a moment, then I said, "I don't know—isn't it kind of the same thing? Not that I'm saying anything, but you know the way people are, you know what they say."

"No," she said, "what *do* they say?"

I looked down the row of desks, past Tammy and her meatball wedge and diet soda, to where Roger's desk stood empty. "I don't know—same thing they say about Roger."

"You know what?" She balled up her half-eaten sandwich and flung it in the wastebasket in the same motion.

"What?"

"Screw people," she said. "Really, screw them."

We had a succession of sunstruck days that fall, Indian summer, but nobody had a chance to enjoy them because we were all stuck inside, racing like gerbils around the academic wheel—and on the weekends, without fail, it rained. I met a girl or two along the way—in bars, where else?—but nobody I could talk to. They were secretaries, receptionists, waitresses, the ones left behind after graduation when their cohort went off to college. Not that I was looking for anything long term, but no matter how compelling their faces were, their hair, their bodies, or how enormous my need, nothing seemed to click. Rob, out of desperation, had begun making the long, dark, hurtling journey up the Thruway to be with his girlfriend on weekends, so most of the time I didn't even have him there to distract me from myself. And yes, there were girls in my classes who were as smart and funny and well put together as you could ask for, girls not much younger than I, but nothing happened there either, though I had Suzanne's example before me, not to mention Roger's and the drama teacher's and god knew who else's. Was I a rock? A saint? A model teacher? Would I have slipped if the opportunity had presented itself? I don't know. Truly, I don't.

The weeks piled up like drift. Somebody told me Mrs. Leitner was never coming back, and it was as if I'd been given a life sentence for crimes I'd never committed. The students wrote essays, I corrected them. I gave up smoking and started in again a week later. Beers, multiples of them, in six-packs or served up in foaming glasses on one bar top or another, were my counters. Then there came a night in November, another Friday, the leaves gone from the trees and a cold rain rattling the gutters, when things suddenly shifted on me.

By the time I got home Rob was already gone, charging up the Thruway while radio stations faded in and out and the tires hissed beneath him. He was on a mission, and the thought of that—and of his girlfriend, Lee Ann, with her pouting underlip and swollen brassieres, just depressed me. I had a beer. Ate something out of a can. I was watching TV with the sound off, killing time till it was late enough to make the rounds of the bars—albeit alone, like some sort of outcast—when the bell rang. This was an unusual circumstance. The bell never rang—it was just Rob and me in the apartment, and I couldn't imagine anybody actually mounting the front steps and depressing the buzzer, unless it was some official, a cop, that is, alerted to the smell of marijuana or fielding a noise complaint because the stereo was cranked up to the maximum. But I wasn't smoking marijuana (not that night anyway, or at least not yet) and I hadn't put any music on, preferring to sit in silence and watch the shapes shift on the screen in a parody of desolation.

It was Suzanne at the door. Her hair was wet, her mascara smeared, and her coat hanging open to display her legs in that same dress she'd worn at the bar—or one just like it. She didn't say hi or apologize for barging in on me or explain that she'd found my address in the faculty listings, just brushed by me the minute I opened the door, stalked to the middle of the room, and swung round on me. "Have you got anything to drink?" she asked, her voice strained and theatrical. "Please tell me you have something, anything, because—" She broke off, as if suddenly aware of how intrusive all this was—or maybe that was play-acting too. "I just—can I sit down?"

"Yes, sure," I said, "of course," and watched her wriggle out of the wet coat before crossing the room and sinking into the couch. She didn't seem to know what to do with the coat—I should have offered to take it, but a fog of confusion had settled over me. After a moment, she dropped it discreetly on the floor at her feet. "I've got beer," I said. "You want a beer?"

"You don't have anything stronger?"

"I think that's about it. Rob had a bottle of vodka in the freezer, but I think we—"

She waved me off. "Beer's fine."

When I came back into the room with the beer she was sitting cross-legged on the couch, working her fingers through her wet hair. She took the bottle from me and drained half of it in a gulp, then gave me a self-referential smile as if she'd just realized where she was. "You wouldn't have a towel I could borrow, would you? And maybe a hairbrush?"

What had happened—what had brought her here, to me—was

potentially catastrophic. Libby's parents had begun to field rumors about their daughter's relationship with the debate coach, which both Libby and Roger denied out of hand, but the principal was involved now and the chair of the English Department and, last Suzanne had heard, even the police. "They could get him for rape, you know that, right?"

I was seated in the armchair across from her, my own beer propped up on one knee. "Rape? I thought they were—I mean, it's consensual, right?"

"*Statutory*. She's under eighteen."

I didn't really know what that meant or how to make the distinction, but Roger Hinckley's haphazard face suddenly rose up before me, and I felt a dark surge of joy. I didn't dislike him, but I didn't really like him either.

"Tammy's saying he's going to have to take a leave of absence." Suzanne patted her hair with the towel I'd fetched from the bathroom, a towel that could have been cleaner and could have smelled better too, but I was doing the best I could. "Really," she said, her voice gone hollow, "I don't know what to do."

I wanted to say, *What do you care?* but I could see where this was going and I liked the way she looked sitting there on my couch—Rob's couch—in her moment of extremity. I said, "Alec's eighteen, right? So you don't have anything to worry about."

"Except my job. Roger's got tenure, but me? They could just fire me."

"For what?"

"There's a morals clause in our contract, isn't there?"

"I don't know, I never read it. You mean the 'Don't-Fuck-the-Students' clause?"

"It's not funny."

"I'm not trying to be funny."

There was a moment then in which we both tried to gather

ourselves, a moment we needed to get past. It was raining still. The images flickered across the TV screen. I took a sip of my beer, then set it back down on the coffee table. "What does Alec have to say about it?"

"We broke up. Over the phone, if you can believe it. He said we couldn't risk it—he said *I* couldn't risk it—and all I could say was 'I love you' over and over. Isn't that pathetic? I mean, he's being more mature about it than me."

"Maybe nothing'll happen," I said.

She got up and crossed the room to me then, perched on the arm of the chair, and leaned in close so I could feel the wet strands of her hair curtaining my neck and shoulders. "It already has," she said.

On Monday, there was a stranger sitting at Roger's desk, a hammy old man with a long nose and rheumy blue eyes who was probably gay, though I didn't know anything about gay in those days either—I'm not even sure the term had been repurposed yet. But there he was, Phil Leicester, looking and sounding like a bit player from A *Midsummer Night's Dream*, the traveling production, propped up in Roger Hinckley's chair and talking nonstop to anyone who would listen. I wasn't listening. We'd made our introductions when I came in and then I'd gone straight to my desk, trying frantically to put something together for my first-period class, which I should have done the night before, but hadn't.

The night before I'd been at a bar—at several bars—and stayed late, drinking alone. I wouldn't admit to being depressed over what had happened Friday night, or worse, Saturday morning, but that was the fact. Suzanne had stayed over and we'd made love (or had sex, that is) in Rob's bed, which was all right, which was fine—I liked her, we were friends, I was needy and so was she—until the next morning. The minute she opened her eyes she said, "Oh my God, what am I doing?" She was up out of bed before I could so much as reach out to her, pulling on her dress with her back to me. "I'm so sorry," she said. "I didn't mean—forgive me, will you? Please, please, please?"

I wanted to say, *There's nothing to forgive*, wanted to say, *Let me take you out for breakfast at least* or *I've wanted to do that for a long time and let's do it again, now, right now*, but she was already gone. Out the door, down the steps, and into her canary-yellow VW Bug with the heart sticker on the rear bumper.

And now, on this morning when a total stranger, wearing a bow tie of all things, had taken Roger's place, Suzanne wasn't at her desk. Which seemed ominous. Not that I was all that eager to sit there elbow to elbow with her—what had happened Saturday morning filled me with shame and anger—but the fact was she could lose her job too. Or already had lost it. And what would they do to her—tar and feathers? Criminal charges? What did the morals clause say anyway? And where was she? It wasn't like her to be late.

As it turned out, she'd taken a sick day and driven up to Rhinebeck with Alec, who'd likewise skipped school, and they'd stayed overnight at the hotel there, where nobody would know them. The next day she was back at her desk, making notes in her copy of *The Odyssey*, which was required reading for her world literature class, acting as if nothing had happened. She didn't avoid my eyes, just glanced up with a smile, said hello in her soft puff of a voice, and caught me up on the details as if Friday night and Saturday morning had never happened. She was in love with Alec, and that was all there was to it, and she was sorry if she'd given me the wrong idea. "Anyway," she said, "I was in a state. I mean, all I could think was the worst—"

I didn't have anything to say to this.

"But really, the focus is on Roger—what he was doing was wrong. And I hate to say it, but he should have known better. Have you ever met his wife? No? Well, she's pretty, very pretty, and the kids are, I don't know, *kids*."

I watched her lips move. She wasn't talking to me, she was talking at me, talking as if I cared—and I didn't care, not anymore. I said, "What about you—aren't you afraid you're going to be next?"

She shook her head, dropped her eyes to the page. I watched her make a notation in the margin, as if the Greeks were what moved her. "We're going to go underground, at least till after graduation." A complicit smile. "No more Brennan's. Or any other place within twenty miles of here."

I was bitter—I couldn't help it. She wasn't my type, as I said, but four nights ago she had been. "Just stay at home, huh?"

Her smile widened till I could see the glint of a gold-capped molar. "Yeah," she said, and her eyes never left mine, even when Tammy and two of the other teachers came in the door and brought all the racket of the hallway with them, "that's the best part."

The department chair, whose office was separate from ours and whom we hardly ever saw except during meetings, was out shoveling snow in his driveway after an early December storm when his left side went numb and he pitched face-forward onto the frozen pavement. He might have lain there till he froze to death but for the quick thinking of his next-door neighbor, who saw what had happened and went out and cradled him in her lap till the ambulance came. The upshot was that Tammy, who was a forty-two-year-old divorcée and wore her hair in coppery beauty-parlor ringlets, was appointed temporary chair, nominally in charge of us and our affairs, though the real power was invested in the principal, and beyond him, the superintendent, who'd put Roger Hinckley on unpaid leave till things could be sorted out. As far as I knew, Roger hadn't been arrested, so there was that at least, but the administration was aroused, and what had once been an open secret was buried so deeply even the drama teacher was forsaking after-school activities—beyond rehearsing the plays themselves, that is.

All this had a chilling effect, to say the least. Suzanne and Alec wouldn't so much as glance at each other in the hallway, and in the class he was taking from her—creative writing—they kept things on a strictly formal basis. Or that was what I'd heard. The fact was, I didn't get to talk with her all that much at this juncture—she'd asked to switch to Tammy's desk, once Tammy had vacated it for the chair's office, and why she'd asked I could only speculate, since she was done confiding in me. Did she feel as uncomfortable around me as I felt around her? Did she feel guilty? Like a slut? A hypocrite? All the above? She tried to make a joke of it—"I just need to be closer to the door in case they come for me with a lynch mob"—but it was bogus and we both knew it. "We can still have our miserable crumbs of lunch together once in a while—it's not like I'm moving over to the math department or anything," she said, but I wasn't having it. "Yeah, sure," I said.

What I want to make clear here, for the record, is that I was not the one who typed up the anonymous note on the IBM Selectric in Tammy's office and slipped it in the principal's mail slot in the main office after everyone had gone home one afternoon, though no one believes that, least of all Suzanne. She had some explaining to do (lying, that is), and so did Alec when they were called separately into the office and grilled by the principal, Mike Blumenthal, who had a thug's face and was as innocent of intellect as anybody I've ever met. What happened? Nothing, as far as

I could see. Suzanne was a woman and women got a free pass in those days.

I kept my head down. I found I needed the job because the job meant money and the money was like a drug. I started helping Rob out with the rent and saving up for my own place because when Lee Ann graduated at the end of the year, she was planning on moving in with him, which left me precisely nowhere. Thanksgiving found me at my mother's house, bored right down to the soles of my feet. There was a hard freeze. Everything smelled of exhaust fumes. Then it was Christmas, and what Christmas meant, beyond the onslaught of syrupy tunes tinkling out of every speaker in existence and the conundrum of what to get for my mother, who already had enough perfume to float a canoe, was the department Christmas party.

A Friday night, yes—one more Friday night. Tammy, as acting chair, hosted the affair at her house, which was at the dead and final end of a rat maze of unlighted streets and looked no different from the two hundred or so exact replicas I had to drive past to get there. I was twenty-two. I didn't know protocol—or even good manners, for that matter. I brought nothing but myself to the party, though the others, I saw, had offered up various dishes—a tuna casserole, chili beans, a mold of Jell-O with grapes embedded in it—and even flowers for the hostess. I knew at least half the people there, my colleagues, but most of them had spouses with them, and that was a kind of ordeal I hadn't factored in when I made my calculations as to whether to attend or not. The attraction was the free food and booze—everybody drank in those days, and drank heavily—and I figured I'd get tanked at the party and then go on out and make the rounds of the places where somebody might have registered an actual heartbeat.

I was well into it, having put away two plates of food and

three or four scotch and sodas and politely endured the posturing of the various spouses, one of whom took me for a student, when Suzanne came hurtling through the front door in a pair of high heels and an ankle-length coat wrapped around one of her extracurricular dresses. She was late, the last one to the party, and she whirled around the room spouting jokes and excuses until she was sure everybody was watching her before she slipped off her coat to reveal the dress. Which looked good on her. Very good. My perceptions were dulled, but when she went up to embrace Tammy over the makeshift bar with its punch bowl and dented ice bucket, I saw that Tammy was wearing the same dress—or one that wasn't much different, though Tammy's was red and Suzanne's green, as if they'd color-coordinated beforehand. It was just a moment, a quick embrace of the two women while people turned back to whatever they were saying and one of the endless corny records provided a musical backdrop, but it registered on me—or Tammy did—in a way that just left me confused. She was my mother's age and here she was wearing the same dress as the girl who'd slept with me in Rob's bed and avoided me ever since, and what was all that about?

Eventually, after she'd made the rounds, Suzanne did come up to me, as if it were an afterthought—or worse, an obligation. She was wearing a serene smile that told me Alec was waiting for her back at the apartment and that the reason she was late didn't have anything to do with Christmas shopping or traffic or the ice on the roads. "Having fun?" she asked, the old edge of sarcasm in her voice.

"It's better than Woodstock," I said. "Have you met all the spouses yet? Like"—I nodded to a man across the room who was wearing a sweater that looked as if it had been knitted by the blind—"*Mr.* Kathy McCaffrey?"

She laughed. "No, but before it's over, I'm sure I will." She gave me a look then that rose from my scuffed boots to my jeans and the leather jacket I'd been affecting lately, and let her face go serious a moment. "And how are you? Everything okay? I mean, I hardly get to see you anymore, what with the rush around the office and the holidays coming on—"

I shrugged. What did she want me to say? That I missed her? Was she really that venal? "I didn't write that letter, you know," I said.

She kept her eyes on me, the steadiest gaze in the world. I didn't want to flinch, because I was innocent, I was, but I had to look away. Across the room, one of the other young teachers, Matt Ricci, was mouthing the words to "White Christmas," the song that was just then laboring through the speakers of Tammy's ancient hi-fi like some sort of tribal dirge. "Yeah," she said finally, "okay," and she was already turning her back on me, her bare shoulders, hair in motion, her thighs. "You take care," she said. "And Merry Christmas."

I should have left then, but inertia had set in and the next drink sat like a barbell across my shoulders. Suzanne found her coat, thanked Tammy in dumb show while Bing Crosby or one of his accomplices—Nat King Cole—obliterated all sense and meaning, and then vanished into the night. The party began to wind down. Phil Leicester, who'd been lighting one cigarette off another all night and laughing at his own jokes in the register of a wounded animal, finally took his sagging face out to his car, then the McCaffreys left, and I pushed myself up from the couch in a kind of panic, counting only six people left standing. It was almost nine o'clock. I had appointments to keep—or at least make. I was wondering how to extricate myself, debating whether to hit the bathroom and slip out the back door or suck it up and thank our hostess, who would after all be evaluating me at some point in the coming term, for the great time I'd had, when there she was, Tammy, standing right beside me in her dress with the thin shoulder straps that was just like Suzanne's but for the color.

"You're not leaving, are you?" She waved a watery cocktail in one hand, then brought a cigarette to her lips with the other.

I told her I was meeting somebody at Brennan's. "At"—I made a show of looking at my watch—"nine-thirty?"

"Bullshit," she said. "I know you—you're just going home to what, didn't you tell me, a couch? Come on," she said. "One more drink. And if you want to know, I could use some help cleaning up too."

"No, really, I'm supposed to meet somebody—"

"A girl?"

My mind was full of sludge. The lie couldn't break free of it. "Yeah," I said.

"What's her name?"

I couldn't think. She was right there, watching me. "Suzanne."

"Suzanne? Not *our* Suzanne?"

"No," I said, and I didn't know how much she knew, "another Suzanne."

"Okay," she said, "but she can wait, can't she? It's not even nine yet—and I really could use some help here." She slipped an arm around my waist as if we were out on a dance floor, and it was the first time we'd ever made physical contact, beyond maybe a handshake when we'd first met, if that. "Come on, one more drink?"

After the others left I went dutifully around the room, dumping ashtrays, gathering up bottles and cans for the trash, and hauling trays of dishes, glasses, and silverware out to the kitchen, where Tammy stood at the sink, a pair of yellow rubber gloves clinging to her bare arms. She'd fixed me a final drink—for the road—and I'd stationed it on the bar, where I could refer to it as I went back and forth. I was drunk enough so that my thought processes pretty well shut down and everything became usual, as if all my life had narrowed to this point of rudimentary usefulness. The music persisted, "O Little Town of Bethlehem" and the like, but it operated on me now like a kind of anesthesia, the world washed free of pain, loneliness, hurt, anger. Tammy was in the kitchen. The music flowed. I transported objects, one after another, until the only thing left was the punch bowl, a cut-glass receptacle the size of a birdbath identical to the one my mother kept on the top shelf of the pantry at home. I took it in both arms, lifted it from the bar with all its dregs of brutalized lemons and limes and discolored fruit juice sloshing merrily against my chest, and backed my way in through the swinging door to the kitchen, where Tammy, craning her neck over one shoulder, admonished me to be careful. "That was my mother's," she called out, and in the next moment she was coming across the room, her arms outstretched, to take it from me.

I didn't drop it. That would have been too easy. No, I shifted it gently into her arms, her face inches from mine—both of us on the same page, concentrating hard—but the physics of the transaction caused some of the liquid, viscid with its load of citrus and sugar, to splash over the rim and dribble down the front of her dress. She let out a soft curse, and then the bowl was on the counter and we were looking at each other in a way that might have been hilarious under other circumstances. But this wasn't hilarious, this was something else I was just in that moment beginning to understand. I watched her drop her chin to peer down the front of her dress in disbelief. The liquid had darkened the material in a spreading stain that was shading from red to maroon, and my first impulse was to make amends, dab at it with something, paper towels, a wet cloth, but I just stood there watching her as her eyes rose gradually to mine. "I guess I'll be making a trip to the dry cleaner's after work Monday," she said.

"What about a wet cloth? Isn't that what you're supposed to—"

She sighed, peeling back the rubber gloves. "And I really liked this dress too. The minute I tried it on I said to myself, 'Tammy, this is you, it really is,' and with my figure it isn't always easy to find something to fit right, believe me—but here, help me, will you?"

She'd turned around, fumbling with the zipper the way my mother did when she got home from work and couldn't decide whether to change first or make herself a drink. I did what I was told. Under my fingers, her skin seemed hot to the touch, though maybe that was my imagination. It took me two tries, but then I got the zipper down to the point where she could reach back and manipulate it herself, which she did with a soft frictive release that was the only sound in the whole house, because the Christmas records—I realized it in that instant—had finally played themselves out. I took a step back, just to give her space, but she turned to face me, to look into my eyes, before she eased the dress down to her waist and I saw that she wasn't wearing anything under it.

The truth? I did what I had to, what was expected, though when it was over I pulled on my jeans and went straight out to my car. Yes, I was drunk, but it seemed I was always drunk in those days, and nobody ever thought twice about driving under the influence, least of all me. The headlights were a revelation: they opened up the road to me and the road took me home. To Rob's.

Where I poured out a beer I couldn't finish, tried to watch something on the TV, and fell down hard into a black, dreamless sleep. The next day my head hurt and I stayed in the shower so long the water began to go cold, after which I flipped through the channels, stared at a book I couldn't concentrate on, and went to the movies, alone. I didn't go out that night, though it was Saturday and Saturdays were almost as precious as Fridays. Sunday was gray, cold, bleak. Then it was Monday and Rob was in his bed, snoring, when the alarm went off. I spent a long time staring into the bathroom mirror in my underwear thinking of what it was going to be like to see Suzanne and Tammy there in the office or the hallway, and the students too—Libby, who'd never missed a class though her coach was in exile, and Alec, who fingered his beard and carried himself like an astronaut just setting foot on earth again. Then I went to the phone and called in sick. I called in sick the day after that and then the following day until there was no point in calling anymore.

It was no great tragedy. I hadn't wanted to be an educator in the first place—it was just a job, that was all. What I missed most was the paycheck, but that took care of itself in a way that wedded need and serendipity. It happened that one of the bartenders at Brennan's quit to go back to school, and since by that point I'd become not only a regular but a kind of prodigy of drink, hyperbole, and free-form bar banter, the manager took me on as second bartender, three nights a week. It was hardly a career, but I accepted it for what it was—a place marker—and on most nights, even the slow ones, there were usually a couple of girls sitting at the bar gossiping over their Brandy Alexanders and tequila sunrises, watching my every move.

The Apartment

Who was to know? She might have outlived most of her contemporaries, but she was so slight and small, almost a dwarf really, her eyesight compromised and her hearing fading, and if she lived a year or two more it would have been by the grace of God alone. Yes, she was lively enough, even at ninety, wobbling down the street on her bicycle like some atrophied schoolgirl and twice a week donning her *épée* mask and fencing with her shadow in the salon of her second-floor apartment overlooking rue Gambetta on the one side and rue Saint-Estève on the other, but his own mother had been lively too, and she'd gone to bed on the night of her seventy-second birthday and never opened her eyes again. No, no: The odds were in his favor. Definitely. Definitely in his favor.

He turned forty-seven the year he first approached her, in 1965, which meant at that point he'd been married to Marie-Thérèse for some twenty years, years that had been happy enough for the most part—and more than that, usual. He liked the usual.

The usual kept you on an even keel and offered up few surprises. And this was the important thing here, the thing he always liked to stress when the subject came up: he was not a gambling man. Before he'd made any of the major decisions in his life—asking for his wife's hand all those years ago, applying for the course of study that would lead to his law degree, making an offer on the apartment they'd lived in since their marriage—he'd studied all the angles with a cold, computational eye. The fact was, he had few vices beyond a fondness for sweets and a tendency to indulge his daughters, Sophie and Élise, sixteen and fourteen respectively that year (or maybe they were seventeen and fifteen—he never could quite keep that straight; as he liked to say, "If you're very, very fortunate, your children will be twelve months older each year"). He didn't smoke or drink, habits he'd given up three years earlier after a strenuous talk with his doctor. And he wasn't covetous, or not particularly. Other men might have driven sleek sports cars, leased yachts, and kept mistresses, but none of that interested him.

The only problem—the sole problem in his life at that point—was the apartment. It was just too small to contain his blossoming daughters and the eternally thumping music radiating from their bedroom day and night, simplistic music, moronic even—the Beatles, the Animals, the Kinks, the very names indicative of their juvenility—and if he wanted a bigger apartment, grander, more spacious, *quieter*, who could blame him? An apartment that was a five-minute walk from his office and a cathedral of early morning light? An apartment surrounded by shops, cafés, and first-class restaurants? It was, as they say, a no-brainer.

He put together a proposal and sent Madame C. a note wondering if he might see her, at her convenience, on a matter of mutual interest. Whether she would respond or not, he couldn't say, but it wasn't as if he were some interloper—he knew her as an acquaintance and neighbor, as did just about everyone else in Arles, and he must have stopped with her in the street half a dozen times in the past year to discuss the weather, the machinations of de Gaulle and Pompidou, and the absurdity of sending a rocket into space when life here, on terra firma, was so clearly in need of *immediate attention*. A week went by before he heard back from her. He'd come home from work that day to an empty apartment—Marie-Thérèse out shopping and the girls at rehearsal for a school play, but the radio in their room all too present and regurgitating rock and roll at full volume (*We gotta get out of this place*, the singer insisted, in English, over and over) until he angrily snapped it off—and he was just settling down in his armchair with the newspaper when he noticed her letter on the sideboard.

"Cher Monsieur," she wrote in the firm decisive hand she'd learned as a schoolgirl in the previous century, "I must confess to being intrigued. Shall we meet here at my residence at four p.m. Thursday?"

In addition to the contract he'd drawn up in advance—he was an optimist, always an optimist—he brought with him a bouquet of spring flowers and a box of chocolate truffles, which he presented somberly to her when she met him at the door. "How kind of you," she murmured, taking the flowers in one all-but-translucent hand and the box of chocolates in the other and ushering him through the entrance hall and into the salon, and whether by calculation or not she left him standing there in that grand room with its high ceilings, Persian carpets, and dense mahogany furniture while she went into the kitchen to put the flowers in a vase.

There was a Bösendorfer piano in one corner with a great

spreading palm—or was it a cycad?—in a ceramic pot beside it, and that, as much as anything, swept him away. To think of sinking into the sofa after work and listening to Bach or Mozart or Debussy instead of the Animals or whoever they were. And so what if no one in the family knew how to play or had ever evidenced even the slightest degree of musical talent—they could take lessons. He himself could take lessons, and why not? He wasn't dead yet. And before long the girls would be away at university and then married, with homes of their own, and it would be just Marie-Thérèse and him—and maybe a cat. He could see himself seated on the piano bench, the cat asleep in his lap and Debussy's *Images* flowing from his fingertips like a new kind of language.

"Well, don't these look pretty?" the old lady sang out, edging into the room to arrange the vase on the coffee table, which he now saw was set for two, with a blue-and-rose Sèvres teapot, matching cups and saucers, cloth napkins bound in silver rings, and a platter of macarons.

He sat in the armchair across from her as she poured out two cups of tea, watching for any signs of palsy or Parkinson's—but no, she was steady enough—and then they were both busy with their spoons, the sugar and the cream, until she broke the silence. "You have a proposition for me, is that it?" she asked. "And"—here a sly look came into the flickering remnants of her eyes—"I'll bet you five francs I know what it is. I'm clairvoyant, Monsieur, didn't you know that?"

He couldn't think of anything to say to this, so he just smiled.

"You want to make me an offer on the apartment, *en viager*—isn't that right?"

If he was surprised, he tried not to show it. He'd been prepared to condescend to her, as with any elderly person—politely, of course, generously, looking out for her best interest as well as his own—but she'd caught him up short. "Well, yes," he said. "That's it exactly. A reverse annuity."

He set down his cup. The apartment was absolutely silent, as if no one else lived in the building, and what about a maid—didn't she have a maid? "The fact is, Marie-Thérèse and I—my wife, that is—have been thinking of moving for some time now." He let out a little laugh. "Especially with my daughters growing into young women and the apartment getting smaller by the day, if you know what I mean, and while there are plenty of places on the market, there's really hardly anything like this—and it's so close to my office . . ."

"And since my grandson passed on, you figure the old woman has no one to leave the place to, and even if she doesn't need the money, why wouldn't she take it anyway? It's better than getting nothing and leaving the place for the government to appropriate, isn't that right?"

"Yes," he said, "that was my thinking."

As far as he knew—and he'd put in his research on the subject—she had no heirs. She'd been a bride once, and a mother too, and she'd lived within these four walls and paced these creaking floorboards for an astonishing sixty-nine years, ever since she'd returned from her honeymoon in 1896 and moved in here with her husband, a man of means who owned the department store on the ground floor and gave her a life of ease. Anything she wanted was at her fingertips. She hosted musical parties, vacationed in the Alps, skied, bicycled, hunted and fished, lived through the German occupation and the resumption of the Republic without noticing all that much difference in her daily affairs, but of course no one gets through life unscathed. Her only child, a daughter, died of pneumonia in 1934, after which she and her husband assumed guardianship of their grandson, until first her husband died unexpectedly (after eating a dish of fresh-picked cherries that had been dusted with copper sulfate and inadequately rinsed), and then her grandson, whom she'd seen through medical school and who had continued to live with her as her sole companion and emotional support. He was only thirty-six. Killed in an auto accident on a deserted road not two years ago. It was Marie-Thérèse who'd seen the notice in the paper; otherwise he might have missed it altogether. They sent a condolence card, though neither of them attended the funeral, which, given the deceased's condition, would have been a closed casket affair in any case. Still, that was the beginning of it, the first glimmer of the idea, and whether he was being insensitive or not ("ghoulish," was the way Marie-Thérèse put it), he couldn't say. Or no, he could say: he was just being practical.

"What are you offering?" the old woman asked, focusing narrowly on him now as if to be certain he was still there.

"Fair market value, of course. I want the best for you—and for me and my family too. Here," he said, handing her a sheet of paper on which he'd drawn up figures for comparable apartments in the neighborhood. "I was thinking perhaps twenty-two hundred francs a month?"

She barely glanced at the paper. "Twenty-five," she said.

It took him a moment, doing a quick mental calculation, to realize that even if she lived ten more years he'd be getting the place for half of what it was worth, and that didn't factor in appreciation either. "Agreed," he said.

"And you won't interfere?"

"No."

"What if I decide to paint the walls pink?" She laughed, a sudden strangled laugh that tailed off in a fit of coughing. She was a smoker, that much he knew (and had taken into account on the debit side of the ledger). Yes, she could ride a bicycle at ninety, an amazing feat, but she'd also been blackening her lungs for seventy years or more. He watched her dab at her eyes with a tissue, then grin to show her teeth—yes, she still had them. Unless they were dentures.

"And the ceiling chartreuse?" she went on, extending the joke. "And, and—move the bathtub into the salon, right there where you're perched in my armchair looking so pleased with yourself?"

He shook his head. "You'll live here as you always have, no strings attached."

She sat back in her chair, a tight smile compressing her lips. "You're really throwing the dice, aren't you?"

He shrugged. "Twenty-five hundred a month," he repeated. "It's a fair offer."

"You're betting I'll die—and sooner rather than later."

"Not at all. I wish you nothing but health and prosperity. Besides, I'm not a betting man."

"You know what *I'm* doing?" she asked, hunching forward so that he could see the balding patch on the crown of her head and the slim tracery of bones exposed at the collar of her dress, where, apparently, she'd been unable to reach back and fasten the zipper.

"No, what?" he said, grinning, patronizing her, though his stomach sank because he was sure she was going to say she was backing out of the deal, that she'd had a better offer, that she'd been toying with him all along.

"I'm throwing the dice too."

———

After he left that day, she felt as if she'd been lifted up into the clouds. She cleared away the tea things in a burst of energy, then marched around the apartment, going from room to room and back again, twice, three times, four, pumping her arms for the sake of her circulation and letting her eyes roam over the precious familiar things that meant more to her than anything else in the world, and not just the framed photos and paintings, but the ceramic snowman Frédéric had made in grammar school and the mounted butterflies her husband had collected when they first married. She'd been blessed, suddenly and unexpectedly blessed, and if she could have kicked up her heels, she would have—she wasn't going to a nursing home like so many other women she'd known, all of them lost now to death or the straitjacket of old age. No, she was staying right here. For the duration. In celebration, she unwrapped the box of chocolates, poured herself a glass of wine, and sat smoking by the window, looking out on the street and the parade of pedestrians that was the best show on earth, better than any television, better than *La Comédie humaine*—no, it *was La Comédie humaine*. And there were no pages to turn and no commercials either.

She watched a woman in a ridiculous hat go into the shop across the street and immediately come back out again as if she'd forgotten something, then press her face to the glass and wave till the shop girl appeared in the window and reached for an equally ridiculous hat on the mannequin there, and here came a boy on a motor scooter with a girl clinging behind him and the sudden shadow of a black Renault slicing in front of them till the goat's bleat of the boy's horn rose up in protest and the car swerved at the last minute. Almost an accident, and wouldn't that have been terrible? Another boy dead, like her Frédéric, and a girl too. It was everywhere, death, wasn't it? You didn't have to go out and look for it—it was right there, always, lurking just below the surface. And that was part of the *Comédie* too.

But enough morbidity—this was a celebration, wasn't it? Twenty-five hundred francs! Truly, this man had come to her like an angel from heaven—and what's more, he never even hesitated when she countered his offer. Like everyone else, he assumed she was better off than she was, that money meant nothing to her and she could take or leave any offer no matter how extravagant, but in fact, if you excluded the value of the apartment, she had practically nothing, her savings dissipated in paying for Frédéric's education and his clothes and car and his medical degree, and Frédéric lost to her now and forever. She got by, barely, through paring her expenses and the reduced needs that come with having lived so long. It wasn't as if she needed theater tickets anymore. Or concert tickets either. She never went anywhere, except to church on Sundays, and that didn't cost anything more than what she put in the collection box, which was between her and God.

After Frédéric's death she'd reduced the maid's schedule to two days a week rather than the six she'd prefer, but that was going to change now. And if she wanted a prime cut of meat at the butcher's or *l'écrevisse* or even *le homard* at the fish monger's, she would just go ahead and order it and never mind what it cost. *Bless the man*, she thought, *bless him*. Best of all, even beyond the money, was the wager itself. If she'd been lost after Frédéric had been taken from her, now she was found. Now—suddenly, wonderfully—purpose had come back into her life. Gazing out the window on the bustle of the street below, bringing the cigarette to her lips just often enough to keep it glowing, she was as happy as she'd been in weeks, months even, and all at once she was thinking about the time she and her husband had gone to Monte Carlo, the one time in all their life together. She remembered sitting there at the roulette table in a black velvet evening gown, Fernand glowing beside her in his tuxedo, the croupier spinning the wheel and the bright shining silver ball dropping into the slot for her number—twenty-two black, she would never forget it—and in the next moment using his little rake to push all those gay, glittering chips in her direction.

————

He went to visit her at the end of the first month after the contract had gone into effect, feeling generous and expansive, wondering how she was getting on. He'd heard a rumor that she'd been ill, having caught the cold that was going around town that spring, which, of course, would have been all the more severe in someone of her age with her compromised immune system, not to mention smoker's cough. A steady rain had been falling all day and it was a bit of a juggling act for him to balance his umbrella and the paper-wrapped parcels he was bringing her: a bottle of Armagnac, another box of chocolates (two pounds, assorted), and a carton of the Gauloises he'd seen her smoking on his last visit. This time a girl met him at the door—a woman, that is, of fifty or so, with sucked-in cheeks, badly dyed hair, and listless eyes. There was a moment of hesitation until he realized that this must be the maid he'd wondered about and then a further moment during which he reflected on the fact that he was, in a sense, paying her wages. "Is Madame in?" he inquired.

She didn't ask his name or business, but simply nodded and held out her arms for the gifts, which he handed over as if they were a bribe, and then led him into the salon, which as far as he could see remained unchanged, no pink walls or chartreuse ceilings and no bathtub either. He stood there awhile, reveling in the details—the room was perfect, really, just as it was, though Marie-Thérèse, who'd yet to see the place from the inside, would want to do at least some redecorating, because she was a woman and women were never satisfied till they'd put their own stamp on things—and then there was a noise behind him and he turned round to see the maid pushing the old woman down the hall in a wheelchair. *A wheelchair!* He couldn't suppress a rush of joy, though he composed his features in a suitably concerned expression and said, "Madame, how good to see you again," and he was about to go on, about to say, "You're looking well," but that was hardly appropriate under the circumstances.

The old woman was grinning up at him. "It's just a cold," she said, "so don't get your hopes up." He saw that the presents he'd brought were arranged in her lap, still wrapped in tissue paper. "And I wouldn't have caught cold at all, you know, if someone"— and here she glanced up at the maid—"hadn't carried it home to me, isn't that right, Martine? Unless I picked it up dipping my hand in the font last Sunday morning at church. You think that's it, Martine? Do you? You think that's likely?"

The maid had wheeled her up to the coffee table, where she set the gifts down, one by one, and began unwrapping them, beginning with the Armagnac. "Ah," she exclaimed when she'd torn off the paper, "perfect, just what a woman needs when she has a head cold. Fetch us two glasses, will you, Martine?"

He wanted to protest—he didn't drink anymore and didn't miss it either (or maybe he did, just a little)—but it was easier to let the old woman take up the bottle by the neck and pour them each a dose, and when she raised her glass to him, cried *"Bonne santé!"* and drained it in a single swallow, he had no choice but to follow suit. It burned going down, but it clarified things for him. She was in a wheelchair. She had a head cold, which, no doubt, was merely the first stage of an infection that would invariably spread to her lungs, mutate into pneumonia, and kill her sooner rather than later. It wasn't a mercenary thought, just realistic, that was all, and when she poured a second glass, he joined her again, and when she unwrapped the chocolates and set the box on the table before him, he found himself lifting one morsel after another to his lips, and if he'd ever tasted anything so exquisite in his life, he couldn't remember it, especially now that the Armagnac had reawakened his palate. He'd never liked Gauloises—they were too harsh—preferring filtered American cigarettes, but he found himself accepting one anyway, drawing deeply and enjoying the faint crepitation of the nicotine working its way through his bloodstream. He exhaled in the rarefied air of the apartment that was soon to be his. And though he'd only intended to stay a few minutes, he was still there when the church bells tolled the hour.

What did they talk about? Her health, at least at first. Did he realize she'd never been sick more than a day or two in her entire life? He hadn't, and he found the news unsettling, disappointing even. "Oh," she said, "I've had little colds and sniffles like this before—and once, when my husband and I were in Spain, an episode of the trots, but nothing major. Do you know something?"

Flying high on the cognac, the sugar, the nicotine, he just grinned at her.

"Not only am I hardly ever ill, but I make a point of keeping all of my blood inside my body at all times—don't you think that's a good principle to live by?"

And here he found himself straddling a chasm, the flush and healthy on one side, the aged, crabbed, and doomed on the other, and he said, "We can't all be so lucky."

She was silent a moment, just staring into his eyes, a faint grin pressed to her lips. He could hear the maid off in the distance somewhere, a sound of running water, the faint clink of cutlery—the apartment really was magnificent, huge, cavernous, and you could hear a pin drop. It was a defining moment, and Madame C. held on to it. "Precisely," she said finally, took the cigarette from her lips, and let out a little laugh, a giggle, actually, girlish and pure.

Three days later, when the sun was shining in all its power again and everything sparkling as if the world had been created anew, he was hurrying down the street on an errand, a furtive cigarette cupped in one palm—yes, yes, he knew, and he wouldn't lie to his doctor next time he saw him, or maybe he would, but there was really no harm in having a cigarette every once in a while, or a drink either—when a figure picked itself out of the crowd ahead and wheeled toward him on a bicycle, knees slowly pumping, back straight and arms braced, and it wasn't until she'd passed by, so close he could have touched her, that he realized who it was.

———

For the first eighty-odd years of her existence, time had seemed to accelerate, day by day, year by year, as if life were a bicycle race, a kind of Tour de France that was all downhill, even the curves, but in the years after she'd signed the contract, things slowed to a crawl. Each day was a replica of the last, and nothing ever happened beyond the odd squabble with Martine and the visits from Monsieur R. At first he'd come every week or two, his arms laden with gifts—liquor, sweets, cigarettes, foie gras, quiche, even a fondue once, replete with crusts of bread, marbled beef, and *crépitements de porc*—but eventually the visits grew fewer and farther between. Which was a pity really, because she'd come to relish the look of confusion and disappointment on his face when he found her in such good spirits, matching him chocolate for chocolate, drink for drink, and cigarette for cigarette. "Don't think for a minute you're fooling me, Monsieur," she would say to him as they sat at the coffee table laden with delicacies, and Martine bustled back and forth from the salon to the kitchen and sometimes even took a seat with them and dug in herself. "You're a sly one, aren't you?"

He would shrug elaborately, laugh, and throw up his hands as if to say, *Yes, you see through me, but you can't blame a man for trying, can you?*

She smiled back at him. She'd found herself growing fond of him, in the way you'd grow fond of a cat that came up periodically to rub itself against your leg—and then handed you twenty-five hundred francs. Each and every month. He wasn't much to look at really, average in height, weight, and coloring—average, in fact, in every way, from the man-in-the-street look on his face to his side parting and negligible mustache. Nothing like Fernand, who'd been one of the handsomest men of his generation, even into his early seventies, when, in absolutely perfect health and the liveliest of moods, he'd insisted on a second portion of fresh-picked cherries at a *ferme auberge* in Saint-Rémy.

She'd gotten sick herself, but she really didn't care for cherries all that much and had eaten a handful at most. Fernand, though, had been greedy for them, feeding them into his mouth one after another, spitting the pits into his cupped palm and arranging them neatly on the saucer in front of him as if they were jewels, pausing only to lift the coffee cup to his lips or read her the odd tidbit from the morning paper, joking all the while. *Joking*, and the poison in him even then. He spent the next six weeks in agony, his skin drawn and yellow, the whites of his eyes the color of orange peels, and his voice dying in his throat, till everything went dark. It was so hard to understand—it wasn't an enemy's bullet that killed him, wasn't an avalanche on the ski slopes or the failure of an overworked heart or even the slow advance of cancer, but cherries, little round fruits the size of marbles, nature's bounty. That had been wrong, deeply wrong, and she'd questioned God over it through all these years, but He never responded.

When she turned a hundred, people began to take notice. The newspaper printed a story, listing her among the other centenarians in Provence, none of whom she knew, and why would she? She was photographed in her salon, grinning like a gargoyle. Someone from the mayor's office sent her a commendation, and people stopped to congratulate her in the street as if she'd won the lottery, which, in a sense, she supposed she had. She really didn't want to make a fuss over it, but Martine, despite having fractured her wrist in a fall, insisted on throwing a party to commemorate "the milestone" she'd reached.

"I don't want a party," she said.

"Nonsense, of course you do."

"Too much noise," she said. "Too many busybodies." Then a thought came to her and she paused. "Will he be here?"

"Who?"

"Monsieur R."

"Well, I can ask him—would you like that?"

"Yes," she said, gazing down on the street below, "I think I'd like that very much."

He came with his wife, a woman with bitter, shining eyes she'd met twice before but whose name she couldn't for the life of her remember, beyond "Madame," that is. He brought a gift, which she accepted without enthusiasm, his gifts having become increasingly less elaborate as time wore on and his hopes of debilitating her ran up against the insuperable obstacle of her health. In this instance, he came forward like a petitioner to where she was seated on the piano stool preparatory to treating her guests to a meditative rendition of "*Clair de lune*," bent formally to kiss her cheek and hand her a bottle of indifferent wine from a vineyard she'd never heard of. "Congratulations," he said, and though she'd heard him perfectly well, she said, "What?" so that he had to repeat himself, and then she said "What?" again, just to hear him shout it out.

There were thirty or more people gathered in the salon, neighbors mostly, but also the priest from the local church, a pair of nuns she vaguely recognized, a photographer, a newspaperman, and the mayor (an infant with a bald newborn's head who'd come to be photographed with her so that his administration, which hadn't even come into existence till three years ago, could take credit for her longevity). They all looked up at the commotion and then away again, as if embarrassed for Monsieur R., and there wasn't a person in the room who didn't know of the gamble he'd taken.

"Thank you," she said. "You can't imagine how much your good wishes mean to me—more even than the mayor's." And then, to the wife, who was looking positively tragic behind a layer of powder that didn't begin to hide the creases under her eyes, "And don't you fret, Madame. Be patient. All this"—she waved a hand to take in the room, the windows, and the sunstruck vista beyond—"will be yours in just, oh, what shall we say, ten or fifteen years?"

If Marie-Thérèse had never been one to nag, she began to nag now. "Twenty-five hundred francs," she would interject whenever there was a pause in their conversation, no matter the subject or the hour of the day or night, "*twenty-five hundred francs.* Don't you think I could use that money? Look at my winter coat—do you see this coat I'm forced to wear? And what of your daughters, what about them? Don't you imagine they could use something extra?"

Both their daughters were out of the house now, Sophie married and living in Paris with a daughter of her own, and Élise in graduate school, studying art restoration in Florence, for which he footed the bill (tuition, books, clothing, living expenses, as well as a room in a pension on Via dei Calzaiuoli, which he'd never laid eyes on and most likely never would). The apartment seemed spacious without them—and lonely, that too, because he missed them both terribly—and without the irritation of their rock and roll it seemed more spacious still. If there'd been a time when he needed Madame C.'s apartment—needed, rather than hungered for—that time had passed. As Marie-Thérèse reminded him every day.

It would be madness to try to break the contract at this point—he'd already invested some three hundred thousand francs, and the old lady could drop dead at any minute—but he did go to her one afternoon not long after the birthday celebration to see if he might persuade her to lower the monthly payment to the twenty-two hundred he'd initially proposed or perhaps even two thousand. That would certainly be easier on him—he had his own retirement to think about at this point—and it would mollify his wife, at least for the time being.

Madame C. greeted him in the salon, as usual. It was a cold day in early March, rain at the windows and a chill pervading the apartment. She was seated in her favorite armchair beside an electric heater, an afghan spread over her knees and a pair of cats he'd never seen before asleep in her lap. He brought her cigarettes only this time, though the maid had let slip that Madame didn't smoke more than two or three a day and that the last several cartons he'd given her were gathering dust in the kitchen cupboard. No matter. He took the seat across from her and immediately lit up himself, expecting her to follow suit, but she only gazed at him calmly, waiting to hear what he had to say.

He began with the weather—wasn't it dreary and would spring never arrive?—and then, stalling till the right moment presented itself, he commented on the cats. They were new, weren't they?

"Don't you worry, Monsieur," she said, "they do their business in the pan under the bathroom sink. They're very well-behaved and they wouldn't dream of pissing on the walls and stinking up your apartment. Isn't that right?" she cooed, bending her face to them, her ghostly hands gliding over their backs and bellies as if to bless them.

"Oh, I'm not worried at all, I assure you—I like cats, though Marie-Thérèse is allergic to them, but there is one little matter I wanted to take up with you, if you have a moment, that is."

She laughed then. "A moment? I have all the time in the world."

He began in a roundabout way, talking of his daughters, his wife, his own apartment, and his changed circumstances. "And really, the biggest factor is that I need to start putting something away for my retirement," he said, giving her a meaningful look.

"Retirement? But you can't even be sixty yet?"

He said something lame in response, which he couldn't remember when he tried to reconstruct the conversation afterward, something like *It's never too soon to begin*, which only made her laugh.

"You're telling me," she said, leaning forward in the chair. "Thanks to you, I'm all set." She paused, studying him closely. "But you're not here to try to renegotiate, are you?"

"It would mean so much to me," he said. "And my wife too." And then, absurdly, he added, "She needs a new winter coat."

She was silent a moment. "You brought me an inferior bottle of wine on my birthday," she said finally.

"I'm sorry about that. I thought you would like it."

"Going on the cheap is never appealing."

"Yes, but with my daughter in graduate school and some recent reverses we've experienced at the office, I'm just not able"—he grinned, as if to remind her they were on the same team—"to give you all you deserve. Which is why I ask you to reconsider the terms—"

She'd already held up the palm of one hand to forestall him. The cats shifted in her lap, the near one opening its jaws in a yawn that displayed the white needles of its teeth. "We all make bargains in this life," she said, setting the cats down on the carpet beside her. "Sometimes we win," she said, "and sometimes we lose."

———

When she turned a hundred and ten, she was introduced to the term *supercentenarian*, the meaning of which the newspaper helpfully provided—that is, one who is a decade or more older than a mere centenarian, which, if you searched all of France (of Europe, America, the world) were a dime a dozen these days. Her eyes were too far gone to read anymore, but Martine, who'd recently turned seventy herself, put on her glasses and read the article aloud to her. She learned that the chances of reaching that threshold were 1 in 7,000,000, which meant that for her to be alive still, 6,999,999 had died, which was a kind of holocaust in itself. And how did that make her feel? Exhausted. But indomitable too. And she still had possession of her apartment and still received her contractual payment of twenty-five hundred francs a month. One of the cats—Tybalt—had died of old age, and Martine wasn't what she once was, but for her part, Madame C. still sat at the window and watched the life of the streets pulse around her as it always had and always would, and if she couldn't bicycle anymore, well, that was one of the concessions a supercentenarian just had to make to the grand order of things.

Monsieur R. didn't come round much anymore, and when he did, she didn't always recognize him. Her mind was supple still even if her body wasn't (rheumatism, decelerating heartbeat, a persistent ache in the soles of her feet), but he was so changed even Martine couldn't place him at first. He was stooped, he shuffled his feet, his hair was like cotton batting, and for some unfathomable reason he'd grown a beard like *Père Noël*. She had to ask him to come very close so she could make him out (what her eyes gave her now was no better than the image on an old black-and-white television screen caught between stations), and when he did, and when she reached out to feel his ears and his nose and look into his eyes, she would burst into laughter. "It's not between you and me anymore, Monsieur," she would say. "I've got a new wager now."

And he would lift his eyebrows so she could see the exhaustion in his eyes, all part of the routine, the comedy, they were bound up in. "Oh?" he would say. "With whom?"

Martine hovered. A pack of the cigarettes he always brought with him lay on the table before him, and a smoldering butt—his, not hers—rested in the depths of the ashtray. "You can't guess?"

"No, I can't imagine."

"Methuselah, that's who," she would say, and break into a

laugh that was just another variant on the cough that was with her now from morning till night. "I'm going for the record, didn't you know that?"

The record keepers—the earthly record keepers from the Guinness Brewing Company, that is, who were in their own way more authoritative than God, and more precise too—came to her shortly after her hundred and thirteenth birthday to inform her that Florence Knapp, of the state of Pennsylvania in the United States of America, had died at a hundred and fourteen, making her the world's oldest living person. The apartment was full of people. The salon buzzed. There were lights brighter than the sun, cameras that moved and swiveled like enormous insects with electric red eyes, and here was a man as blandly handsome as a grade-A apple, thrusting a microphone at her. "How does it feel?" he asked, and when she didn't respond, asked again. Finally, after a long pause during which the entire TV viewing audience must have taken her for a dotard, she grinned and said, "Like going to the dentist."

———

Marie-Thérèse, who'd been slowed by a degenerative disc in her lower back that made walking painful, came clumping into the kitchen one bleak February morning in the last dwindling decade of the century—and where had the years gone?—to slap the newspaper down on the table before him. "You see this?" she demanded, and he pushed aside his slice of buttered toast (the only thing he was able to keep down lately) to fumble for his reading glasses, which he seemed to have misplaced until he discovered them hanging from the lanyard round his neck. Marie-Thérèse's finger tapped at the photograph dominating the front page. It took him a moment to realize it was a close-up of Madame C., seated before a birthday cake the size of a truck tire, the candles atop it ablaze, as if this, finally, were her funeral pyre, but no such luck.

Whole years had gone by during which he daily envisioned her death—plotted it, even. He dreamed of poisoning her wine, pushing her down the stairs, sitting in her birdshell lap and crushing her like an egg, all eighty-eight pounds of her, but, of course, because he was civilized, he never acted on his fantasies. In truth, he'd lost contact with her over the course of the years, accepting her for what she was—a fact of nature, like the sun that rose in the morning and the moon at night—and doing his best to ignore all mention of her. She'd made him the butt of a joke, and a cruel joke at that. He'd attended her one hundred and tenth birthday, and then the one four years later, after she'd become the world's oldest living human, but Marie-Thérèse had been furious (about that and practically everything else in their lives), and both his daughters had informed him he was making a public spectacle of himself, and so, finally, he'd declared himself *hors de combat.*

Besides which, he had problems of his own, problems that went far deeper than where he was going to lay his head at night—the doctor had found a spot on his lung, and that spot had morphed into cancer. The treatments, radiation and chemotherapy both, had sheared every hair from his body and left him feeling weak and otherworldly. So when Marie-Thérèse thrust the paper at him and he saw the old lady grinning her imperturbable grin under the banner headline—WORLD'S OLDEST LIVING PERSON TURNS 120—he felt nothing. Or practically nothing.

"I wish she would die," Marie-Thérèse hissed.

He wanted to concur, wanted to hiss right back at her, "So do I," but all he could do was laugh—yes, the joke was on him, wasn't it?—until the laugh became a rasping harsh cough that went on and on till his lips were bright with blood.

Two days later, he was dead.

———————

At first she hadn't the faintest idea of what Martine was talking about ("Dead? Who's dead?"), but eventually, after a painstaking disquisition that took her step-by-step through certain key events of the past thirty years, she was given to understand that her benefactor had been laid to rest—or, actually, incinerated at the crematorium, an end result she was determined to avoid for herself. She was going to be buried properly, like a good Catholic. And an angel—her guardian angel who had seen her this far—was going to be there at her side to take her to heaven in a golden chariot. Let the flesh rot, dust to dust, her spirit was going to soar.

"So he's dead, is he?" she said in the general direction of Martine. She was all but blind now, but she could see everything in her mind's eye—Martine, as she'd been five years ago, hunched and crabbed, an old woman herself—and then she saw Monsieur R., as he was all those years before when he'd first come to her to place his bet. Suddenly she was laughing. "He made his bet, now he has to lie in it," she said, and Martine said, "Whatever are you talking about? And what's so funny—he's dead, didn't you hear me?"

Very faintly, as if from a distance, she heard herself say, "But his twenty-five hundred francs a month are still alive, aren't they?"

"I don't—I mean, I hadn't really thought about it."

"*En viager.* I'm still alive, aren't I? Well, aren't I?"

Martine didn't answer. The world had been reduced. But it was there still, solid, tangible, as real as the fur of the cat—whichever cat—that happened to be asleep in her lap, asleep, and purring.

These Are the Circumstances

"We're animals," she said, "never forget that," and he said, "Speak for yourself," and she said, "I'm serious, because we're just not made to sit around all day in an artificial environment staring into two-dimensional screens—which is why everybody's so unhappy and so neurotic and maladjusted and basically *unhealthy*," and he said, "Speak for yourself," and she said, "No, really, I'm serious."

At the time of this discussion they were seated in an artificial environment—a red faux-leather banquette at Pizza Napoli—sipping Chianti and clutching their phones, into which they'd been separately staring just seconds before. Laurel, under the influence of Irina Chertoff, who owned and operated the local health-food emporium, had become fascinated with the concept of *shinrin-yoku* (or nature-bathing, as it roughly translates from the Japanese) and was launching a campaign to convince him to attend a session with her.

He set down his phone and bent forward to draw a series of tight concentric circles on the place mat with one of the crayons the management provided. There was music in the background, barely audible, a robotic thump and wheeze that was designed specifically to be ignored. Everybody else in the place was either texting or emailing. "I don't have anything against the basic concept," he said finally. "We could all use a little more fresh air, that's a no-brainer. It's just that the notion of needing a guide, an *expert*, to take you five hundred yards into a nature preserve so you can sit there for two hours and stare at a leaf is patently ridiculous. Why can't we dispense with the expert—and the fee, whatever she's going to charge—and just do it in the backyard, in the garden?" He tapped the rim of his glass. "With wine as our guide?"

"You're missing the point, Nick. The garden's artificial too. And we never just sit there because your mind is always, 'Oh, the rosemary needs to trimmed back,' or 'Did I remember to water the begonias?' or 'Mulch, is there enough mulch?'"

"You think the Peter and Esperanza Quiñones-Thatcher Preserve is any different?"

"'Forever Wild,' that's their motto."

"Right," he said, leaning across the table to tease a slice from the pizza. "Forever since when?"

"Nineteen ninety-three, which is what the plaque out front says. It's all organic, okay? A tree falls, they let it lie. Humus, think humus."

"And what about poison oak? Snakes? Yellow jackets? Are they part of the experience or do you have to pay extra?"

"That's extra," she said. "But really, what have we got to lose?"

The nature walk—or *bath*, he corrected himself, since a walk has a purpose and this had no purpose or destination or goal other than to show up and remit fifty dollars apiece for the privilege— was on Saturday, from ten in the morning till noon, though of course you were welcome to stay on beyond that, albeit without the continuing services of your guide, who was being paid for two hours only. There were eight in their group, including him and Laurel, and their guide was Irina Chertoff herself, who'd taken on a new employee to free her up for these critical Saturday morning excursions. Irina (forty-five, ropy blond hair, her figure concentrated just above her hips) had them sit in a circle in the dirt at the entrance to the preserve, while she explained the basic concept to them.

"This is not a hike," she said. "And it's not bird-watching or species counting or anything like that—and it's definitely not a way of getting from Point A to Point B. What we're going to do is shut down our conscious minds, as if we were meditating, but with the difference being that I'm encouraging you all to move, even if it's within a five-foot radius, so you can dwell in the moment and see and feel and *appreciate* the ordinary, the natural radiance that's right there before our eyes if we can only just stop long enough to recognize it. When was the last time any of you looked at an insect, really looked at it, whether a fly or an ant or a monarch butterfly? Or a leaf? The veins, the symmetry, the perfect unalloyed beauty of its design?"

No one responded. The other six—two couples and two singles, all in their thirties and forties, like him and Laurel—took the question for what it was, a chastisement that required no answer. He wanted to raise his hand and point out that he'd closely observed a cockroach in the shower stall just that morning, both in its animate state and its even more radiant moribund one, but he restrained himself. He was doing this for Laurel, and the tenor of the proceedings didn't admit for humor or sarcasm or even freethinking. It was an exercise in the obvious, and that meant it had to be a kind of masquerade or else the obvious would send them all back to their own suburban gardens.

"I encourage you to take off your shoes—and as much of your clothing as you feel comfortable with, so you can let your skin, your biggest organ, make contact with the real world and *absorb* the touch of nature." As she said this, Irina was working at the straps of her sandals, which she removed before wriggling on her bottom a moment to shrug out of her shorts and remove her blouse, revealing a black one-piece swimsuit beneath, as if this really were an exercise in bathing. "I'd rather go au naturel," she said with a little laugh, "but the authorities frown on it," and as if to demonstrate the advantages of natural contact, she stretched out on her back and rolled over once, just enough to coat her limbs in dust.

"There, now that feels better," she said, rising to her feet without deigning to pat herself down, which, he supposed, would spoil the effect. "Everyone?" No one moved, though they threw sheepish looks at one another, till finally one woman—a kink of black hair tied up in a kerchief, camo shorts, T-shirt, gold cross conspicuously dangling from a chain round her neck—edged off her hiking boots, slipped out of her socks, and stood, her feet as white as two bars of soap. As if that were the signal, they all removed their shoes and rose uneasily, the dirt soft and compressed between their toes. "Good honest dirt," he said in an aside to Laurel, but she didn't respond: her eyes were fixed on Irina.

"Okay," Irina said, "good. Just a few things—first, I'm going to lead you to a place no more than ten minutes from here, where I'm going to stop leading and you'll all just lead yourselves. Think five years old. Think what it was like for you the first time you went out into the woods, even if it was only a city park or an orchard or what, a Christmas tree farm? All right?" She stood there, arms akimbo, her belly a prominent swell against the grip of the swimsuit. "Now, the second thing—and if we had blood pressure cuffs here with us we could verify it—is that after a few minutes you'll begin to feel the benefits of woodland immersion. Your parasympathetic nerve activity will increase and your anxiety—*and blood pressure*—will decrease correspondingly, because this is all about achieving inner peace. And wonder. Remember wonder?" She let her eyes roam over them. "I want you to feel, smell, see—and listen, really listen to the low-threshold sounds of the little lives lived all around us, the sounds we normally block out with our phones and radios and earbuds. Agreed? Are you with me?"

A few people, Laurel and the woman in the camo shorts among them, said, "Yes," in a soft evangelical hiss, and they all turned their heads to gaze on the well-beaten path that led into the preserve. He'd actually started moving toward it when Irina stopped abruptly. "Oh, I almost forgot," she said. "I want everyone to pick up a stone—any size, any color, it doesn't matter—and then set it back down in place again. Why? Because you are going to imprison your troubles right there in that negative space between the stone and its bed." And now the smile, and the joke: "You're welcome to pick them up on the way out and take your troubles right back home with you—but trust me, you're not going to want to do that. I mean, *really* not."

If he'd felt faintly ridiculous to this point, like one of the children Irina Chertoff wanted them all to revert to, now he felt only shame—was anybody listening to this, anybody watching him to see how he would react? *Put your troubles under a rock?* Was she kidding? He was in the process of ignoring their guide's injunction when Laurel gave him a sharp jab with one elbow, which reminded him of why he was doing this in the first place, and so he bent randomly to a rock and pried it from the earth, thinking to drop it right back in place, but then he stopped himself. There was something there beneath it, an insect as big as his thumb, its bloated abdomen decorated in alternate bands of black and mahogany. "Jesus," he murmured, "what the hell is that?"

Irina Chertoff had come to him the moment he uttered the question, and she stood there beside him, staring down at the thing. "I don't know," she said. "A bug. We don't need names here, common or scientific—we want wonder, that's all, wonder and nothing short of it."

"Jerusalem cricket," a voice said over his shoulder. The voice belonged to Josh, the man who'd come with the woman in the camo shorts. "Don't touch it. Those things'll bite the shit out of you."

Very slowly, very carefully, he put the rock back in place as if he were fitting the lid to a pot. "All right," Irina was saying, "we've seen the first wonder—just think of what's to come." And then she turned, wide-beamed and splay-footed, to lead them into the forest.

If there were snakes, they were taking a holiday. Ditto the yellow jackets. He did, however, recognize a clump of poison oak from the coppery sheen of the leaves, which meant, of course, that he'd already contracted a case of it, and his wonder in nature necessarily took a back seat to thoughts of colloidal oatmeal and calamine lotion. Laurel was oblivious. As soon as they arrived at the stream, she'd waded into the murky water and eased herself down on a rock, parting the current with her feet and studying the redirected flow with as much concentration as if she were sitting over a crossword puzzle with her morning coffee. He suspected her of faking it—for Irina's sake, if not his. There she was, plunked down on a rock in a slow-moving excuse for a stream, staring at nothing, at a cost of twenty-five dollars an hour. Still, he decided to give her space and moved upstream a bit, away from the others, the whole thing increasingly humiliating—if he was going to give himself over to wonder, he was going to do it where nobody could see him.

The stream was shin-deep at most, but he made the best of it, settling down on the bank and idly tossing twigs and bits of leaf into the water as if he really were five years old again, and the activity kept him occupied for all of three minutes. After which, he was bored. Deeply, profoundly bored, and he wished he'd sneaked his cell phone along or at least a book, but Laurel had strictly forbidden it because that would defeat the whole purpose, wouldn't it? He'd agreed, reluctantly, but now as he sat there staring into the dull ranks of the bushes and the trees that overhung them, he couldn't help thinking of the more productive things he could be doing, like balancing his checkbook or changing the oil in the Subaru. Or just taking Laurel to the local bistro and sitting out on the patio to watch the way the filtered sunlight played across her features, while the waiter brought them a mezze platter and tall glasses of iced tea.

Time passed. Nature condensed. And then a voice seemed to be calling to him, a distant voice that took a long while to sort itself out from the trickle of the stream and the gentle rasp of the breeze stirring the leaves overhead. It was Irina Chertoff's voice and she was saying, "Time's up, wanderers, so if we could just gather here by the stream a moment . . ." He looked around him. He seemed to be stretched out on his back in a bed of leaves. In the next moment he propped himself up on his elbows and peered through the scrim of vegetation to see Irina standing there on the bank beside Laurel and the woman in the camo shorts, who both wore rapturous expressions, as if this had been all they'd hoped for and more.

"Of course you're all welcome to stay on as long as you like," Irina called while birds feebly cheeped and the distant sound of traffic reasserted itself. "But I"—a little laugh—"do have a business to run and a whole life to lead, though certainly these two hours of wonder will last me all week and underscore everything I do."

Someone murmured a thank-you. The others were all emerging from wherever they'd found themselves in their unconscious states, while Irina—he was moving toward her now, slashing through the bushes—reminded them that she'd be leading another session next Saturday, same time, same place.

The snake, as it turned out, was in the garden—where else would it be? Whether it had been there all along or taken advantage of their absence to slither down out of the preserve and take up residence where resources were more plentiful—rabbits, mice, gophers—was a matter of conjecture, but the reality was that it was there. And that Laurel's sharp contralto cry discovered it for him. She was in the garden, binding up the tomato plants with strips of cloth to prevent them from breaking under the weight of their bounty, and he was sunk into the chaise longue on the patio with a book and a beer. It was late in the afternoon, the shadows had begun to lengthen, and from somewhere the aroma of outdoor cookery drifted across the yard to them. Earlier, they'd gone from the preserve to the bistro for the lunch he'd envisioned (mezze platter, iced tea), and after washing up in the unisex restroom and checking their phones, they sat down to eat. "I didn't realize wonder could be so exhausting," he said, lifting a wedge of pita and baba ghanoush to his lips, "or that it would build such an appetite either."

"You had leaves stuck to the back of your head when you came out of the bushes," she said, glancing up at him. "In fact"— and here she reached across the table to pluck something from his hair, which turned out to be a fragment of dried leaf—"you still have leaves in your hair."

He shrugged. "Twenty-five dollars an hour to experience the wonder of sleep in a natural setting, mosquitoes, ticks, poison oak, and all. And leaf mold."

Her voice was sharp-edged. "Well, I, for one, enjoyed it. And I'd like to go back and do it again."

He set down the pita, took a moment to pat his lips with the crisp white linen napkin. He studied her a moment to see if she was joking—she wasn't—and abruptly changed the subject.

And now, back at home, this new wonder had appeared—not in a state of nature, not on the banks of a muddy stream, but right there beneath the gently nodding leaves of the tomato plants in their dedicated suburban garden. Laurel had sung out, "Nick, oh my god, *Nick!*" and he vaulted out of the chaise longue to charge across the lawn and down the slight declivity to the vegetable garden, not knowing what to expect till he saw it coiled there beneath a cluster of ripening heirlooms. It blended in with the dirt, and then it didn't, vivid suddenly and glittering, thick as his arm and perfectly motionless. Laurel, her face bleached of color, stood well back from it, saying, "Don't hurt it, whatever you do, because it has every right—"

That was when it began to buzz like an overworked alarm clock and it became apparent just what sort of snake this was. He could feel his heart pounding in his chest. The thing was out of place here, clearly out of place, and it was a danger in the moment and into the future too—it could bite them, poison them, every time they went out to pick a tomato or cucumber. Worse, it could breed, establish a nest, a turf, a territory. Without answering her—and without thinking, that too—he ran to the garden shed, snatched up the shovel, and raced back to confront the thing.

There it was, still coiled, its eyes like hot embers and the bright fork of its tongue flicking in and out to decode the information on the air. His first impulse was to prod it with the blade, as if that would encourage it to slither back across the yard, out onto the sidewalk, and up the three blocks to the preserve, where it belonged. That didn't happen. What did happen was that it whipped forward to strike the blade with its white hooklike fangs and instantly recoil itself to strike again, which was when instinct took over and he brought the blade down just below the thing's head with all the strength in him. The cut was clean. The decapitated body suddenly jumped and writhed and twisted on itself, knocking tomatoes to the ground in a thumping flurry, till after a moment it lay still. And the head? There it was, the locus of all this violence, lying quietly in the dirt, as inanimate as the stone he'd trapped his troubles beneath.

"You killed it," Laurel said. "Did you have to kill it?"

It took him a moment to answer, his heart paradiddling in his chest. He felt tight all over, the shovel still clenched in one hand. The thing had meant nobody any good, that was for sure. And now it was dead, now the crisis was over and they could bury it or toss it in the trash and mold its brief appearance into a lively tale for their friends and intimates—and for Irina Chertoff, whose view of the benignity of nature could use a little revising. "Of course I killed it," he said, his voice tight in his throat. "What did you expect me to do—wrap it around my neck? Or what, bring it in and drape it across your pillow?"

He watched her eyes roam from the long, intricately patterned strip of muscle and flesh to the severed head beneath the tomato plant. "It's so, I don't know, *beautiful*—isn't it?" she said.

He was going to say that *beautiful* was the last adjective he'd apply to the thing, but when he looked at it, really looked at it in the way Irina Chertoff looked at the bugs and the trees and all the rest, he had to admit there was something in what she was saying. The scales gleamed in the low slant of sunlight, imbricate and sharply defined, the eyes shone like glass buttons, and the fangs were a stark, unblemished white. It was a trophy, that was what it was. He'd put it in a jar of formalin, along with the rattles, and display it on the mantelpiece as an illustration of the story that was just then gelling in his head. Yes. Sure. And then he reached down to pick it up.

At the hospital, they told Laurel they were going to have to transport him by helicopter to the larger regional hospital, where he could be treated with antivenin obtained from the blood of horses injected with the very venom he'd just been injected with himself. He'd never been in a helicopter before, but then he'd never been bitten by a rattlesnake either, so these were unique experiences, even if he didn't recall much of them. What he remembered, though it was necessarily hazy and reconstructed from what Laurel later told him, was that the moment he touched the snake's head it had somehow, in a death reflex, clamped down on his right hand, its fangs penetrating the middle and ring fingers and clinging there for a full ten seconds before he was able to prise it off. In that time it had managed to empty out its glands, injecting him with a dose far more potent than a rattlesnake would have delivered under normal circumstances, an all-or-nothing revenge dose meant to ensure mutual destruction.

In the car on the way to the emergency room, Laurel on the

line with the 911 dispatcher and speeding in a blind panic of blaring horns and screeching tires, he began having seizures, his entire body jerking spasmodically and then freezing up so that he couldn't see or hear or feel anything but the burning in his hand, which was already swollen to three times its normal size and erupting in ugly black blisters. Inside him, the hemotoxic venom was destroying blood cells and fomenting internal bleeding, but he didn't know that, or not yet anyway. He wasn't aware of much of what was happening, aside from the fact that the windshield of the car exploded with sun till it was like a supernova, and the sirens began tangling themselves around his brain like tentacles, and then he was out.

He awoke four and a half days later in a bright antiseptic room with no memory of snakes, nature baths, or helicopter rotors, and the first thing he said to Laurel when he saw her there sitting at his bedside in a stiff plastic chair and wearing a face molded of dough was, "Where am I?"

The doctors told him he was lucky, but of course luck is relative. None of them (there was a revolving team of them, all so alike he couldn't tell them apart) had lost a finger or any other body part as far as he could see, but they all kept insisting on his luck as if he'd won the lottery. He hadn't won the lottery—he'd lost it. His middle finger, the one he was used to employing in an instructional way when somebody ran a red light or went out of turn at a four-way stop, had been amputated because the tissue was irreparably damaged and gangrene had set in, despite the doctors' best efforts to combat it. In fact, he'd very nearly lost his life, suffering from septic shock and bleeding internally despite twenty-six doses of antivenin, and the doctors had had to put him in a medically induced coma to stabilize him.

What came next was a period of adjustment. He had to re-learn how to use his right hand, tasks as basic as turning a door-knob, tying his shoes, or using a fork and knife presenting their own difficulties, at least at first. They were very understand-ing at work, giving him a full month off, with pay, but when he did get back and sat down for the first time at his computer, it hit him pretty hard. The fact was that he was maimed, and when his hand wasn't glancing awkwardly across the keyboard or locked around the steering wheel of the car—when it wasn't in use—he kept it buried in his pocket. At home, the garden withered, the tomatoes blackening and dropping to the ground where something—raccoons?—came to gorge on them at night. From the chaise longue, where he spent most of his time these days, he could glance up and watch the rot creep across the garden in daily procession, the flowers wilting, cucumber vines browning and drying out till they were like sticks, melons and zucchini gone to pulp, peppers shriveled. Weeds took over. The lawn reverted. He wasn't about to go down there, that was for sure, and Laurel, despite her enthusiasms, was in no hurry her-self.

One afternoon she came home from work, poured them each a glass of wine, and crossed the patio to him with as bright a smile as she could manage, given the circumstances. "Listen," she said, sinking into the chair beside him and handing him his wine (which he took with his left hand, the one he had confi-dence in), "why don't we call the exterminator?"

He gave her a puzzled look. "What are you talking about—termites?"

"No, no," she said, impatiently waving her glass. "They exter-minate whatever, you know, squirrels, gophers—you remember the time that gopher got into the garden?"

He nodded, not quite catching on. Gophers? He welcomed

them—they were part of nature's bath, weren't they? And they didn't have fangs.

"Because this is ridiculous. It's like we can't use half the property anymore. I mean, isn't it time we moved on with our lives?"

As it turned out, the local exterminator employed a snake man, whose job it was to inspect and snake-proof properties, and two days later he was ringing the doorbell at eight a.m., just after Laurel had left for work. Nick had taken a personal day to be there to greet him—by his way of thinking, this was as personal as it got. "I'm Raymond," the man said, when Nick pulled open the door, "from Cal's Pest Control? I'm Cal's brother." He was in his forties and affected a military style, close-cropped hair, khakis, black lace-up boots. He grinned. "The better-looking brother, that is."

Nick didn't offer his hand. He just thanked him for coming and led him through the house, across the patio and—though it cost him an effort—into the high grass that had overtaken the yard and the garden too.

Raymond let out a low whistle. "Well, there's your problem right there—they love this high grass. It's cover for them. And all this vegetable garden here? That's like a rodent supermarket—and they do love rodents, all kinds of snakes, from your king snake to your racers to the diamondbacks. You've got to clean this up."

"I know. I got bitten." He had an impulse to show him the evidence of it, the shiny annealed flesh over the stub of the knuckle, the absence there, but he didn't, he couldn't.

"Yeah?" Raymond raised his eyebrows. "Rattler?"

Nick could only nod. He had to bite his lip. Tears of self-pity started up in his eyes, another kind of humiliation, and he roughly wiped them away.

"Shit." Raymond was studying him carefully. "I been bit nine times myself, hazard of the trade, you know? The trick is not to piss them off—they want to conserve that venom just as much as you want them to. But I'll tell you, you build up a resistance after a while."

This information landed with a thud—to build up resistance, he'd have to be bitten again. And again. "Yeah, well, I'm really hoping I never get the chance to find out. But can I ask you something? I mean, while you're here?" He felt as if his voice were going to crack, everything boiling up in him now, the whole sequence of events, the shovel, the thrashing whip of the body, the naked head, the fangs. "Why don't they stay up in the preserve—isn't that where they're supposed to be?"

Raymond gave him a wide, pitying smile and very slowly shook his head. He gestured to the yard as if presenting it in evidence, the garden, the fruit trees, the birdbath and feeder, the seed heads of the grass swaying in the breeze that just then came up. "They're here for the same reason you are."

The days came and went. High summer slipped gradually toward fall. He and Laurel contracted with Cal's Pest Control to install a three-foot-high electrically charged fence around the entire property, they pruned the fruit trees, let the garden go fallow, and hired a man to come in twice a week and cut the lawn till it had the character of a putting green and you could see from one end of the yard to the other at a glance. In the beginning, people at work had been morbidly curious—rumors went around, of course they did—but all that faded away in time and the new circumstances were the only circumstances now, but for the fact that he still couldn't bring himself to shake hands with anyone, even his boss, and when he was in public he kept his hand firmly entrenched in his pocket.

They were at Napoli's one night, sharing a pizza margherita and a bottle of Chianti, when Irina Chertoff came in with a man so pale and reduced he looked as if he'd barely been out of doors, let alone prancing through the forest. Nick dropped his gaze, but she'd already made eye contact, and in the next moment she was standing over their table, introducing the man as her husband and making small talk. The husband—Sergei—didn't have much to say, but he nodded and smiled as Irina went on about her sessions and how popular they'd become. Then she paused and looked straight at Nick. "I haven't seen you two out there in a while—you do know I'm offering a special five-session discount to my regulars, don't you? And the Lattimers, remember the Lattimers? They were with you that first time, Josh and Julie? Well, they've really—"

"Nature's all around us," he said, cutting her off. "We're bathing in it now."

She made a face. "All this artificiality, all this noise—there's nothing to embrace."

"You'd be surprised," he said, and he took his right hand from his pocket and laid it flat on the table, right beside the plate that held his half-eaten slice of pizza. "In fact, did you hear about that woman in Yorba Linda, I think it was?"

Irina looked down at his hand and then back into his eyes. Laurel said, "Nick," but he ignored her.

"She was in her own living room, vacuuming the rug, when she felt the slightest little pinprick on her ankle, and by the time she looked, whatever it was that had bitten her was gone. You know what it was?"

"Nick," Laurel said.

"A brown recluse spider. They have them in the preserve, I'm sure, just like that bug I found under the rock. But this woman. Two days after that she went into a coma, and when she woke up *five months later* she was minus all four limbs and—here's the kicker—her nose too, just for good measure. And you know what she said?"

Laurel's hand was on his arm now, but he shrugged it off and held up his own hand, his right hand, and peered through the gap his missing finger had left as if he were sighting down the barrel of a rifle. "She said, 'I was lucky.' Can you believe that? *Lucky.*" He was laughing now, laughing hard, and he couldn't help himself, he had to repeat it, just to hear it one more time.

The Thirteenth Day

The ship was monumental, like Atlantis risen from the depths, its own island, its own nation, a miracle of every kind of human labor and ingenuity. Even the sea was impressed. The waters calmed to make way for it, and when it slashed across the horizon, the pelagic creatures appeared in their slippery legions to disport themselves in its wake. Dolphins rocketed alongside. Sea lions barked. Whales bobbed up like corks to salute its monumentality, then dove deep to escape the crushing impact of its bow. In port—and it was in port now, indefinitely—its vast hull attracted the attentions of mollusks and crustaceans and its decks the loose-boweled gulls whose excreta would have buried them knee-deep but for the unceasing attentions of the ship's crew. Can you say Yokohama? I can. *Yokohama*. There, see?

When the passengers boarded the *Beryl Empress* in Yokohama Harbor, none of them—none of *us*—expected to be there longer than it would take for everyone to settle into their staterooms and the massive engines to crank the screws and compel the shore to fall away behind the taffrails of its fourteen decks. The itinerary, lavishly laid out in the cruise line's brochure, had us at sea for a fortnight, with ports of call at Hong Kong, Taiwan, Phu My, and Sihanoukville, among others, locales where the 2,666 of us could absorb Asia through our five senses and browse the wares of the local artisans and trinket purveyors. Unfortunately, that wasn't to be. And what resulted was hard on us, hard on me and Amarita, my ageless and serene bride of forty years, but so much harder for the newlyweds in the cabin across from ours, Scott and Bunny, who, despite their impressive size and the solidity of their limbs, weren't much more than children in our eyes. As if their youth wasn't enough of a liability, they also happened to be Americans, which further complicated things. Americans, in my experience, are unused to privation of any kind, expecting this great spinning globe we communally ride to deliver up exactly what they want, when they want. Poor Scott. Poor Bunny. Poor me.

The ship departed right on schedule, at 3:00 p.m. on a day of high ceilings and sea-glitter, banners flying, the trumpets, saxophones, and electrified guitars of one shipboard band or another crying out joyously, and the ship's horn delivering up a shattering salvo that resonated in every passenger's solar plexus, whether he or she was confined to an inner cabin or an outer, like ours, in which you actually had room to breathe and savor the fluidity of the air and the stately creep of the water below. It was a fine celebratory moment, and Amarita and I enjoyed it with a bottle of complimentary champagne from the high-flown perch of our private balcony, which measured one hundred and seventy-five square feet and adjoined our two-hundred-square-foot cabin, numbers which would become increasingly significant as events unfolded. In all, that is, we enjoyed three hundred and seventy-five square feet of space, room in which to drift in our complimentary fleece-lined slippers from the sofa to the vanity to the bed, to stretch out, indulge ourselves, and defeat even the slightest fleeting thought of claustrophobia. Snug, that was what it was, and snugness was what the cruise line was selling, part of the charm of being at sea in your own individual stateroom. Battening down—isn't that the term?

Clicking her glass to mine, Amarita, her lips creased with the softest of smiles, asked, "Aren't you glad we came?"

Well, I was—in that moment anyway. The cruise had been her idea, her fixation, actually. I was considerably less inclined than she to abandon the comforts of our home in the Recoleta quarter of Buenos Aires, where my work absorbed me, every comfort was at our fingertips, and we did not have to share space— precious living space—with hordes of strangers in costumes I can only call *bizarre,* from the young *güera* who wore two bikinis, one conventionally, the other facing backward, to the man of my own age who slathered himself with coconut-reeking grease and sang continuously into his mobile in a fluid baritone, as if he were trying out for a role in *Pirates of Penzance.*

In any case, the great ship rolled magnificently on over the waves until the shore receded from sight and the clamoring gulls along with it, and Amarita and I clicked glasses again while I wished her a felicitous fortieth wedding anniversary, even as the ship's captain was receiving the command over the radio to return to port. And why? Because it had been discovered that one of the passengers—a *Chino* from Wuhan who'd just been one more anonymous face among our 2,666—had come down with a fever.

A fever, can you imagine! At first, when the news came to us that night at dinner, where Amarita and I were seated at our assigned table in the 5-Star Red Beryl Celebrity Dining Saloon with twelve other guests, including Scott and Bunny, none of us could believe it. Turning a boat around for a fever? A few hours later, however, a new term entered my vocabulary, an acronym that was as bland as any other until it wasn't. Can you say COVID-19? I can. And I've said it all too many times since that first day, though, like you, I presume, I'd never before even heard of it, let alone spoken it aloud. Forgive me, but even now, even after all that's transpired (or, as Scott and Bunny would say, "gone down"), I can't help thinking that the term sounds more like some version of linoleum tiling you might install in the kitchen than a contagious disease that could burn through the world of humanity and force a ship as unconquerable as the *Beryl Empress* to become a floating prison.

In a ship as vast as this, it was impossible to perceive any maneuver the captain may have made, even, I imagine, in the highest of seas, in a typhoon or hurricane or anything else the sea might get itself up to, and so none of us had the slightest intimation that he had turned us around until the second dessert course was served and the waiters began handing out printed notices as if they were petit fours. To that point, we'd had a grand gay time, everyone in high spirits and the food beyond superb (I had the foie gras powdered with pistachios and the grilled suckling lamb, Amarita the venison shoulder, after a starter of lacquered Jerusalem artichokes in a black truffle sauce). We'd already met Scott and Bunny, who, as I've mentioned, occupied the cabin across from ours, and over dinner we had a chance to get acquainted with the others, all of them charming, including a podiatrist and his wife from Singapore, who were the only couple besides me and Amarita in formal dress. He was a wit, this podiatrist, diverting us with a seemingly endless array of anecdotes about the alignment of great toes, the aesthetics of bunions, and the treatment of onychomycosis, and the fact that he was Chinese had no more bearing on the way Amarita and I viewed him than if he was a fellow Argentine.

At any rate, we were all captivated not only by the podiatrist's stories but by the amatory antics of the newlyweds, who couldn't seem to keep their hands off each other, constantly snuggling and smooching and feeding morsels of one delicacy or another into each other's mouth, until the gentleman across from me, Konrad Pohnert, of Düsseldorf, snatched up the notice the waiters had just passed round and cried out, "What's this?" and we all stared at him.

"What do you mean?" I stammered, and now I too had the notice in hand, and the martialed lines of harsh black letters were infesting my brain, the harshest of them composing the supercharged word, QUARANTINE, and then everything, as the Americans say, fell to shit.

We retraced our route in darkness, the suspense sutured in place by threads of rumor—there'd been a second case, a third, an albatross had landed on the bridge and been promptly dispatched with a single gunshot, the lobsters in the ship's twenty-seven industrial-size coolers had taken on an odd greenish glow. It wasn't panic. At least not on my part. Panic was undignified, and throughout my life I'd always abjured it in times of stress, and so it was now. Amarita and I calmly finished our coffee and the chef's selection of cheeses from the seven continents (which was an odd designation, considering that presumably there was no cheese in Antarctica), then retired to our cabin and watched the stars from our private balcony as they subtly shifted their alignment with the progress of the evening. When the anchor dropped right back where we'd started in Yokohama Harbor, it was like a great rending of the heartstrings of the ship itself, defeated before it had a chance to demonstrate its mastery of the high seas. There was a volcanic groaning that reverberated through every square inch of the ship, then silence. Sea and sky were a uniform black behind us, while the shore exploded with the myriad lights that fanned out over the face of the land to Tokyo, a city of 38 million souls, not a single one of them infected. What's more, as we'd soon come to understand, the Japanese government intended to keep it that way, even if it meant sacrificing every one of us aboard.

But I'm getting ahead of myself. At the table that evening, after the waiters had distributed the printed notices, a lively discussion started up among the dinner guests. The first thing we all did was try to break down this term *quarantine* and make it conform to our hopes and expectations, the podiatrist assailing the captain's judgment while another man, whose name I never did catch, assured us that it was all a mistake, a case of the flu and nothing more. Herr Pohnert, who, as it turned out, was a medical doctor, asserted that the quarantine would necessarily be absolute and that most likely it would have to extend over a period of fourteen days, typical for a viral infection of the type this was most likely to be. "At the end of fourteen days, if no one else on the ship shows signs of infection, then the incubation period for the virus will have expired and it will be safe to assume that it is no longer active and transmissible."

"Fourteen days!" Bunny wailed. (She was a kind of Amazon, actually, a broad-shouldered, heavy-breasted blonde whose hands were bigger than mine and must have stood six feet tall in her heels.) "Stuck here, you mean? Jesus, what are we going to *do for fourteen days*?"

Here, her husband, Scott, the newlywed, lifted his eyebrows facetiously and said, "Oh, I don't know, I think we'll find something, don't you?" and we all laughed, though, admittedly, it was nervous laughter. We were all adrift at this juncture, and each of us was privately trying to answer Bunny's question for himself—would we be bored to the point of stultification? Would the captain confine us to quarters or would we have the ship (and its attractions) to enjoy as we saw fit? Would the ship's eighteen restaurants, bistros, sushi bars, hot dog stands, and coffee dispensaries remain open? And what of the nightclub, the casino, the floor shows and internationally celebrated crooners we'd come to hear? Of the disease itself as yet we knew little, except that it was highly infectious and that it disproportionately endangered the elderly. I was sixty-eight years old, Amarita sixty-two. Did that, I wondered, qualify us as elderly? Or were we merely, as the Americans would label us, senior citizens?

I felt the first thin knife blade of fear insert itself then, even as Bunny, in a uvular squeak, demanded of the table at large, "Are they going to refund our money, then?" and, without waiting for an answer, "What about helicopters? Can't they send helicopters out from the, I don't know, embassy or something?"

Herr Pohnert was slowly shaking his head. "That would defeat the purpose. A quarantine must be airtight unless you would risk the whole world for your own individual comfort."

Scott made a fist and thumped the table. "What are you saying? Are you saying my wife isn't, what, *patriotic*?" Another thump. "You know, I don't like your tone, dude, not one bit—"

It was a childish thing to say and who knows what it might have led to—tempers already fraying, apprehension in the air—if it weren't for the reappearance of the waiters, these men and women who till this moment had been the very avatars of servility and good nature, treating each and everyone aboard as if he were a visitant from the heavens who'd sat at the foot of Jesus of Nazareth Himself. Now it was different. They were wearing surgical masks and nitrile gloves, as if they'd come to lay us out on the operating table and pick through our organs like the diviners of old.

I woke in the morning with a scratchy throat, but I didn't think anything of it—it was a condition that sometimes afflicted me after a late night and too much to drink, even when I wasn't in a strange place, amid strangers. The boat was immobile beneath me, down through all its multiple decks to the cowed sea that had no choice but to support it, and a trio of gulls was perched on the rail of our private balcony, delighted to see us back again. Since Amarita was still asleep and I didn't want to disturb her (no rush: we could order breakfast anytime we liked in a floating empire such as this, even at midnight), I decided to take a stroll around the deck.

The first thing I observed, up and down the passageway, were the notices taped to the doors of the cabins, notices that would also appear on our individual flat-screen TVs in electronic array. "NO CAUSE FOR ALARM," the notices read. "AS A PRECAUTION, HOWEVER, WE WILL REMAIN IN PORT UNTIL FURTHER ADVISED. NO ONE, PASSENGERS OR CREW, WILL BE PERMITTED INGRESS OR EGRESS DURING THIS PERIOD, WHICH WE EXPECT WILL BE BRIEF." And, in smaller print: "Your comfort and safety are our sole concern."

No one else was in the passageway, and when I went out on deck there were few people about, though admittedly it was early yet and rather brisk, even for February. The man who sang into his phone was there, huddled in a bathrobe and gazing out over the rail at the serried buildings of the shore, the phone clutched in one hand, a surgical mask dangling from its cord in the other. When he saw me approaching, he swung round and demanded, "Can you believe this shit?"

All I could see in that moment was the mask, which focused my attention to an alarming degree. "What shit?" I asked, though I already had a pretty good idea.

He shook the mask as if it were some living thing he'd snatched out of the air and throttled. "If they think I'm going to wear this goddamned thing day and night and sit here paying"—he named a figure considerably below what we had paid—"a day to look at some floating junkyard, well then, then—"

"Then what?" I asked, wondering where he'd gotten the mask and why he wasn't wearing it—and, more to the point, why I wasn't wearing it, or rather, one just like it.

"Fuck," he said, using the term as a kind of placeholder. "I'll fucking jump overboard."

We both peered over the rail. The pier, which was the size of three or four city blocks in itself, stretched out below us in dwindling perspective. "It's a long way down," I observed, and was about to turn round and continue my stroll when a scrum of crewmembers dressed in white hazmat suits rushed up to us. "Please, sir," the man nearest me cried out in a harried voice, handing me a mask and a pair of gloves still sealed in their plastic packaging. "You must put these on and wear them at all times. And while you're free to move about the ship, the captain advises you to stay confined until such time as we get a better read on the situation."

At the same time, another crewmember was admonishing the cell-phone man to put his mask back on, but the cell-phone man wasn't having it. "Bullshit," he shouted. "You think I'm afraid of germs? You want germs, I'll give you germs!" He made a series of kissing noises, then reared back and flung the mask out over the rail, where the currents of the air carried it, tumbling end over end, into the vast gulf below.

I watched a pair of gulls briefly squabble over it before realizing it was of no use to them and lifting themselves back into the air even as two of the crewmembers, chanting a litany of apologies, hoisted the cell-phone man under his arms and frog-marched him down the deck at the very moment a nautical term I must have come across in a book or heard spoken in some film came to me. Can you say brig? I can.

Thus began our Calvary. There was to be no more dining in the 5-Star Red Beryl Celebrity Dining Saloon, no more strolls round the deck, no shuffleboard, no blackjack, no musical theater, no films showcased in the 5-Star Red Beryl Celebrity Theater of the Seas. By noon, we were no longer merely being advised to remain in our quarters, but ordered to do so.

Amarita was unfazed. On returning from my truncated stroll that morning, I found her sitting up in bed watching images of our very ship on the flat-screen TV, while the news crawl below bristled with arcane Japanese characters. "Remember SARS, MERS, Y2K?" she asked without even glancing up at me. "It's the same sort of hysteria, the hounds of the press playing it up in order to sell deodorant and self-cleaning toilet cartridges. Or, in this case, Handi Wipes and hand sanitizers."

"Yes," I said, as gently as I could, "but we weren't locked in a cabin on a ship full of strangers when all that"—and here I used the Americanism—"went down. But why are you watching it in Japanese?"

I bent for the remote and clicked on the channel we'd watched the night before after climbing into bed in weary resignation. Immediately the same footage of our ship dominated the screen, but with the crawl in Spanish. *El Barco de la infección*, the banner read, even as the camera played over the immensity of the vacant decks and the cold sunless sky above. Soon, statistics appeared enumerating the cases confirmed in China, the red-hot glowing epicenter of the outbreak, followed by a Mercator projection of the world indicating the spread of the virus to Europe and the Mideast. And then, abruptly, there was our ship again, a white wall rearing against the sky, and a newsman in an inset was reporting that the initial case on the *Beryl Empress* had succumbed to the disease, which was chilling enough to hear, but nothing like what he revealed next—there were already sixty-seven confirmed cases aboard and many more expected because of the close cohabitation characteristic of cruise ships. "It's one big floating petri dish," he averred, reading from a Teleprompter, "and the chances of contagion are magnified by—"

Suddenly I was staring into the broad blue-eyed face of Doris Day, film star of my youth. She was in a white strapless gown that might have been stapled to her breasts, singing some banal tuneless song on a set that was made to look like the saloon of a cruise ship. I swung round on Amarita, who'd snatched up the remote the instant I'd set it down. "What are you doing?" I demanded, gesturing helplessly at the screen as Doris Day threw up her arms and kicked out her heels.

"I don't want to hear it," Amarita said.

I have to admit I was tempted in that moment to use an expletive, but I restrained myself. "What are you saying—*Que sera, sera?*"

"Yes, and I believe Doris Day sang that one too, didn't she?"

"Of course she did, why wouldn't she? But she's dead and we're not, at least not yet." Our cabin, made all the smaller with the sliding door to the deck shut against the chill, began to feel like a coffin. "Our lives could be at stake," I said, "and you're watching a dead actress in a third-rate film?"

Amarita shrugged, even as a knock came at the door and we both jumped.

It was the steward, bringing us breakfast, though we hadn't ordered it. He was dressed in what seemed to have become the official uniform of the crew—a hazmat suit—and he solemnly handed me two paper bags that contained not the selection of fresh fruit, gravlax, chilled shrimp, eggs Benedict, and crisply fried *Peregrino Ibérico de bellota* bacon that comprised just the smallest fraction of the choices at the 5-Star Red Beryl Celebrity Breakfast Saloon buffet, but rather two Styrofoam boxes of scrambled eggs and two Styrofoam cups of coffee sealed with plastic lids.

The ensuing days were difficult, each one climbing grimly out of the grave of the one we'd laid to rest the night before. We watched the full catalog of films available gratis to 5-Star passengers, then started in on them again. Cheese sandwiches were delivered each day at noon, burgers and BLTs in the evenings. I ordered two bottles of pisco from room service (within forty-eight hours they'd run out of scotch, vodka, gin, brandy, tequila, and Jägermeister) and Amarita made us pisco sours to enliven (or perhaps deaden) our mornings, afternoons, and evenings. I read through the complete works of Filéncio Salmón on my Kindle, though science fiction isn't really my cup of tea (after a point, the planet Pentagord seemed more tangible to me than our cabin, which had become increasingly unreal, as if it weren't a stateroom on the 5-Star *Beryl Empress* at all, but a coat closet in an anteroom of hell). We made love three times that week, which, at our age, was something of a feat, testimony not so much to the fact that love never dies, but that boredom is a potent aphro-disiac. Who would have guessed? Of course, as Amarita pointed out, "We have to do something, don't we?"

It was on the fifth day when we did have our first bit of good news. Just after breakfast, the ship's doctor (Schumann, another German) stopped by to take our temperature and collect sam-ples of our sputum to test for exposure to the virus. Dr. Pohnert, though he was a passenger, had volunteered to help with the rather daunting task of testing each of the crewmembers and the 2,666 passengers (excuse me: 2,665, after the unfortunate passing of patient zero), and he was there too, accompanying Schumann on his rounds. Neither man was dressed in a hazmat suit, which made them seem less intimidating, but both, of course, wore pro-phylactic gloves and face masks. Dr. Schumann asked how we were feeling, and though I'd had that scratchy throat the first day, it seemed to have gone away, and so I chimed in with Amarita to say, "Fine."

I spat in a vial. Dr. Schumann plied the nasopharyngeal and oropharyngeal swabs, secured the samples and was just turning to go when Amarita took hold of his arm and asked, in an un-certain voice, "Is it spreading?" This, of course, was our biggest worry, aside from developing the infection ourselves, because if it continued spreading, there was the very real possibility that we could find ourselves confined to our 5-Star cabins eternally, or at least until everyone aboard was either cleared or dead.

"No new cases since the second day," Dr. Schumann informed us. "Don't you worry—we're closely monitoring all the passen-gers who did test positive and we're confident, or at least fairly confident, that at the end of the two-week incubation period, the crisis will have passed and we'll all be allowed to disembark. Does that sound good?"

In answer, Amarita broke into a grin and clapped her hands

like a schoolgirl, but I was less sanguine. "Is that counting from the second day—or today?" I asked.

Dr. Schumann exchanged a look with Dr. Pohnert, as if hesitating, but then he nodded decisively and said, "From the second day."

I pulled out my phone and consulted the calendar. "So that means, since we boarded on the first of the month, our fourteen days, counting from the second, will be up on the sixteenth?"

"Yes, that is correct," Dr. Schumann said, his lips squirming beneath the fabric of his mask like larvae trapped in a gauze net.

"Unless," Dr. Pohnert put in, "another case should arise, in which eventuality we would have to reset the clock."

"But that's not going to happen," I said. "Is it?"

As that moment we were all distracted by a shriek from across the passageway, and without thinking, I pulled open the door. Bunny was standing at the open doorway of her own cabin, her back to us, shoulders heaving. "I hate you!" she screamed, even as we saw Scott's face recede into the depths of the room, which was dark and cramped, and at 168 square feet and lacking a private balcony, wasn't much bigger than the average restroom ashore. We watched as Bunny wrestled with something in her left hand, which turned out to be her diamond wedding ring. She had her hair drawn back in a ponytail and was dressed in gym shorts and a halter top that left her shoulders bare, so that we could see the muscles working there as she twisted off the ring, reared back, and flung it at her husband.

The recoil of the motion had carried her out into the passageway, sans mask or gloves, and both doctors, alarmed, marshaled themselves to restrain her, but she shook them off, her eyes exophthalmic, her face twisted in fury. "No," she cried, "no, get away from me!" For a moment, there was a standoff, Bunny, even in her bare feet, taller than either of the men and her whole body one tense cord of muscle. "If you think I'm going to stay in this *cage* for one second more with this, this *shitbird* that I can't believe I actually went out and married—"

It was an epic breakdown, shameful and sorrowful, and when Scott suddenly reappeared and reached out to take hold of her arm, she shrieked, "I want a divorce!" and bolted down the passageway, both doctors in pursuit.

As if it weren't trial enough to be confined to our cabins and denied use of the ship's cornucopian amenities, the weather turned bitter on us as well. After the morning of Bunny's breakdown, it began to rain, a steady dispiriting downpour that erased our views of the harbor and rendered our 5-Star private balcony all but unusable. We tried a game of pinochle to pass the time, but found we couldn't concentrate. I clicked on one of the films we'd already seen twice—a prison picture from the 1940s featuring a brutal warden, a riot, and an elaborate escape plan thwarted by an informer—but under the conditions it wound up being worse than staring at the wall, so I turned it off. When the steward came by with our lunch (peanut butter and jelly on rye accompanied by two blackening bananas and Styrofoam cups of what appeared to be Hawaiian Punch), I asked if he had any news, as starved for information at this point as any castaway. He wasn't particularly forthcoming, and in any case what he might have known must necessarily have been at third or fourth hand, but he did say, rather enigmatically, "Word is we'll be moving soon."

"Does that mean we'll be evacuated?" Amarita wanted to know. She was in bed, the covers pulled up to her throat. She'd barely been out of bed since our ordeal began. Nor, for that matter, had I. After all, where was there to go? Why even bother to get dressed?

The man, like most of the crew, was Greek, or had been before he donned the hazmat suit—at least that was my recollection of him—and he stood no taller and had no more authority about him than a twelve-year-old. He didn't say yes and he didn't say no. Through his mask, he murmured, "All I hear is we're going to move."

"Ashore?" I asked, feeling a wave of relief wash over me. The TV news had speculated that we'd be moved to a containment facility ashore to wait out our quarantine, and though that was hardly ideal—I pictured walled courtyards, barbed wire, sanitized cells—at least we'd be off the ship.

He was slowly shaking his head even as he turned to go, leaving us to wonder at his meaning, until not ten minutes later it became clear. We were just sampling our sandwiches and doctoring our drinks with pisco (can you say Hawaiian Pisco Punch?) when we felt a thunderous shiver run through the ship as it weighed anchor and pushed back from the pier, heading out to sea.

What had happened—and I'm sure you must have seen accounts in the press—was that the Japanese government, in response to the emergency, revoked whatever permits or contracts the 5-Star Red Beryl Cruise Line might have had with the Port Authority of Yokohama and not only refused to allow any passenger or crewmember to set foot ashore but demanded that the ship vacate Japanese waters altogether. The irony here was that although we didn't know it yet, we were about to continue our cruise after all, though not in the manner we'd anticipated when we'd first come aboard.

Our cabin was the last one on our passageway, so that there was no one to our right, which helped ease our growing sense of constriction—Amarita, who'd booked the trip, had planned it that way for the sake of privacy, or as much privacy as you could expect from what had already become a kind of seagoing *favela*. The cabin to our immediate left was occupied by a single passenger, a woman in late middle age of whom we couldn't help catching glimpses as she moved about on her private balcony, which was separated from our own only by a laminated white plastic panel. She hadn't been at dinner that first night, or at least not at our table, and so to this point all we knew of her was what was printed on the placard attached to her door: *Mrs. Amelia Knob. Homeport: Bath, England.* I mention it because she soon became central to the drama playing out on board, or at least to our little portion of it.

We were rolling right along, the Japanese shore long faded from sight and the great ship flattening the waves like a steamroller, when the TV screen suddenly went dark in the middle of the sole remaining movie we'd seen only once, a Disney confection about a misappropriated poodle finding its way home to a suburb of Paris from what appeared to be Lac Léman at the foot of the Alps, and I got up to check the connections. Amarita, who never uses foul language, let out a curse, then pulled the covers over her head and refused to emerge for the rest of the afternoon. I called down to the desk but got no answer, and having nothing else to do, I unhooked everything, cleaned the connections, and reattached the cables, but to no avail—the screen remained dead. Finally, after twenty minutes or so, a message appeared. "WE ARE HAVING TECHNICAL DIFFICULTIES," it read. "WE WILL RESTORE SERVICE AS SOON AS POSSIBLE. THANK YOU FOR YOUR PATIENCE." And, in smaller letters: "Your comfort and safety are our sole concern."

For some time I'd been hearing a tapping or thumping that began to separate itself from the usual noises of a ship at sea, and when I looked up, my eyes were drawn to our private balcony, the sliding door of which was shut against the blow. An arm appeared over the top of the plastic panel to the left, then a shoulder and a face framed in wind-whipped hair the color of rainwater. It was Mrs. Knob, and she was beckoning me, her face wearing an expression of extreme urgency. "Do you see what they've done?" she demanded without introduction when I stepped out onto the balcony. She wasn't wearing a mask. Neither was I.

"What do you mean?"

"The telly. They've cut the cable."

"Oh," I said, and here came that knife thrust of fear again, "it's just a technical glitch, that's what the message said. They'll have it up and running any minute now. How difficult can it be on a ship like this?"

"You are so naïve. They're isolating us, don't you understand? They don't want us to know what's happening." And then she began to cough, a deep, dredging, explosive cough that silenced the wind and chased the dolphins all the way down to the bottom of the sea.

I didn't answer her. Shielding my face, I fled inside and slammed the door shut behind me. Then I went to the sink and scrubbed my face and hands like a surgeon heading into the operating room.

By the twelfth day (counting from the last known incidence of infection, that is), conditions had become increasingly dismal. Back at home, our maid, Esmerelda, who has served us cheerfully and hygienically for thirty years now, customarily changed our bedding three times a week, whether it was strictly necessary or not, but here, needless to say, all maid service had been indefinitely suspended, so that we were forced to wash our sheets, towels, and underthings ourselves in the sink and hang them to dry on the rail of our 5-Star private balcony. As you can imagine, this gave rise to a new set of difficulties altogether, including the vagaries of the winds and the depredations of the gulls we encountered at the next port of call, Hong Kong, which left me entirely bereft of undershorts for the duration. Meals, such as they were, began to appear at the oddest hours, the crew strained to the breaking point with the exigencies of providing what amounted to bag lunches for 2,665 passengers three times a day, so that the breakfast waffles might come at noon and the evening's macaroni and cheese at two in the morning. Still, we managed as best we could, though we were sunk in lethargy and victimized by a slow creep of apprehension as the quarantine period counted down and we awaited word from the authorities at Hong Kong as to whether we would be allowed finally to disembark and put an end to our ordeal.

We'd taken to leaving our door open as a way of expanding our space, at least psychologically, as did most of the other passengers on our deck, especially those confined to the inner cabins. Like Bunny and Scott, who we could observe lying motionless on their bed, as if they'd already been stricken. After her outburst, Bunny had been subdued, though Amarita, whose eyesight is a good deal sharper than mine, observed that she was definitely not wearing her wedding ring. For the most part, as far as I could see, Bunny just stared at the ceiling, though every so often she'd prop herself up on her elbows and call out to us across the passageway in odd disconnected phrases like, "Enjoying the ball game?" and "Five'll get you ten."

Once a day the crew escorted her and Scott and the others occupying inner cabins out onto the deck for a spot of exercise and fresh air, and from our doorway we got to exchange greetings with them—and rumors too; rumors proved more contagious than the virus itself. One man, trudging by in the passageway, claimed that there had been three suicides already and as many as a dozen people rescued after jumping overboard. We heard that the lobsters had again changed color, which explained why the chef had eliminated them from culinary consideration, and that a woman on the twelfth deck, after having tested negative for the virus, was being treated for demonic possession by one of the three priests aboard. Not that we believed any of it. Rumors were rumors, nothing more. But in the absence of cable news and service for our mobiles, we were left in the dark, which only stoked our fears, which in turn gave rise to new flights of rumors.

On the morning of the thirteenth day, Dr. Schumann stopped by to test us for the final time. Dr. Pohnert was conspicuously absent, and though I could barely summon the energy to put two words together, I did manage to sit up and inquire after him. "Can we assume he's off doing tests separately, so as to expedite matters? Or is he"—and here I attempted a joke—"busy arranging the shuffleboard tournament?"

"Oh, I've got a whole crew under my wing now," the doctor said, waving a hand as if to indicate that the situation was well under control. "As it turns out, there are twelve other physicians among the passengers—and so many nurse practitioners it's almost as if they were attending a convention."

Amarita, who was sipping a cup of watery tea brewed from a thrice-used tea bag, looked up and smiled. "And how is Dr. Pohnert? Is he bearing up?"

Dr. Schumann frowned. "I'm afraid he's indisposed."

"No," I said, my heart sinking, "don't tell me—?"

"Oh, no, no, no, nothing like that. It's just a head cold, that's all. But under the circumstances . . . ," and he trailed off.

From across the passageway, Bunny called out, "You know what the ducks say—quack, quack, quack."

———

Both Amarita and I tested negative for the virus, as we had the first time around, which was a relief on many levels, but the unremitting tension of being at the center of the contagion and having to fret over every slightest palpitation, every tickle in the throat or stifled sneeze, had worn us down till we were nearly as debilitated as the initial sixty-seven victims themselves, all of whom were now out of danger and displaying no further signs of infection, according to Dr. Schumann. That evening the captain sent round complimentary bottles of something called Miller High Life, "the Champagne of Beers," and Amarita and I sat outside on our private deck and sipped from them as we gazed out on the night-spangled waters and the infinity of individual lights faceting the jewel of Hong Kong, each of them signifying some private refuge, whether it be an apartment, an office, or a Chinese restaurant throwing open its doors to travelers from the four corners of the earth.

All seemed well, and as we dined on Cup Noodles and prepackaged cheese and crackers and washed them down with the beer, our spirits began to rise. I found myself grinning over nothing in particular, and was about to reprise one of the podiatrist's better jokes, when Amarita, wrapped in a blanket against the chill of the night, let out a sigh and murmured, "I suppose it could have been worse."

"Worse?" I said. "How could it possibly have been worse?"

"At least we didn't hit an iceberg," she said, and in the next moment we were both laughing despite ourselves. It was a companionable moment, one that only reaffirmed what we'd built together over forty years of marriage, which stood in stark contrast to Scott and Bunny, who'd gone directly from exchanging vows to their cramped economy cabin on the grandest ship in the fleet, assuming that the waterslides and the casino and romantic interludes in the 5-Star Red Beryl Celebrity Theater of the Seas would provide the essential glue to bind them. When I'd last looked, Bunny was still lying there stretched out on her back, staring at the ceiling. Scott, perched in the doorway, had given us a thumbs-up, and when I asked how she was doing he'd pinched his lips together, shot a look both ways up and down the passageway, and said, sotto voce, "She's just depressed, is all."

This was when Mrs. Knob came back into the picture. We hadn't seen any sign of her on her balcony, and when I'd glanced idly down the passageway from time to time I saw that the steward had left her bag lunch outside her door, only to remove it and replace it with a fresh one at the next meal cycle. I didn't think much of it—she was English, after all. No doubt she'd brought kippers and Marmite and the like aboard with her, distrustful of the French-Asian fusion the ship's 5-Star kitchens were renowned for. Mrs. Knob. The Englishwoman. She'd occupied her cabin and we'd occupied ours and we were all, equally, available to contagion, which, I suppose, is the most basic form of democracy. If she didn't want to eat her meals, didn't want to expose herself, didn't want to chat at her doorway or over the laminated plastic panel of her private balcony, that was her privilege.

But now there seemed to be some sort of commotion in the passageway, colliding voices, the tattoo of rushing feet. Curious, I pushed myself out of bed and went to the door. Behind me, Amarita lay curled up beneath the covers, softly snoring, though it was three in the afternoon—she'd taken to napping at all hours as a way of defeating time, as I had myself, both of us drifting into a kind of self-willed narcolepsy. Across the hall, Scott and Bunny had shut their door, and what that might have meant I didn't have a chance to consider because my attention was caught by the two crewmembers outside Mrs. Knob's cabin. One of them was rapping on the door and persistently calling Mrs. Knob's name, while the other applied a master key to the lock, which didn't seem to be having the desired effect. "Mrs. Knob?" the first man called. "Mrs. Knob?" The second, his features shrouded by the mask, let out a curse. "She must have jammed something in the lock."

At that moment, they both shifted their attention to where I stood leaning out into the passageway. "Do you know the woman in this cabin?" the first man asked.

I shook my head. "Not really," I said.

"When was the last time you saw her?"

I shrugged. "Maybe two days ago? I'm not sure."

At that, the second man produced a battery-powered drill and applied it to the lock, which, after a moment, did the trick: there was a clunk, then the thump of something dropping to the deck, and the door pushed in. From where I was standing I could just barely see a fraction of the room, and so, curiosity getting the better of me, I stepped out into the hall and peered through the doorway. Did I touch the doorframe? Breathe the air? Allow my bare, unslippered feet to contact the threshold? I don't know. But the world is a tactile environment, composed of atoms, and what we touch and what we breathe in is not always subject to our will: Mrs. Knob was lying supine on the floor while the two crewmembers knelt over her, the beak of her nose thrust up like the sail of her own private barque, her eyes fixed on the ceiling.

So there was to be another fourteen days at sea, news that came down to us via our flat-screen TVs within an hour of the discovery of Mrs. Knob's body. Sequestered now in a rippling black 5-Star body bag, Mrs. Knob was wheeled away on a gurney even as hazmat-clad crewmembers thumped up and down the passageway, wielding sprayers of disinfectant. "Will they bury her at sea, do you think?" Amarita wondered aloud, her eyes roving over my face.

I was sitting on the bed beside her, idly flipping through the pages of an overstuffed novel I'd read three times already and knew so well I could have recited it aloud from memory. "I don't think they do that sort of thing anymore. Most likely they'll lay her out in one of the coolers next to the Chinese man and the green lobsters—till we get to shore, that is."

"If we ever do get to shore," Amarita said, and she slid over on the bed and wrapped her arms around me. "I'm so sorry for putting you through this," she whispered. "I just"—and here her voice scraped—"thought it would be an *adventure*, that's all."

From across the hall, even through the airtight door, we could hear Bunny's high, fractured voice singing, "Mama's little baby loves short'nin', short'nin', Mama's little baby loves short'nin' bread."

The great ship gave a shudder then, and the distant groan of the anchor revealed the sequel: we were heading back out to sea, rejected by Hong Kong and its 7.4 million inhabitants before we had a chance even to breathe its air. "It's not your fault," I told my wife, though of course it was, and all I could think of in that moment was the leather sofa in front of the fireplace back at home, and the very old Jerez brandy I kept in the cut-glass decanter in the polished teak cabinet beside it.

I'm sure anyone reading this account will be aware of our plight over the course of the subsequent days, during which we were rejected by any number of ports in succession, including Sihanoukville, where the Cambodian prime minister, Samdech Techo Hun Sen, desperate for favorable publicity, had initially invited us to dock, then at the last minute withdrew the invitation because the ship before us had unleashed the virus on the city despite the fact that all the disembarking passengers had ostensibly tested negative for it. You might know that, but you're probably not aware of the degree of privation to which we were all subjected at this point, everyone alike, including the Americans. As if the food hadn't been bad enough as it was, now we faced shortages of the essentials—wine, macaroni, picante sauce, creamer packets for our morning coffee. Stevedores had refused to attend the ship at Yokohama, and we hadn't got close enough at Hong Kong for it to matter, but the cruise line had arranged for a helicopter drop of various foodstuffs and medicines off of Sihanoukville, including test kits for the virus, though ultimately the supply proved inadequate and testing was reserved only for those who might be showing symptoms.

But the worst thing, the degrading thing, was the filth we were forced to abide. Some sort of mold had made every surface of the cabin sticky, and though we complained repeatedly, the best the crew could do was pass us a sponge, a bucket, and half a cup of Clorox (itself in short supply) through the door of our cabin. Then there was the bedding. We washed the sheets as best we could in the shower, using those diminutive bottles of shampoo in lieu of detergent, and there was of course the problem of my lack of undergarments, which necessitated the frequent washing of my Dockers and being reduced to wearing my tuxedo trousers while they were drying over the shower rail. The weather continued foul. The whales and dolphins vanished. The bands did not take up their instruments, the roulette wheels sat idle, and the 5-Star Red Beryl Celebrity Saloon gathered dust. No matter—the ship, grand monument that it was—quelled the waves and humbled the seas even while the authorities tried in vain to find a port that would take us when our second round of days had counted down to the finish.

And Bunny? On the morning of the second thirteenth day, after the steward had arrived with our bag breakfast (two balls of rice darkened with soy and two cups of creamless coffee), I glanced across the passageway and saw that Scott was alone in his cabin. I was astonished. And terrified, that too. Had she somehow come down with the infection? Did this mean that we would not be disembarking tomorrow at whatever port for which the captain was now heading? Would we have to endure two weeks more of this purgatory? Was the world uninhabitable? Was normalcy a joke? A sudden rage seized me—*Bunny*. What a ridiculous name. What a ridiculous person. I was ready to don my mask and gloves and drag her out of the sick bay or wherever she was and fling her overboard myself if that would spare us.

"Where's Bunny?" I called to him. Amarita, who'd been asleep—always asleep now, even at mealtimes—roused herself at the sound of my voice and peered blearily over my shoulder.

"They had to take her away. And no, it's not the virus, thank god—she's just, well, feeling the strain. She's very sensitive."

That afternoon our screens came to life again, first with an announcement that we were on a course for Phu My, in Vietnam, where we would be allowed to disembark, as no one had tested positive for the malady since the unfortunate loss of a passenger two weeks earlier, and then with the full array of news programs, movies, and games we'd been deprived of in the interim. And there it was, like a miracle—the image of our ship steaming across the screen under a banner reading, COVID CRUISE SHIP CLEARED TO DOCK, while various talking heads clucked over our predicament, as if they could begin to know the half of it. The sun rose up suddenly out of the clouds to bathe us in a rhapsodic light, and the sounds of electric guitars and saxophones began to drift down to us from the promenade deck above. Gulls material-ized out of the ether to beat their white wings round our private balcony like angels sent out from shore to guide us in. The sea fell away. I was so moved I took Amarita in my arms and pulled her to me for a long lingering kiss, the kind of committed and passion-ate kiss we'd rarely given ourselves over to since the early days of our marriage. The moment held and it was exquisite. But then, and perhaps it was because I'd been breathing through my nose while we pressed our lips together, I couldn't catch my breath. In the next moment I was coughing and I couldn't seem to stop.

"Jorge, what's the matter?" Amarita asked, the urgency in her voice like a new force gathering on the earth. "Are you all right?"

My eyes were clouded, my chest ached. The cough stopped then, as abruptly as it had begun, but the itch lingered, digging in its claws. I felt dizzy, everything in motion around me, as if the great ship had finally given way through all its fourteen decks and left me floating suspended in the void. The next cough was there, already scratching at my throat, but I shook my head, looked into my wife's eyes, and said, "It'll pass."

(March 2020)

Key to the Kingdom

He had a glass in his hand when he answered the door. By this point—his third drink—it might as well have been grafted to his fingers. His problem was boredom, Caroline away for an extended visit with her mother, who was dying of a cancer so rare it didn't even have a name, and the afternoon suspended in a haze of midsummer sun while the clocks stood still and all the dogs in the neighborhood held their breath. His deeper problem, of course, was far vaster than a touch of ennui on a stifling summer's day—it wore a face of self-pity and despair, compounded by alcoholism, though he wasn't about to admit that, not even to himself. The cure for boredom was alcohol, and the cure for alcoholism was death. As he'd said somewhere once in one of the interminable email interviews he found himself responding to on sleepless nights when his fingers seemed to function on a higher level than his brain, "All writers are drunks, drug addicts and betrayers of trust, any trust, on any level." He'd meant it as a joke, or at least partly, but as he crossed the living room in his bare feet, the furniture lurching at him and the shadows infested with ghost images of the past, the joke didn't seem all that funny.

The doorbell rarely rang, and when it did, invariably at one or two in the afternoon when he'd overcome his fear and vapidity and was just beginning to enter into the tranced world of his work, Caroline would deal with it. On the odd occasion when he did answer the door, if he didn't instantly recognize the face of the person standing there on the pressure-treated boards he'd personally nailed down himself in a time when his knees and back were more cooperative, he slammed it shut before whoever it was could make his plea or pitch or whatever it was going to be. If that was rude, well, he wasn't the one doing the doorbell ringing, was he?

This time it was different. This time he was drunk. And bored. And there was something in the face of the kid at the door that gave him pause. The kid (midtwenties, testimonial haircut, Levi's jacket with the collar turned up, and a pair of eyes that were already holding a conversation with him) said, "Hi, um . . . Mr. Riley?"

Riley didn't say yes and he didn't say no. He was standing at the front door of his own house, the number of which was clearly indicated in the custom-made wrought-iron numerals Caroline had selected from a catalog and he'd set in place with the screws in the cellophane packet they'd come in. Really, who else would he be?

"F. X. Riley?"

That was when he should have slammed the door, but something held him back. The eyes. And the nose that had the slightest out-of-plumb twist at the tip of it, a familiar nose, intimately familiar, maddeningly familiar, though he couldn't quite place it—or not yet anyway. "I don't know what you're selling," he said, "but whatever it is I don't want it."

"I'm not selling anything. I just wanted to, I don't know, see what you looked like—"

"Let me guess—you've got a problem with something I wrote somewhere? Or no: I stole your life story, plagiarized your whole life from birth on and never gave you proper credit, right? Let alone a check."

The sun was intense. There was a smell of process, compost working in the flower beds, the funk of nature that kept on churning through its generations, renewal saturated with the promise of death. Out on the main road, a motorcycle blatted past, and when he glanced up to track it with his eyes, he saw a gleam of metal that coalesced into a bicycle propped up against the front gate. A bicycle. The kid had come all the way out here and he didn't even have a car.

"No, but that would be great—I mean, the check part, anyway." The kid smiled to indicate the joke, then dropped his eyes and brought them up again. "It's about my mother," he said.

Everybody had a mother. And for that matter, a father too. And it was true that Riley had been on the campus in question a quarter century ago, or thereabouts—it was his alma mater, after all—but then he'd been on so many campuses since even his biographer would have been hard-pressed to provide any definitive evidence. Still, he remembered the occasion, not only because it marked the first reading he'd given for his debut book, but because of what happened to Dave Davits in the aftermath. Professor Davits, that is. The man who'd been his mentor and advocate and who'd arranged for the reading, replete with a fifty-dollar honorarium, round-trip airfare, and two nights at a motel in the howling wastes four miles outside of town.

The time was winter. The college, located in the far northern reaches of New York State, was not the sort of place anyone who wasn't already dead and buried six feet deep would elect to be in that relentless season. There were stretches when for days at a time the temperature never rose above twenty below. Radiators froze. Engine blocks cracked. Birds plummeted from the sky like stones, their wings jacketed in ice. Winter. Upstate winter. What better time and place to bring out your first book?

Professor Davits had himself picked Riley up at the regional airport. He looked substantially the same as when Riley had last seen him at graduation six years earlier, his hair the color of soap powder, worn long and swept back, the scholar's bifocals clamped over the bridge of his nose, his features vivid beneath a permanent alcohol burn. Riley had been his student, not his colleague or friend or drinking buddy, and he didn't know what to expect when he came off the plane and saw his professor standing there in the cold wind, hatless, grinning, the muffler flapping round his throat like the wings of a flightless bird. There was an awkward moment when his professor's body language (a shifting of the booted feet, a widening of the gloved hands) seemed to indicate he was maneuvering in the direction of a hug, but Riley, cold even then, even when he was twenty-eight years old and not yet impacted by all that was to come, thrust out his own gloved hand for a shake. He squeezed his professor's hand and his professor squeezed back, and that squeeze communicated something to him, something proud and sentimental and hyperinflated, and in the next moment his professor was extracting a flask from the breast pocket of his parka and holding it out in offering.

They shared hits from the flask as frozen fields and derelict farmhouses slid past the windows, the heater roaring, the tires rhythmically slapping at the metallic patches of ice that periodically gave way to wind-scoured blacktop. The scene was rural, more rural than he'd remembered it, and everything had shrunk, even the sky, which seemed barely able to lift itself from the ground. Though this stretch of road meant little to him—he'd hardly ever left town, with its student bars and burger joints, the movie theater and lecture halls and the girls, especially the girls—he was already choked with nostalgia, as if his essential self had been molded from the snow-streaked dirt alongside the road. "Thanks for picking me up," he said. "Really, thanks for everything."

That was all right. That was good. It was Dave's pleasure, because rarely had a former student rocketed so high, and it was a special joy to have him back here again, especially after that novel, and what a book it was . . .

So the subject was Riley and that was all right too, as was the bourbon he sucked from the flask till it mounted the back of his throat and climbed right on up to the highest peaks of his brain, crampons and all, and when the motel appeared in a depression cut out of a stand of pines on the left—TRAVELERS REST, the sign out front proclaimed, sans apostrophe, as if it weren't so much denominative as aphoristic—he had to speak up and say that if it wasn't too much trouble he'd like to check in and dump his bag before . . . what, lunch? That was where they were going, right? Lunch?

Dave had looked startled, as if the lunch with faculty for which they were already late was the last thing on his mind, and he suddenly jerked his shoulders, tugged the wheel hard left, and cut a screeching U-turn directly in front of the only other car on the highway—a rust-scrawled pickup with two stricken faces shrinking behind the windshield. It was a moment in which the worst could have happened, but didn't—the scenery lurched, two sets of tires squealed, and the pickup skittered coquettishly out of the way, vanishing with a blare of its horn. There was another lurch, another squeal, and then his professor tamed the wheel and fought the car down the sloping driveway to the motel, slaloming to an uncertain halt before a gray clapboard building with the neon VACANCY sign in the window.

"Here he is!" Dave roared to the moon-faced woman behind the desk. "Odysseus returned from the wars. Give him anything he wants!"

The woman—thirtyish, wearing a name tag that read *Toni*— worked up a grin and said, "That's great, that's really great. Two nights, right?"

Even then, even as he signed his name in the ledger and received the key to his room—number 2 of the twelve apparently deserted units lined up under a single long roof that cut away from the office at a right angle—he was congratulating himself on his decision to stay two nights rather than one. After all the work he'd put in—grad school, teaching, the three years of daily terror that had resulted in the novel with its glossy cover and his name inscribed in the center of it in shining inch-high letters—he thought he could get used to the idea of reveling in the glory of himself, at least for one extra day. Why not? There was nothing back at his apartment in the city but an accusatory typewriter and a mountain of blank paper (and Janine, the girl who would ineluctably become his first wife, as if it were a law of nature). He dropped his bag in the room, spent a critical moment in the bathroom, during which he discovered he'd forgotten both toothpaste and his electric razor, then stepped back into the winnowing blast of the wind and slid into the car beside Dave, who promptly offered him another hit from the flask. Which he accepted. As his due.

The lunch was a dreary proposition, held in a special room off the main dining hall where the students shuffled back and forth with trays held out before them like offerings for the dead. He drank iced tea and a glass of white wine, declined the soup, declined the salad, and wound up staring into a half-eaten plate of Salisbury steak, mashed potatoes, and wax beans while various people chatted him up, professors, that is, and two students, one male and one female, who'd been selected on the basis of their essays on his book to participate in what began to feel more and more like an inquisition. For his part, the male—his name was either Harley or Harlan, he never did get that straight—sat hunched over his plate, elbows spread wide on the table, and looked up slyly from time to time with the name of some obscure Eastern European writer on his lips, wondering what Riley thought of him. Which wasn't much, since he'd never heard of any of them, let alone read them. The female, the girl, was named Heather, and she wanted to know about the symbolism of the pair of stainless-steel pruning shears that kept cropping up in the novel—were they meant to reflect the protagonist's castration complex?

Afterward—he didn't need to rest up, did he?—Dave took him over to his own house to sit by the fire and have a real drink and say hello to the Mrs.—Did he remember her? No? Well, here she was, "Margaret, meet Frank, or do you go by F. X. now? Which admittedly, has a whole lot more gravitas than Frank, don't you think so, Margaret?"

He had a drink in his hand. The fire was a fire, snapping and hissing appropriately. His professor's wife was what you'd expect, physically anyway (fifty, jeans and sweatshirt, a face that might once have been more or less attractive), but something else altogether when it came to theories on art, politics, and nature, who in the half hour he was there must have used the phrase "Don't you agree?" half a dozen times till it became a verbal punji stick poking at him every time he lifted the drink to his lips. At some point, Dave glanced at his watch and said, "Well, this was nice—thank you, Margaret—but we've got to be off."

"Off where?" Margaret looked from Dave to him and back. "It's only quarter past four and dinner's not till seven, didn't you say?"

Dave was already on his feet and reaching for his parka. He gave a little shrug. "You know, make the rounds of the campus, indulge in a little nostalgia for Frank here—F. X., I mean—and check out some of the improvements we've made since his time, the arboretum, the new wing of the library, that sort of thing." Dave gestured to him now, as if in evidence. "You did say you wanted to have a tour, didn't you?"

He hadn't said so, but the idea appealed to him, especially after draining his second glass of Dave's special private-label XO bourbon, and so he said, "Yes, that would be great."

But when they backed out of the drive, Dave didn't turn right, in the direction of the campus, but left, toward town, where the bars were.

"So you're saying your mother knew me?"

They were outside now, out back, sitting at the glass-topped picnic table on the patio, he with a refreshed drink, the kid with a sweating black bottle of Guinness that had been marooned on the back shelf of the refrigerator since St. Patrick's Day, at least. Or maybe the last time he'd made corned beef and cabbage, which, come to think of it, would have had to have been St. Patrick's Day, the only time anybody would even want to think about boiling meat in a pot, let alone eating it. The fact was, he hated corned beef and he didn't drink Guinness anymore, just vodka.

The kid sniffed the aperture of the bottle, took a swig, sniffed again, took another, longer swig. Riley forgave him the sniffing—it was a habit he himself had, an animal gesture that served to assay the condition of whatever was about to go down, whether it was a piece of cheese you'd scraped the mold off or a silky black stout bottled in Dublin. He forgave him the intrusion too, because he was half drunk and terminally bored and the kid *was* in possession of those eyes and that nose, which was at least interesting. And there was something else too, an intuition as thunderous and spookily foreordained as Laius blundering into Oedipus on the road to Thebes. The kid looked up and said, "Yeah, something like that."

"She was a classmate?"

Shaking his head, the kid slowly set the bottle down, as if the weight of it was suddenly more than he was capable of supporting. "My mom—Heather? Heather Mastafiak?—was always a single mom. And, I don't know, I guess I'm getting older now and I just got curious, so I did 23andMe?"

The bars—the Albion, the T&R, Blanche's—weren't much different than he remembered, smaller maybe, less crowded, arenas of student lust and sexual display smelling of perfume, beer, and peppermint schnapps served in shot glasses to mediate the cumulative sourness of the beer after the first pitcher went round. And yes, you always sniffed it between sips, just for the *elevation* of it. Of course, he and Dave weren't drinking peppermint schnapps, which along with Jägermeister and rum and coke were beginner's drinks, student drinks, rungs of the ladder ascending to the top shelf of XO bourbon and single-malt scotch, the Manhattan, the martini. An example of the last of which they both ordered at the Albion, sitting companionably, elbow to elbow, at the very same pitted and gouged bar top where he'd propped himself up night after night through his senior year, scrawling his thoughts on the yellow legal pad he carried with him everywhere—ostentatiously, affectedly, hopefully. Dave said, "You heard about Bill Barrigan, I guess?"

"Who?"

Dave leveled a fierce squint on him through the magnifying lenses of his bifocals. The pores round his eyes looked like craters on the moon. He ran a hand through his hair and his nostrils flared and flattened again. "Barrigan," he repeated, a wounded tone creeping into his voice, as if not recognizing the name was a personal insult, and beyond that, a dereliction of everything the college and even the world of scholarship itself stood for. "Our medievalist? You never took his Chaucer course?"

Riley shook his head.

"Hanged himself."

Riley wasn't much of an actor, and the afternoon's drinking had numbed him to the point at which he couldn't have worked up the appropriate facial expression in any case, so he just lifted his glass as if in honor of the departed spirit of the medievalist he'd never known and waited for Dave to fill in the details and supply the homily. "Despair, Frank. Can you imagine that, anybody despairing of anything up here in the Athens of the North with the dog shit frozen on the sidewalks half the year and even the last fading smears of culture on permanent hiatus? Can you?"

Then it was on to dinner at another professor's house, one he did know and remember with a degree of fondness that seemed to intensify as the evening wore on and an unending procession of bottles of a full-bodied California Zin circulated round the table. They were ten at dinner, including Dave's wife—Margaret, wasn't it? Yes, Margaret—and a poetry professor he vaguely remembered who wore her hair bound up on top of her head with a pair of what appeared to be lacquered chopsticks holding it in place and who asked him, at least three times in the course of the evening, what he was working on now.

That was all right. That was fine. He was feeling no pain. In fact, he was filled with a golden, awakening glow of humble gratitude toward all these bright, articulate people who kept fêting him and toasting him and praising him, till at one point he stood and announced to the table that he was so overcome he was afraid he was in danger of becoming untethered from reality. And Dave quipped that it wasn't a problem because they'd hired the Goodyear Blimp to hover over campus all day tomorrow and advertise the reading, which was not only a reading, but a homecoming too. Raising his glass, he intoned, "To F. X., our own wandering star!"

Afterward, at the door, when they were all shuffling round in the anteroom, wrestling with their down vests and overcoats and fleece-lined gloves, Margaret pulled Dave into the corner behind the coat tree and said something to him under her breath that must have run to a paragraph or more. Her face was animated—or no, agitated—and she seemed to be spitting the words at him as if she'd already stripped them of their essence and had nothing left but the pits. What she was doing, and it was apparent to everyone, though no one acknowledged it, was reading him the riot act over a pattern of behavior that had roots in scenes that Riley, the first-time novelist, could only begin to sketch in his mind.

Then he and Dave were out on the frozen sidewalk watching the taillights of Margaret's car recede down the street. The cold was crippling. The wind came up again. He tried to light a cigarette just to take the sting out of his lungs, but his fingers were made of stone. Dave had trouble getting the car door open, finally rearing back and giving it three savage kicks with the rippled sole of his left hiking boot, the last of which caused him to lose his footing and go to his knees on the hard crust of compacted ice in the gutter. Riley briefly wondered whether he should reach down and offer his professor a hand, which would have been awkward, an acknowledgment of the older man's feebleness in the face of his own youth and strength and promise, but no matter, Dave sprang up like an acrobat, and in the next moment they were both in the front seat, the heater blowing super-chilled air in their faces.

They listened to the roar of the fan a moment, and then Dave let out a sudden cascading laugh that ended in a series of hoots. "You've got to forgive Margaret," he said, shaking his head comically. "Poor woman thinks we're going out for a nightcap, but she's wrong, isn't she? That's not the sort of thing we'd do, two scholars reunited after all these years, is it?"

So there was a nightcap at some country bar where everybody knew Dave but seemed wary of him, keeping their distance, and while Dave had another bourbon, he ordered a beer, only a beer, by way of drinking himself sober. Then they were back in the car again. There was ice. There was instability. Objects— parked cars, streetlamps, naked trees—loomed and fell away again. At some point the motel appeared. It was dark, every room of it, black dark, no light anywhere but for the neon VACANCY sign in the window of the closed and locked office. This time, as they parted, Dave did reach over and hug him, and he returned the gesture as best he could before stepping out into the blast of the wind and hustling toward the door of his room.

Caroline had planted salvia in hanging baskets as an attractant for hummingbirds, and one came into the picture now, hovering just over the kid's left shoulder, as if it were a messenger from some deep generative well of being. Riley, who cultivated an abiding distrust of technology in all its forms and arrays, knew of the existence of 23andMe only because Caroline had sent in a sample of her own body fluids so she could discover that in addition to her French-German ancestry, she was 0.5 percent Fijian or Laplander or some such, as if it mattered. She'd badgered him to send in a sample as well, but he'd refused categorically. "What," he'd countered, "you mean voluntarily provide my genetic code to some corporation so the NSA can track me down all the quicker when the fascist takeover's complete? Or so some scam artist can direct-market me cures for genetic disorders I didn't even know I had?"

He remembered a news article a few years back, when DNA testing was in its infancy and used primarily in forensics, and it had fortified his determination never to allow anyone access to his under any circumstances, not even if he was lying on his deathbed. It involved a career criminal who was a suspect in a series of rapes but refused to provide his DNA and had walked free in the absence of evidence. Which prompted a detective to follow him around discreetly, waiting for him to slip up. One afternoon the detective watched the suspect order a cheeseburger, fries, and Coke at a McDonald's around the corner from his apartment and waited for him to enjoy his meal, crack his knuckles, finish reading his Craigslist or racing form or whatever it was, and then finally push himself up from the table and deposit his trash in the bin just inside the front door. It was the simplest thing in the world. All the detective needed was to retrieve the straw from the soft drink and the rapist was history.

The kid tilted the empty bottle over his compressed lips and made a series of soft sucking noises. Some sort of tic or twitch had invaded the right side of his face, but Riley attributed that to nervousness. This was a big moment for him. It was a big moment for both of them, or potentially so, though the cards were not yet on the table and Riley hadn't been near a McDonald's since he was in high school.

"So the nearest match," the kid said, setting down the bottle and grinning weirdly at him so that the nose tilted even more noticeably, "was your brother Connor."

Riley was drunk, it was true, and the moment at which he could have extricated himself from whatever was about to happen was long past, but he just sat there, and as if he couldn't help himself, grinned back. "So what are you telling me, I'm an uncle?"

The kid gave an abrupt laugh, a self-deprecating laugh, and in that moment Riley saw him for what he was: a goofball, a nerd, awkward and unsteady in a multiplicity of ways, the kind of kid who didn't have a girlfriend. Or a job. Who probably lived with his mother and jerked off six times a day. A kid sitting here across the table from him with a pained look, who wanted knowledge, certainty, connection, just like anybody else. "I already checked," he said. "Your brother's never been to the college and my mother's never been in California, which is where he's been living since before . . . before all this happened? Isn't that right?"

What could he say, *Prove it to me? You got a lawyer?* It was probably just some scam, that was all, the sort of thing that happened to celebrities all the time, not that he was a celebrity himself, or not especially—books were too obscure in this age to register to that degree on the social scale, especially literary books. Like his. Oh, he received fan letters now and again, especially if he published a story in one of the magazines, but they were exclusively from cranks wanting to correct some recondite point regarding whatever field he didn't properly understand the nuances of . . . and yet what sort of scammer would pick his name out of a hat—or off the jacket of a book? But no, no, no, it couldn't be, it just couldn't—he was the patron saint of antinatalism. He was an environmentalist. The world had too many children in it as it was. Sex was not for procreation. Sex was for recreation, for scratching an itch. He looked the kid in the eye and said, "You've got the wrong man."

The kid—his grin had never faded—stared right back at him. "I don't think so," he said. He laid his hands flat on the table, his fingers shapely and thin, his wrists delicate, his biceps strung tight under the uniform chalk line of his skin. "You see these arms?" he asked, holding them out a moment before bringing both index fingers to his nose as if he were taking the drunk test. "You see this nose? And my hair, look at my hair. My mother? Not that it would mean anything to you—you don't even remember her, isn't that right?—but she has the straightest hair in the world. Blond hair. Still long and beautiful and parted in the middle, hippie style."

How great a leap is it from suspicion to conviction? What *did* Laius think when Oedipus came at him? Or did he think at all, because in that moment he wasn't the king protected by his bodyguard and all the perquisites and privileges of his royal ascension but just a sorry human being fighting for his life?

"Tell me your name again?" Riley peered down into his glass, which was now vodkaless and sweating out the last dying slivers of ice. "I must have missed it."

"Frank," the kid said, and then repeated it in a harsher voice, a voice that was almost a snarl. "*Frank*, my name's *Frank*, short for Francis. I mean, what else did you expect?"

Someone, somewhere, had once come up with the metaphor of a wind that stabs at you, a knifing wind, and it was so apposite it had long since become a cliché, but Riley, even back then, didn't deal in clichés. No, the wind that came at him as he stood there outside the door of his motel room, patting down his pockets for the key that was inexplicably and fatally missing in the grip of an ambient temperature that was 28 below, even without any additional help, was simply death in another form, the kind of death that doesn't need to resort to manufactured blades, that existed before blades or the hominids that contrived them. He had never been so cold in his life. And where was the goddamned key? If he wasn't so drunk he'd be dead already, that was what he was thinking as he balled up his fist and pounded at the door in desperation, then, hunched against the wind, darted to the office and pounded on the door there too. In his extremity, he saw that there was a notice in the window, just visible in the faint neon glow of the VACANCY sign. It read, "We are closed. Office hours are 7:00 a.m.–Midnight. For emergencies, dial 315-265-2672." All right. Great. But where was the phone? He hurled himself round back of the building, made a quick tour of the parking lot, squinted his eyes against the faint, pale band of the deserted highway, but there was no phone, phones did not exist, and of course, this was long before cell phones (another technology he hated) came into existence.

Shivering violently, he went through his pockets again, his fingers numb, his breath frozen even before he exhaled it, then went back to the room and put a shoulder to the door, but it didn't give, and then he kicked it the way cops are always doing in the movies, but that didn't work either. How ridiculous he was. How drunk. How richly deserving of the fate awaiting him. Four miles to town. Twenty-eight below zero with a stiff wind. Even if he ran the whole way, he'd never make it, and even if he did, he'd certainly lose a few fingers, and what was he going to do, type with his toes? But then they'd be gone too.

He was right on the verge of panic, utterly helpless, utterly lost, when suddenly the door to the room next to his cracked open and a woman's voice called softly, "Who's there?"

The wind! *Jesus!*

"I'm locked out," he said, hearing the note of weakness in his own voice and hating it. "I lost my key? And the office is *closed—*"

He could see her face now, a pale oval hung there in the crack of the door like a dangling cameo. Behind her, in the flickering glow of the TV, he glimpsed a pair of twin beds, one of which was occupied by the sleeping form of another woman, a female, a girl. The girl at the door said, "Mr. Riley?"

"Yes," he said, "yes," and recognized her in that instant, the garden shears girl, and what was her name? "But I just—I mean, I'm locked out."

"Okay," she said, "just don't wake up my roommate," and she pulled back the door and let him in, even as she slipped away from him to retrieve a bulky corded sweater from the shelf over the bed and slide something—her own key—from the night table.

He was feeling . . . redeemed. Foolish, but redeemed. "This is huge," he said, "huge, and I can't thank you enough, but I'm going to need *my* key, the key to *my* room—"

"Shhh! Don't wake Sarah." She gave him an uncertain look, then grinned. "I bet anything, in a place like this, any key'll work."

"You've got to be joking."

"Shhh!" She brushed past him and pulled the door back. "It's worth a try, isn't it?"

Shivering, he watched as she inserted the key in the lock of his door and jiggled it, working the handle at the same time, her lips pursed in concentration. Her hair was loose and it fell across her face as she leaned into the task, and the last thing he was thinking about was sexual imagery, but there it was—the key, the lock, the maiden—and then the lock turned and in the next moment he was in and so was she. "I can't believe it," he said, stamping and hugging himself to try to get some circulation going. "Jesus, you just saved my life, that's all—"

And there she was, standing beside his bed in a flannel nightgown and the sweater she'd wrapped round herself in order to survive the ten-step trek from her room to his, and what was she even doing there, anyway? Shouldn't she have been in the dorm? Well, yes, but the pipes had frozen and burst in her room, so the university was putting her and Sarah up here in this exotic, glamorous motel until the repairs could be made, which was a coincidence or serendipity or whatever you wanted to call it, and she was glad she was here, gladder than ever, because what would he have done? He could have frozen out there.

He said, "You want to have a drink?"

Later, after the mosquitoes drove them inside and he'd found another Guinness in the back of the refrigerator for the kid—for Frank—he dug through his blues collection and put a Josh White album on the turntable, just to see how the kid would react. Did he like the blues? Did he know the blues? Or was it all rap or hip-hop or whatever? Plus, the blues calmed him and he was at a point—five drinks in—where he needed calming. A stranger had knocked at his door. And here the stranger was, as familiar now as the dirt under his own fingernails, double helix, deoxyribonucleic acid, heritance like a throw of the dice, *Frank*. He sank into his leather armchair and listened to the kid narrate the story of his life, attuned to the tenor and rhythms of his voice as if to some voodoo chant—a son? He couldn't have a son. It was impossible. His second wife, Crystal, had twice gotten pregnant and twice he'd convinced her to eliminate the problem—badgered her, hounded her, bled out his veins, and shouted himself hoarse, *Get rid of it! Get rid of it!*—because that was what it was, a problem. He wasn't cut out to be a father. He was a world unto himself, and there wasn't room enough in it for replicas.

"So I would have—biology, I mean, or better yet, ethology?" the kid was saying. "Because more than anything I wanted to just go out in the field and observe the animals, you know? Whether it was chipmunks in the nature preserve down the street or hyenas on the Serengeti, it didn't matter, it really didn't, but for science you've got to get through math and physics and math to me is just like brain death, the single most boring subject ever invented . . ." He paused, ran a hand through his hair that rode high up off his forehead and had a pronounced kink to it, a feature Riley's mother, in reference to his own hair, which had resisted all efforts to style or even flatten it, had always chosen to call a natural wave. "What about you?" the kid asked. "Were you good in math?"

Despite himself, despite the derangement he was feeling and a kind of sickness in his soul that felt thick and adhesive, like mucilage, like tar, as if his soul had been tarred and feathered by all the outraged generations that had gone down before him, Riley laughed. It was his long laugh, his winnowing laugh, the laugh he used to put people down, but at the moment it seemed almost companionable, and what was happening to him?

"Math?" he repeated. "I can add and subtract, maybe do simple multiplication, divide a very small figure into another very small figure, but why would I ever want to? Why would anybody, unless their ambition is to work for the IRS?" He laughed and the kid joined him. "Talk about drudges, right?"

He became aware of the record then, which must have been playing for the third or fourth time because he'd neglected to put the arm down, thinking he'd get up and pick out another one and another after that, as a kind of test, the kind 23andMe couldn't begin to touch. The arrangement was sparse and primitive, and Josh White's clipped tenor rode up over the beat, *I've got a key to the kingdom and the world can't do me no harm.*

That night, after Dave Davits had dropped him off at the motel and left him to his fate, Dave's adventures were just beginning. There was one more bar, and when he left it he was pulled over by the police because he was driving erratically, because he was drunk, drunk then, drunk for the better part of his adult life, mentor in more ways than he was aware of. Dave had spent the night in jail and in the morning, after Margaret bailed him out, discovered that his face was featured on the front page of the local newspaper, a situation that prompted a call from the dean informing him that he was being relieved of the chairmanship of the English Department, a post he'd occupied since long before Riley was his student.

At the time, Riley knew none of this. He woke in his motel room, all his digits intact and Heather in bed beside him. What he remembered of that encounter at this distant juncture was so close to nothing it wasn't even real, a shattered fragment of all the sexual encounters he'd ever had, the naked body, the heat, the need that was so resolutely and so easily satisfied. Heather. He hadn't even remembered her name. Dave had called him at the motel an hour before the reading to say that something had come up, something that was developing into a major shitstorm, and he was sorry, tragically sorry, catastrophically sorry, but he wasn't going to be able to make the reading. Professor Linniman—the poet—was going to introduce him, and that was about the best he was going to be able to do. "Sorry," he said again, "sorry," and hung up.

That put a pall over things, no doubt about it. But the auditorium was packed and the minute Riley walked onstage he could feel the pulse of the audience, the steady heartbeat of the world he'd come here expressly to inhabit. He thought of addressing the situation or even simply announcing that he was dedicating the reading to Professor Davits, but in the end he just thanked Professor Linniman for her introduction, turned the page, and focused on conjuring the characters he'd brought into being with nothing more complicated or dangerous than his own imagination. There was a subdued dinner with Professor Linniman and a few others after the reading, and when Professor Linniman dropped him off at the motel, he saw that there was a light burning in the window of the room next to his, Heather's room. She'd been at the reading, but not the dinner, and now her presence had been reduced to a light in a window. It was past midnight. It was cold. He slipped the key in the lock and eased the door shut as softly as he could.

In the morning Harley/Harlan drove him to the airport, and he went home and married the girl who was waiting there for him, which was fine, which worked for almost ten years, after which he divorced her and married Crystal, whom he divorced six years after that and married Caroline and bought this turn-of-the-century farmhouse with the hand-hewn hickory beams and fieldstone fireplace, in which this big-knuckled, thin-wristed, kinky-haired kid was now sitting, sniffing at the aperture of his beer bottle.

Josh White sang, scraped his guitar, sang again.

Riley got up and refreshed his drink. "So what do you want from me anyway?" he asked, easing back into the chair that fit him like an upholstered coffin, the chair in which he did his reading at night, and his drinking too.

The kid was like a dog, one of those stray dogs in the shelter ads staring out at you with all the need and heartbreak and longing in the world bleeding out of their eyes. "I don't know—

acceptance? But I can see from the look on your face I'm not going to get that, am I? How about information? Like who my grandfather was and did he have this"—he tapped the bottle in his hand—"what is it, weakness for alcohol, because let me tell you, it's fucked up my life . . ."

So Riley sat back and revealed what he knew—about his own father and his father's father, about his uncles and aunts and his mother's side too, family stories, history, his history and nobody else's, the book of his life he'd never written because the pain was always right there at the surface. The windows darkened, but he didn't turn on the lamp. The drink had gone warm in his hand. He was thinking of asking the kid to stay for dinner, nothing fancy, salad, cheese sandwiches, a gesture that needed defining—an omelet, he could make an omelet—but the kid was already on his feet. "Okay," he said, already moving toward the door. "Thank you. Really, thank you."

Riley got up and came across the room to him. "No, yeah," he said, "it's nothing, my pleasure." They were at the door now, the night solidifying behind the screen, cicadas buzzing, the smell of ferment heavy on the air. "You need anything? Want me to call a cab? Or money, you got enough money?"

"No, I'm good." The kid's face hung there in the doorway, floating free against the dense shadow of his torso. He pushed open the door, and then, as if he'd forgotten something, leaned back in. "You want to see a picture of my mother?"

Riley was already shaking his head. It was going to rain, he was sure of it. "No," he said, "no, I don't think so."

SCS 750

At first, we tried wearing masks to throw off the facial-recognition algorithm just to see what would happen, but the cameras were able to identify us by our body movements, the way we walked, held our shoulders, flicked our fingers to the brims of our caps when the wind came hurtling down Zhima Credit Street. The whole thing—charade, whatever you'd like to call it—was Devin's idea, and I do want to emphasize this point: it was Devin's idea, not mine. Trust me on that.

It happened like this: we were sitting around my apartment one afternoon not long after the rating system went mandatory, wondering if we could buy alcohol, Juul pods, and video games without them keeping track of just how much we were using, and Devin said, "We wear masks, that's all—and maybe baggy old clothes from the Goodwill or wherever. What do you think?"

We would have to pay in cash, of course, so there would be no credit record, though cash was frowned upon just about every-where but the black market. And you didn't want to go there. You definitely did not want to go there. If they caught you negotiating for anything on the black market, no matter how innocuous or even socially positive—diapers, Windex, acai juice—your score would plummet out of sight. "I don't know," I said. "Why bother?"

"Because I like to vape? Because I'm bored with Red Dead Resurrection and I want to be able to buy more than two games a month without having to worry about what it's going to do to my score?" He gave me his choking-dog look. "Masks, come on—how are they going to know?"

The masks were state of the art, Second-Skin Silicone, a whole universe beyond the ones you saw in the old movies like *Mission Impossible* and *Face/Off*, each one made individually to conform to your bone structure so that no one who wasn't right there in House of Magic with you when you bought it would have suspected a thing. I chose a generic face, snub nose, balanced ears, lips that weren't nearly as puffy as the ones I'd been born with (and always hated—my nickname through five long years of elementary school was Blowfish). I liked the mask so much I was about to walk out of the store with it on before Devin caught hold of my arm and pointed out that it would defeat the whole purpose—the first street camera would capture the image, check it against the database and my purchase history, and know just whose face underlies the mask inside of thirty seconds.

So we took our masks home in a bag, pulled them on, and played around with them in the apartment all afternoon, trying on different outfits and throwing our voices to confuse the voice recognition systems on the video feeds—we even watched sitcoms for a while, trying to mimic the way this character or that talked. As soon as it got dark we went to Zhima Liquor, where the girl behind the counter tried to act as if she'd never seen cash before (until she didn't, and took it), and then we tried GameStop and got what we wanted without having to jump through too many flaming hoops. It was pretty exhilarating. We got drunk and played games and felt we'd gotten away with something, which made it all the more exhilarating.

Right. Sure. Who were we trying to kid?

The next day when I got home from work—within five minutes of walking in the door—a representative from the Ministry of Public Safety was pushing the buzzer. What did she want? She just wondered if I had a moment to chat, that was all. She was a girl, actually, more or less my age, dressed all in black, with her straight black hair cut so it framed her face like the folded wings of a bird. Her eyes were the same color as her hair, and they gave up nothing.

"So what's this about?" I asked, even as she edged into the room, set her z-Pad on the coffee table, and brought up the video of Devin and me in the liquor store. She didn't say a word, just stared at me.

I wanted to tell her it was Devin's idea, not mine, but I could see from the look she was giving me that it wouldn't have mattered. "It was just a joke, that was all," I said.

Her lips were made of stone. They never moved except when she spoke. "Not a very funny one, I'm afraid."

"Come on, we were just goofing around. No harm done, right?"

"Halloween's in October," she said. She might have been pretty if she smiled, but I got the sense that smiling wasn't part of her job description.

"Come on," I repeated, a whining tone creeping into my voice. "This isn't going to cost me points, is it?"

I was too young to remember a time before our leader became our leader, but I did have enough experience in my teens and now my early twenties to compare the way things were ten years ago and the way they are now. Which didn't make me a critic or rebel or anything even close—I was like anybody else, happy to live in a society where we could all prosper and love one another and work toward a common goal without worrying about getting ripped off or defrauded or attacked in a dark alley (actually, there were no dark alleys anymore, except in the cop shows on TV, but you get the point). Regimes of the past may have used punishment as a way of enforcing laws and regulations, but the Social Credit Score program was more reward/reward, like vying for gold stars on your report card when you were a kid. It was self-regulating, that was the beauty of it, everybody doing everything they could to raise their score and avoid any hint of negativity. As our leader says, "Zhima Credit ensures that all roads are open to the good citizens, while the bad ones have nowhere to turn."

It was a guy, older, in his thirties, who came to Devin's door, and he was no sunny personality either. Devin told me about it the next night when we were shooting hoops at the park, and he seemed genuinely put out when I told him I'd been docked 10 points, my score (which had been on shaky ground anyway after my second jaywalking citation) dropping to 605 on a scale that topped out at 800, a level only our leader and a few celebrities attained, and his problem with it wasn't necessarily that I'd been penalized 10 points but that he'd been docked 20.

"Well," I said, "it was your idea."

He gave me that gagging look again, the ball thumping rhythmically under the wrist action of his right hand. "It's not like I had to twist your arm or anything. And it was just a goof, right? I mean, are you telling me we're living in a society where you can't even have a sense of humor? Or what, tell a joke?"

"Not lame ones," I said. "And that's all you know."

"Did I ever tell you the one about—"

"Yes," I said, and we were both laughing.

The ball thumped, but he made no move to take a shot. A pair of doves, too slick looking to be certifiable, came in low, then made a graceful arc and perched on the electric wires overhead. "You know what? I'm not done yet. There's got to be a way to score what we want, like a case of Sapphire gin or enough Juul pods to last a year, or what, porn, without this constant shitty oversight, because really, so what if I want to jerk off in my own bedroom or play FlexKill III all weekend? How does that hurt anybody?"

I was stunned. His score was already hovering around 550, and if it dropped any lower he could find himself in that gray zone where you had to ride third class on the train and couldn't go to any of the resorts on vacation and might even have a problem just keeping your job. A perfect score was out of sight, but anything in the 700 range put you on the fast track to all the perks, from air travel to renting a car without putting down a deposit to getting prime seats at a concert and discounts on just about everything. I'd never heard of anybody below 500, which was the territory of pariahs and foreigners and other marginal types. Anything south of that and you might as well shoot yourself. "Count me out," I said, and even as I said it, he feinted to my right and drove past me for a perfect lay-up.

That was around the time Jewel came into my life. I was on my way home from work, thinking I'd kick back with this new game I was obsessed with (*WraithQuest*, which seems a thousand years old now, but was the hottest thing going back then) and just microwave something out of the freezer and wash it down with a couple of beers, when I saw her coming up the street toward me, oblivious, her eyes on her phone. I recognized her from work, though I'd never spoken to her and, in fact, hadn't seen her in the building for a while, if she was even still there, and I felt my face flush as I tried to think of what to say to her beyond, "Hi, how're you?" Or, even lamer, "Long time, no see."

She was in a short skirt and white leggings that dropped into a pair of red ankle boots and some kind of satiny blouse that caught the light and threw it back again. I saw that she'd cut her hair in the style of the girl from the Ministry of Public Safety, like that was the thing now—bird's wings—and she had on a pair of eyelashes that must have been fifteen millimeters long, which, I had to admit, I found very sexy. Just as we were about to draw even, she looked up from her phone, stopped right there in midshuffle, and gave me a smile. "I know you, don't I," she said, making it more a statement than a question, as if she'd been aware of me all along and had the phrase right there on her lips.

After I fumbled around a bit—was she still at Alibaba, because I hadn't seen her there like for weeks, or no, months, wasn't it—and she told me she'd gone over to WeChat, which was only like three blocks away and she was making better money and thought she was happier there, not that Alibaba hadn't been good to her—I asked her if she was doing anything and she said no. So we went to a bar I knew where they had a killer sound system and people hadn't started clipping their score badges to their breast pockets yet, which was about as obnoxious a form of self-promotion as I could think of. This was a neighborhood bar, my neighborhood bar, or the closest thing we had to one. The patrons were mostly people our age, so it was cool, very cool, and whoever designed it framed everything—from the bar top to the molding to the mullions on the windows—with thin neon tubing in the soothing blue your phone gave back when you reached a 750 score (not that I'd experienced anything like that yet, but I had aspirations, which, in fact, was the name of the bar itself, looped over the front door in the same cool color only in letters three feet high).

She ordered a watermelon-cucumber mimosa and I had a beer, which was what I would have had if I'd gone home. A minute later I was watching the way her lips—her taut, glistening model-slim lips—pursed in a miniature O over the tip of her striped paper straw, and I was glad I hadn't. The sound system offered up a feast of the music I liked best, and we found we had a common bond there, and then she told me about herself (living at home, one sister, one brother, a cat, a hamster, and a tank of neon tetras), and I told her whatever there was to reveal about my boring life without making it sound so boring as to drive her away. Finally, over the third drink, we revealed our scores, because there was nothing more intimate than that unless you were one of these rawbies that went around wearing them on their shirts.

She was a 715, and I was impressed. And took her word for it, because she didn't offer to display it on her phone. Which would have been rude, right? And because she wasn't rude, wasn't flaunting it, it made me like her all the more. When I told her about the mask adventure she laughed—"That sounds so cool!"—but made an elaborate sad face when I told her what it had done to my score. "That and two jaywalking citations inside of a month," I added, feeling a little surge of panic at the thought that she might get up and walk out the door.

But she didn't. She just waved her forefinger back and forth and said, "You naughty boy. Didn't your mother ever tell you to cross at the light?"

A few nights later I was back at Aspirations, this time with Devin, and if I'd been thinking about Jewel off and on all day, being there brought it back to me in a kind of golden haze, and I couldn't help envisioning her sitting there beside me, instead of him. As if that weren't enough, there were two girls in a booth by the window, both of them sporting bird's-wing cuts and sipping mimosas, and I saw it as a sign. I had to call Jewel, ASAP, before she forgot about me (and in the process maybe see if she was doing anything later tonight). I was working up my courage to go dial her number in one of the stalls in the men's because I didn't want Devin or anybody else hearing what I had to say, when Devin laid a hand on my arm. "You know I'm in trouble, don't you?" he said.

I felt a tick of alarm. He was making one of his tragic faces, the one he liked to call "Death in the Afternoon," his eyes like cue balls and his chin plunging to his chest, only I could see he wasn't putting me on, not this time. "What do you mean?"

"I mean I'm fucked."

The bartender set two fresh beers down beside the ones we hadn't finished yet—without asking. We were regulars, so why not? We were trustworthy. We were known. We had privileges. I drained the old beer, which was still more or less cold, and took a tentative sip of the new one. "Yeah, go on—you're not going to keep me in suspense, are you?"

That was when he slipped his phone out of his pocket, and holding it down out of sight below the bar so nobody could see, showed me the screen.

I don't want to say I was shocked—in reality, I could have seen this coming a long way off, the mask incident and what he'd said about gaming the system on the basketball court like flares shooting off the deck of a ship plowing into a reef—but I couldn't help sucking in my breath when I saw the color. The screen was orange. I'd never seen anybody with an orange screen before except Freddie Cheung, who was expelled from our local branch of Zhima Credit University for bringing a tuna sandwich and a bottle of Snapple into the exam room for Third-Level Finals (somebody claimed he had the answers inscribed in nanoscript on the underside of the bottle cap, which was never proven, not that it mattered—if the camera says you did it, you did it). I wanted to come up with a quip—that was how we related, how we'd always related all the way back to elementary school, when he was the only kid to stick up for me when the bullies came round pinching me till I bruised and calling me Blowfish and Blobber Lips and the like—but I couldn't find the words. "Jesus," I said, "what did you do?"

He shrugged, pressed the new beer to his mouth, swallowed, fought back a belch. The song that was just then playing ("One Drop Bosco Roy," a ska/C-pop tribute to our leader that I usually couldn't get enough of) seemed to disappear down some aural canyon. "They're accusing me of a speech crime."

I felt afraid suddenly—for him, yes, but most of all for myself. In the eyes of the system, you were who you hung out with, and if your friends' scores dropped—or your family's, even your second cousin's—it could adversely affect your own. "You're messing with me," I said.

He shook his head dolefully. "I wish." The beer bottle went to his lips again, but he didn't drink, as if his throat had stopped up, as if he didn't even deserve the consolation of a cold beer after work. "It was last week on the basketball court? The doves, remember?"

It was amazing what they could do with animabots these days—they had feathers, beaks, eyes, their wings even flapped. "Aw, shit," I said, and I was frantically trying to reconstruct our conversation that day. Had I said anything? Had I been complicit?

"They're claiming I have individualistic goals. They're saying I'm a drunk because I want to buy more than one bottle of gin at a time. They're saying I'm a backslider and a traitor to the spirit of Zhima Credit. And Larry Soloso, my boss? He's saying don't bother coming back to work till this screen's as blue as the sky at noon."

Jewel told me to meet her at Plus-Citizens, a dance club on the other side of town. Her voice was whispery and confidential, as if we'd been dating for months, and though the guy one stall over was vomiting with a machinelike gasp and snort that I was afraid she could hear over the line, I felt elated, felt like I was already in love. I got the feeling Devin wanted me to stick around, have a third beer, a fourth, buddy up when he needed it most, but I told him I had a date.

"You? A date?" He dredged up his eyes, grinning, and gave me his Rocket-to-Mars face. "Is it somebody you met online? No, come on, don't tell me you're posting on WeDate?"

I was uneasy, I have to admit, on a number of counts. First and foremost was the knowledge that the surveillance cameras were picking up everything. I wasn't saying anything that could be interpreted as untrustworthy or even remotely negative (dating was a plus, dating could lead to marriage and the production of additional trustworthy citizens, to homeownership and diaper buying), but here I was in conversation, intimate conversation, with a guy who had an orange screen, and what did that say about me? Plus, I wouldn't have wanted to discuss Jewel with him anyway, even if we were sealed in a meat locker or a time capsule. What I felt about her—or what I was beginning to feel about her—was private, strictly private. I said, "It's just some girl from work."

"Really? Is she hot?"

I felt myself blushing. I didn't know what to say so I just nodded.

"You got a picture?"

"Uh-uh," I said, shaking my head, and I don't know why I denied it, because I had seven selfies of the two of us I took the night we were here for drinks, and I must have studied them a hundred times in the interval.

His grin vanished. "Bullshit," he said, "you don't have a date. You just want to get rid of me. I'm a liability now, right? All those years, all the shit that went down between us, what does it mean? Nothing, right?"

I pulled out my phone, which glowed a copacetic lima green, the hue that would give way to forest green and then teal and turquoise as you moved up the scale to powder blue, periwinkle, and finally the deeper blues. I didn't say anything, just brought up a picture of me with my arm around her as she leaned in close for the selfie, her eyes wide and her lips ever-so-faintly aglow with the residue of her third mimosa.

Jewel was waiting for me out front of the club, her shoulders hunched in a tight pink rayon jacket, her purse slung over one shoulder and a cigarette at her lips (which alarmed me, because it could cost her, depending on how many she smoked daily; I didn't smoke myself, but I'd heard from a smoker friend that anything in excess of five per day counted as self-destructive behavior, which was by definition untrustworthy). There was a line of maybe twenty-five or thirty people behind the rope to the right of the door, but she wasn't standing in it. She was slouched against a lamppost, her head down, smoking, as if she had no intention of going inside. "Thank God," she said when she saw me coming up to her, and I thought I should hug her or pat her back or something but her body language said no, so I raised my hand, lamely, in a kind of childish wave.

"I forgot my phone," she said, looking distressed behind the beating fringe of her eyelashes. "I must have left it on the table when I went out the door, because, I mean, I was doing my makeup, and then I changed my outfit like three times because I wanted to look nice for you. You like it?" She twirled round so I could admire her, before casually dropping the cigarette to the sidewalk and grinding it under the toe of one of her pink suede kitten-heel mules. Which, if they were watching—and they were always watching—could have constituted littering. Which made me even more nervous than I already was, so I went down on one knee to retrieve the butt and tuck it into my jacket pocket for lack of anything better to do with it.

"Okay," I said, smiling, "you ready to do a little stanky leg in there?"

She looked at me, puzzled. "What?"

"Dance. I mean, that's what we're here for, right? At a dance club? A little nae-nae? Harlem shake? Wapoo?"

Her face fell. "We have to wait in line, because, like I told you—I forgot my phone? And you're like, what, a six-oh-five?"

"Six fifteen. Didn't I tell you I've been volunteering at the Bosco Roy Oncology Center, and that's been pushing my score up? And within three months the jaywalking thing's going to expire and for sure I'll see an uptick there, plus—"

At that moment, a couple dressed like they'd just stepped out of an AliExpress store glided up to the doorman, who instantly pulled back the rope for them. I only caught a glimpse of them as they went by, but both were wearing score badges, and though I couldn't tell exactly what shade they were displaying, it was blue, definitely blue.

"Yeah," she said, after turning her head to watch them pass through the brassy double doors in a burst of light and a quick pulse of intoxicating music, "but we're shit out of luck now, aren't we?"

I didn't want to point out that she was the one who'd left her phone at home, because that would have spoiled things, and besides which, I didn't mind waiting on line—waiting on line was socially positive, the very foundation of cooperation and selflessness. I didn't like the phrase she'd used either, not that I didn't curse sometimes myself, but it was different for a girl, or at least in my limited experience of girls, who always did what was right and unfailingly garnered points. I told her I didn't mind waiting if she didn't, and actually things turned out fine. We only had to wait for forty-one minutes, and the club was as hot as they come, absolutely destroying us with all the up-to-the-minute songs from z-Tunes and Tencent, and we danced till our legs were like overcooked noodles.

Afterward I asked her up to my apartment, and she said she had to work in the morning. "So do I," I said, "but just for a snack or something—aren't you hungry?" I gave her one of Devin's faces, the one he called the Pleading Hound, all sagging cheeks and bleeding eyes. "After all that dancing, I mean? I could make us, I don't know—scrambled eggs? You like scrambled eggs?"

I watched her eyes run through a series of calculations, and then she said, "Okay, but only for a minute."

Actually, neither of us really wanted to bother with food—or another drink; we'd both had enough—so I popped a couple cans of pomelo Zhima Water and we both had a sip, as if to rinse our mouths before the main event, which was intertwining our tongues and groping each other. We did that for ten minutes or so, till I thought I was going to burst. "You want to go in the bed-room?" I whispered.

She sat up suddenly, looking around her as if she didn't know where she was. After she'd had a moment to gather herself, she said, "You know, I like you. I really do. And your lips—I love your lips, they're so kissable, like big stuffed pillows—but to be honest, I can't really see myself getting serious with anybody under, say, seven hundred?" She smiled. "Minimum."

A month went by. We went out a couple of times, maybe three or four, I don't know, but I made a point of calling her almost every day just to hear her voice and chat about games and music and the comings and goings of various celebrities, especially our leader's teenage twins, Zora and Zofar, who were constantly in the news doing socially positive things like feeding the giraffes at the zoo or cutting the ribbon at the new robotics factory out on Bosco Roy Boulevard. Jewel always seemed happy to hear from me, and when we went out she was upbeat and affectionate—not as affectionate maybe as I'd want her to be, but I was persistent. As our leader says, "Persistence is the superhighway to achieving long-term goals," and my volunteer work at the oncology center—and the fact that I'd taken my grandmother in for her treatments at the Human Performance Hub three times in a single week—was gradually improving my score. And it didn't hurt that in the absence of Devin, who just seemed to have vanished (and no, I didn't try to call or text him, for obvious reasons), I'd begun cultivating two friends at work who maybe weren't as simpatico as he was, but whose scores were bound to elevate my own. Was I sucking up? Yes. Sure. Of course I was. Really, was there an alternative?

And then, just as things were improving for me, Devin showed up out of nowhere. I'd just sat down at the console with a beer and a bowl of kung pao chicken when the buzzer sounded and there he was, looking pathetic and giving me his done-and-done face to underscore what his body language was already telling me. He looked as if he hadn't showered in a week. And his Mavericks jersey was so faded you couldn't even tell it was blue anymore.

I didn't exactly block the door, but I didn't move out of the way either.

He said, "Hey," and I said "Hey" in return. And then—we hadn't moved yet, both of us trying to adjust to this new reality interposed between us—I said, "Did anybody see you coming up here?"

"Are you shitting me? In a country of five hundred million surveillance cameras? Like the ones at either end of the hallway we're standing in and that pinhole lens in the doorframe?" He stamped his foot for emphasis, and I saw that his Nike Hyper-dunks, which used to be his pride, were filthy and abraded. "For shit's sake," he said, "aren't you going to let me in?"

Suddenly I felt ashamed of myself. He was my best friend, or had been. "You want a beer?" I asked, pulling the door open.

So we had a beer and I microwaved a bowl of kung pao for him and we just started playing WraithQuest till we lost all track of time and space. It was half past ten by the time I got up and started putting things away. He was still working the gamepad, wasting wraiths and dire wolves and stockpiling weapons. At that point I started rattling the plates in the sink in a suggestive way, and he set down the gamepad and glanced up at me. "You know, I was just wondering . . ."

"What?"

"Is it okay if I spend the night?"

He lived two stops away, ten minutes or less on AliRail. "What are you talking about—why not just catch the train? I mean, I've got work in the morning . . ."

That was when I found out how low he'd sunk. He'd lost his job and then his apartment, and for the past two weeks he'd been living with his mother out in the ass-end of the suburbs, which was hard enough in itself, but just that morning she'd told him he had to leave. "You know what a shopper she is," he said.

"Grade A, Number One, shop till you drop. And she does love her discounts and the VIP sales and the end-of-the-year plus-point cruises. She told me she loved me, for what it's worth, and she promised to advance me fifteen hundred at the end of the month, but right now I just need a break, you hear what I'm saying?"

I heard him, but I was already shaking my head.

The next night, I took Jewel out again, this time to a restaurant that rated four stars on the WeDine app. I had General Tso's Chicken, sweet and chewy, a dish I'd loved since I was a kid, and she ordered two appetizers and the Angry Lobster (a two-pounder coated with spicy Szechuan chilies and fried garlic and sprinkled all over with black-bean dust). We shared a bottle of French wine the waiter recommended, and when I asked how her lobster was she plucked up a dripping morsel and held it out to me on the tip of her interlaced chopsticks, which was nice. I looked into her eyes as she watched me eat and swallow and then frantically drain my water glass—it was that hot. Her laugh was musical and friendly, though not without a hint of one-upmanship. "Too much for you, big boy?" she asked, then laughed again.

It wasn't until we got back to my place that she realized she'd left her purse at the restaurant. Though I was on tenterhooks to see what would come next, what with my SCS climbing and the way the lobster had set her eyes afire, I volunteered to run back to the restaurant and reclaim it for her. It was eight long blocks, and when I said I'd run I wasn't speaking metaphorically. The girl at the hostess stand had the purse right there—a little black beaded thing hardly bigger than a z-Phone—and I was back out the door before it even had a chance to ease itself shut. By this point my jacket was sweated through, and though I'm in fair-to-average shape, I had to slow to a brisk walk on the way back, which was what gave me the time to contemplate what I was doing—or to contemplate just what it was I had in my hand, that is. Her purse. Jewel's purse. Which contained the only object anybody really needed in this society: her phone. It came to me then that she'd never displayed it for me, though she must have seen mine half a dozen times. Was it trustworthy of me to stop under the big Zhima Credit display across the street from Sesame Appliances and look through her phone? Snoop, that is?

It was an inert slab, black and faceless, but all it took to bring it to life was a single on-off switch. (No need of a code—codes were things of the past, when breaches of trust were as common as flies piling up on a windowsill during the first autumn cold snap; these days there's no reason for anybody to hide anything.) I turned it on, and if by this point you might have guessed what's coming, I tell you, I was stunned. At first, when they were still ironing out the kinks in the system, your SCS was upgraded or downgraded weekly, but now it happened in real time, minute to minute, day by day, so there was no denying or excusing the bright citrusy orange of that display and the harsh black numerals fixed right there in the dead center of it: 515.

There was a scene at the apartment. I handed her the purse and watched her eyes enlarge when she realized from the weight of it that something was missing—and it wasn't her compact either. She didn't look ashamed, only angry. "All right," she demanded, "hand it over."

"Deceit," I said, quoting our leader, "is the ice pick in the kidney of trust."

From next door, through the too-thin wall that separated my apartment from my neighbor's, came the *shush-shush-shush* of the magneto guns in the latest iteration of StarLoper I was dying to purchase when I got my paycheck at the end of the month.

"I was going to tell you," she said, switching to penitent mode.

"Yeah, right. What were you waiting for—till my score dropped to like five hundred? Do you know how . . . how *rude* that is?"

She took the phone from me and zipped it back in her purse as if it were going to infect the whole room, the whole building, but it was already too late for that.

"If it means anything, it was unintentional," she said, her lashes congested with droplets of liquid that might have been tears, that *were* tears, though I didn't believe them. "So my mom got sick," she said, as if everybody in the country should have known about it. "And because she was accused of a speech crime back in her student days, way before the SCS came along to elevate us all, she ranks as a Grade D citizen, which meant she couldn't get proper treatment—it was cancer, cancer of the colon?—and we all pitched in, my brother and sister and I, to nurse her and try to pay for all the tests and her operation . . . In the end, I had to drop out of school and go to work, and I wound up defaulting on my student loans, okay? But my mom's better and I'm paying down my debt, and I tell you Zhima Bank's just *merciless*—"

I was no longer listening. It was an impossible situation. Not only had she deceived me—and been haughty about it too, as if she were doing me a favor by letting me pay for her Angry Lobster and her mimosas, and she was a *drinker* too, let me tell you, and a smoker on top of it—but just knowing her, just having her there in my apartment when the security cameras had watched the way we'd snuggled when I turned the key in the door half an hour ago, put me at risk.

I gave her one of Devin's faces, the one he called the Shroud, and pointed at the door. "You know the way out," I said.

———

It took me a long while to recover—over a year, actually—but at least I knew why my score had been so slow to rise even after the slate had been wiped clean on my second jaywalking offense. I worked hard to be trustworthy, doubling up on my hours at the oncology center and joining the Campaign for a Trash-Free City, which was sponsored by Zhima Credit itself. Most important, I was careful about who my friends were—once burned, you know? For the last two months I've been dating a 750—a *legitimate* 750, who wears her score badge pinned at the neckline of her blouse and isn't shy about it either—and if she isn't absolutely as attractive as Jewel, she has plenty to offer, and I've been thinking about surprising her with an engagement ring, though I haven't quite got around to going to the jewelry store yet. But I will. Soon. That's a promise. Meanwhile, my two friends at work—they're both 700s and both named Bosco, after our leader, which is a plus, and why hadn't my parents thought of that?—have become fixtures in my life, especially after my score topped the magic 700 plateau and they didn't have to worry about me anymore. And give them credit here, because they saw something in me even when I was down. That's loyalty, and you can't really put a number on that.

Big Mary

She wasn't all that big, actually. Five, five six, tops. And what would you call it, being charitable—heavyset? Plus size? Somebody within earshot gave a low whistle when she walked in the door at Gabe's one afternoon and said, "Wow, she's a whole lotta lovin', isn't she?" Which was all right, I suppose, if that was your taste, and it wasn't mine, or not that I was aware of before things started up between us. She was a blonde, or mostly, though sometimes it was hard to tell because she didn't wash her hair all that much. As for her style, it was retro by default—she seemed to have two dresses only, probably from the thrift store, one black with red flowers on it and one red with black flowers. She was drunk on pitcher beer and shots of Southern Comfort about 88 percent of the time, and where she got her money nobody knew, because she'd dropped out of school and didn't have a job, unless it was in the mornings when nobody was stirring except A-types and the guy who chucked the newspaper out the window of his car. "Maybe she delivers newspapers," I quipped when she went to the restroom, which got everybody laughing, and then Stuart chimed in with, "Nah, she probably works down at the Dairy Queen," and I didn't get the reference at first, but then I did: dairy equals milk and milk equals tits. Or udders, anyway.

That was the day she came back to the table, made sure everybody was looking, then hammered her shot and laid both her arms flat out on the tabletop as if she'd just found them lying by the sink in the restroom. Normally she didn't go out of her way to call attention to herself—and she always nursed her drinks, which was a credo of hers ("You should savor your pleasures," she'd say when anybody asked and leave the innuendo floating there in the blue pillar of cigarette smoke that held the roof up over our heads).

"See these arms?" she asked now, and of course we did see them because we weren't blind, but we didn't really want to see them and didn't know why she was showing them off or why she was asking. They were very white, her arms, as if she'd never been out in the sun, but otherwise not much to remark on—no tattoos or bruises or needle tracks or skin cancers or anything like that. She was sitting next to Jadine, the Chinese girl Stuart had picked up two or three days back and who hadn't been out of his sight since, and if Jadine's arms were thin, sticklike almost, it only meant that Mary's were thicker by comparison, but they weren't especially muscular in any way you could see. They were a girl's arms, that was all, and when she asked in a clear, penetrating voice if anybody wanted to arm-wrestle for the next pitcher, we all laughed.

"Laugh," she said, "go ahead. But the offer stands." And she looked at me then and said, "What about you, Doke? You're a big strong man, aren't you?"

All of a sudden everybody was locked in. A minute ago we'd all been doing what we did most afternoons, whether we had a gig that night or not—drinking, that is, passing the time, sometimes getting up to smoke weed in the men's room or in the alley out back or challenging some loser to a game of eight ball on the table we practically owned, or if anybody thought to bring a deck of cards, playing pitch or poker or even crazy eights just for the kick of it. I suppose the boredom factor played into it, but we didn't consider ourselves bored back then, just alive, and if being alive meant sitting at the same table in the same bar with the same people every day, well, that was the way things had been ordained and who were we to rock the boat?

I wasn't big and I wasn't strong. I was a musician, my arms weren't much bigger around than Jadine's, and I'd grown up in a redneck town where your self-worth was entirely predicated on sports, and I hated sports then and I hated them now. I said, "No way—you'd kill me," and everybody laughed again and somebody, I think it was Jeremy, though I don't really remember, let out a hoot and in a rising glissando the whole room could hear accused me of being a wimp, as if we were all back in junior high again.

How did that affect me? In the way that zero plus nothing equals zero. Maybe I wasn't the most confident person sitting at that table—that was Stuart—but I was starting to get a better sense of myself and had begun to feel that being twenty-three and playing music three or four nights a week was like an open window on being twenty-four at some point and maybe twenty-five beyond that. There was half a beer and a bump of rye whiskey on the table in front of me, pretty much all I drank in those days, as if it were the serum I needed to stay alive, and I grinned, picked up the shot glass, and toasted Mary before taking a delicate sip and setting it back down again.

She turned to Stuart. "How about you?"

We were a student band, or, actually, since none of us were

students anymore and one of us never had been, a band that played student bars and had congealed enough to branch out and play non–student bars in a fifty-mile radius or so, and Stuart was our front man. The focal point. The one the girls saw first when they were shaking their accoutrements out on the dance floor. He wasn't big either, or not particularly, but he was strong because he lifted weights out of the vanity that ruled him, and his arms were an advertisement of that fact. "Sure," he said, giving us all a look so we could appreciate how altruistic he was, "I'll take your money."

That was when things turned upside down, because Mary pinned his arm so fast half of us missed it, but then Stuart made some excuse along the lines of *Come on, I wasn't even ready*, and she pinned him again and then one more time for good measure.

The result was that we all drank for free for the next couple of weeks, or at least whenever a sucker could be found, and if a sucker couldn't be found at Gabe's we'd find him at one of the other bars around town. Big Mary never lost, not once. When I asked her about it, about how she could beat guys twice her size, she'd give me her wide-eyed look (her eyes were a pale, filmy blue and they always seemed slightly out of focus, as if she wasn't really looking at what she was looking at) and say it was all in the timing. Or, if she was feeling more expansive, she'd say it was genetic. "One of my genetic gifts, and don't you want to know what the other one is?" And here was the innuendo again, or more than innuendo, because the first time she said it there were just the two of us sitting at the table, while the others were standing around the pool table propped up on their cue sticks, and she reached out and ran one hand from my knee up to my crotch, which, admittedly, caught my attention. Of course,

I didn't have a girlfriend at the time and she knew that, not that I was looking, because I'd crashed and burned with Darla, the girl I'd been living with for almost two years before she stripped the apartment bare while we were off playing a two-night gig in Dubuque, taking not only her own things and all the pots and pans but my Muddy Waters and John Lee Hooker albums and the Skipper Canteen metal mug I'd brought back from Disneyworld when I was fourteen, and moved back in with her parents in Chicago, which was a four-hour drive away, so that was the end of that.

At this point you're probably wondering why I'm telling you all this. Here was Mary, who could have had more style, who could have washed her hair and done something with it, a girl who needed to lose weight and didn't really stand out at all among the other low-level groupies buzzing around us except that she wasn't as pretty, so what was the attraction? I mean, who's going to star in the movie, right? In answer, I'll say that she was smart, smart in a way that lasered through the usual run of doper discourse that was like a thick white paste gluing your brain to the inside of your skull, and I appreciated that even if some of the others wound up being intimidated by her, but the thing that made her stand out, that made her become a minor celebrity in the small-town arena we commanded at that one particular point in time, was her voice.

Nobody even knew she could sing or that she wanted to, or that the reason she was ingratiating herself with us—had made herself indispensable, actually, in terms of free beer and the ritual humiliation of various loudmouths, frat boys, and jocks—wasn't entirely innocent. Or sexual, as it was with the other girls who came sniffing around. No, what she wanted was the microphone, and once she got it she wasn't about to let it go. Of course, we didn't know that, not at first, and if we had we wouldn't have cared one way or the other, at least I wouldn't. Anyway, there came a day in April when the trees were greening, and the way the air smelled made you think life had been created out of nothing (which, come to think of it, it had), and we were rehearsing in the garage attached to the house Stuart and Jeremy rented half a mile out of town, where the farmer's fields began their slow creep out over the world. We didn't rehearse much because we were a blues band at heart, and we had the whole catalog down, from Pinetop Perkins to Howlin' Wolf to Luther Allison, but every once in a while we had to work in a few current tunes just to stay out front of the paying customers.

We cued up the records and played along, jamming our own versions of a couple of new tunes, raggedly at first, but smoothing out the edges by the third or fourth time through, and it was satisfying, the way it always is when you're playing as a group and you know each other's moves as well as you know your own—plus, for the first time in months, the garage, which wasn't heated, was warm enough to make us almost feel like human beings. We took a break. Ate a sandwich. Shared round a couple of six-packs.

The girls were there that day, Mary, Jadine, Jeremy's girlfriend, Megan, and our drummer Richie's wife, Annemarie, because where else would they be—at the mall?—and they'd sat in the corner and provided us with an audience of sorts, which was always good as far as I was concerned—at least we were playing for *somebody*. I was sipping my second beer and working my loose front teeth (more on that later) around a ham-and-cheese sandwich, when suddenly the mic was on and Mary was standing in front of it and her voice, a voice we didn't even know she had, was right there as a presence among us. She was just singing as if that was what was expected of her, as if that was what she'd always done and we'd always been there to take it in, just like the sunshine coming through the skylight or the air circulating in our lungs. She was doing a Big Mama Thornton tune—"Ball and Chain," the one Janis Joplin made famous—but she wasn't singing it like either of them, giving it a phrasing and authority that was all her own, and a cappella, no less. For a minute, nobody knew what to do, then Jeremy picked up his guitar and I strapped on my bass and the afternoon went on for a long time after that, much longer than anybody had planned.

The reason my teeth were loose was because a few nights earlier I'd been blindsided by a punch from Donald Turlock, a mean, skinny bass player who wore his hair in dreadlocks and thought he'd invented reggae all on his own. He was black, which in his mind made him authentic, while we were just parasites sucking the blood out of the blues legends who really knew what it meant to be downtrodden and oppressed and ghettoized and weren't just blowing out their asses about Parchman Farm and getting behind the mule and all the rest. Which was infuriating. We *revered* them, which was what had brought us together in the first place, and what we were doing was homage to them, no different from what he was doing with Bob Marley and Jimmy Cliff and Toots and the Maytals. He didn't see it that way. In his mind he was the real deal, and we were shit. Never mind that the other two guys in his band were students in the music school, who also happened to be white, or that he introduced himself around town as Rasta Selassie, *Because Donald's just a slave name.* I didn't like him. I called him Donald every chance I got, especially if he was at the bar bullshitting a bunch of people—women, especially—with his Rastafari act. He even faked a Jamaican accent, though I knew for a fact he was from St. Louis.

I don't remember what I said to him that night, something

about Donald Byrd, the jazz trumpeter, who *happened to be black*, and he threw it back on me, like Donald *Who*? He got in my face, and I told him if he wanted to know the truth I was blacker than he was and he couldn't play for shit, and when I turned to reach for my beer he rounded on me and knocked two of my front teeth loose, for which I was going to have to go to the dentist—or worse, the dental school, where you could get worked on for free if you valued money over pain. So there was that. All I wanted was to live in the slow-wheeling drift of those dragged-out afternoons at Gabe's like a warrior laying down his shield, all the battles won, or at least averted, but circumstances wouldn't let me.

There was Mary, for one thing. What she did behind that microphone made everything I'd ever done and everybody I'd ever played with seem like filtered water. Darwinian selection, mutation, the coalescing of the genes and the gifts unequally distributed, well, that's not fair and never has been and never will be. I had no illusions about myself, or not any more than anybody else playing in a bar band, though I'd be lying if I told you I never fantasized about something bigger, which everybody does, especially when you're in the throes of it and everything's coming together and you feel like you can lift off the ground like a frictionless bird with a pair of wings bigger than the whole county you're leaving behind, but I was enough of a musician to know a real gift when I saw it. So was Stuart. Which was the other thing.

At first we let her come in and do a couple of tunes in the middle of the second set, just to change things up, just for fun, no money involved, nothing serious, and Stuart sat back and saved his throat and his vocal cords and what was left of the rest of him for the final set and made jokes about how easy she was making it on him. "Shit, I don't even have to gargle anymore, and I'm just going to start leaving my jockstrap at home from now on out, you know what I mean?" He said this with a grin, but eventually, as the weeks went by and Mary, Big Mary, got bigger and bigger in the scheme of things, until she was covering half or more of the tunes on our playlist and the tip jar lost weight because it was all bills instead of coins, his grin fell out of contention.

What happened—and I was there to see it—was that he put the moves on her one suffocating day in June when you could taste every molecule of dirt in every field for miles around and the beer seemed to go stale in the glass before you even lifted it to your lips. There was some pop crap playing on the jukebox that we'd heard sixty thousand times and that functioned as a form of brain death exceeded in sheer pathology only by the song that would come after it. (I'm not complaining, just reflecting on the fact that some musicians who don't even merit the name can get very, very lucky, and by extension, those who do merit the name—like me, for instance—are shit out of luck.) It was late in the afternoon, the hottest time of day, and the place was pretty well deserted except for the four of us and Mary and a couple of thick-necked types presiding over a long procession of tequila tonics at the bar.

Stuart was wearing a sleeveless T-shirt that showed off the muscles he'd been working on and foregrounded the silver crucifix he wore strictly as a goof since he was no more religious than the dog panting in the shade just outside the open door, which must have belonged to one of the thicknecks, because he wasn't ours, and Jamieson, the bartender, didn't have a dog. "Hey, Mare, you're looking hot today, you know that?" Stuart said out of nowhere, and at first we thought he was being sarcastic. "Is that a new dress, or what?"

"I am hot," she said, fanning herself with one of the laminated menus nobody ever looked at. "It must be a hundred and ten out."

"Ninety-two," I corrected. "But the humidity's right up there."

Nobody said anything, so I added lamely, "Going to rain tonight. I hope. Just to cool things down."

Stuart toyed with his glass, making wet rings on the tabletop and then smearing them over again. "No," he said. "I mean it. You look . . ."

Mary supplied the adjective for him, giving it an interrogatory lift: "Fuckable?"

If that took him aback, he didn't let it show. Stuart was all about being cool, or appearing to be. He frowned, toyed with the glass some more, then looked up into her eyes. "You want to go over to the house?"

I got Mary on the rebound. She lasted all of maybe two or three weeks with Stuart, because what he was doing was trying to exert control over her, pure and simple. If he wasn't the focal point of the band anymore, at least he could make her screw for him and whatever else that entailed. Or that's my reading of it, anyway. What they did together I never really knew, but if Stuart had his pick of girls while Jadine was back in San Francisco on summer break, Mary had to wonder why he'd picked her. Especially after he began coming down on her in public. "You really look like shit, you know that, Mare?" he'd say in the low, nasty tone he'd perfected when he wasn't getting his way in every conceivable phase of life. Or, "You know the only sport where they lose weight after they retire? Sumo, Mare. You know what that is?"

She didn't shed any tears. She just took over the band, and then, because she could, she took me over too, and Stuart was the odd man out.

Flash ahead to the fall, when Mary was living with me in the apartment Darla had vacated along with my records and my Skipper Canteen metal mug, and Stuart had quit the band to go up to Minneapolis because there was somebody there who knew somebody in L.A. who wanted to do a demo of a couple of the songs he'd written, which, as far as I was concerned, were primarily crap, but that was what he claimed and that was where he'd gone. I don't want to say his vocals were formulaic or too rock and roll or diminish him in any way, because he had his moments, but Mary gave the band a whole new dimension. There just weren't that many girl singers around and not one who could even touch her, and we started getting bookings that stretched beyond our fifty-mile radius, and we found ourselves playing venues in places like Madison, Rockford, and Milwaukee. Truly, I think it was her gift as a musician I fell in love with as much as anything else. I admired her. Was blown away by her, actually. Plus, she was funny, wicked funny, with a take-no-prisoners attitude, and the way we fit together in bed was just fine too, as if we were working through the first two verses of a slow, sexy, bass-heavy tune where the rhythm was everything. We bought a fan. She made salads. When I cooked burgers or hot dogs, the only things I knew how to make, she ate them without buns because she was trying to cut down on starches.

Then there was the night when I came back from the break and couldn't find her because she was sitting out in the audience with a couple of people, nothing unusual, except that when I went up to the table to join her I saw that one of them was Donald. I stood there a minute, wondering what to do, then pulled out a chair across from her and eased into it. Ignoring him, I tapped my watch to get her attention and said, "It's about that time, Mare," but she was in the middle of a long story about how she'd been pulled over for a DUI and talked her way out of it because it turned out the cop was a blues aficionado—a story I'd heard, in various versions, at least half a dozen times since I'd met her— and she wasn't going to be rushed.

Who else was there? I don't remember. Four or five people

mired in the sludge of their own hipness and feeling privileged to be on intimate terms with her—and with me, don't forget me, because I'd been up on that stage too and was about to go back up there for the final set. Donald just stared at me. When Mary paused to pick up her beer, he said, "I hear you got an appointment down at the dental clinic."

"Don't," Mary said. "Be nice, Ras."

Now it was my turn. "I hear your God died," I said, looking straight into him. This was a reference to Haile Selassie, emperor of Ethiopia, who was the presiding deity of the Rastafarian cosmos. If Nietzsche had declared the Christian God dead, that was theoretical since as far as anybody knew he'd never been alive in the first place, but a month ago Haile Selassie had been a living, breathing, tiny little pint-size Ethiopian dwarf who ate, drank, and shat like anybody else.

"The Lion of Judah is forever," Donald said, pressing his palms together as if in prayer.

"I hear they strangled him," I said, tailing off with a laugh. "Some god—they didn't even bother to nail him to a cross."

Donald asked me, in a high intense voice as if he were being strangled himself, if I'd like another crack in the jaw, and I didn't throw it back at him or try to tough it out because this was Gabe's and this was our gig, not his, and that just made him all the more insignificant. I laughed again and then I got up, took Mary by the hand, and we went back up onstage.

The blues mixes it up, of course—you've got to have up-tempo numbers like "Shake Your Money Maker" to get people out on the dance floor—but it was the slow, grinding, dragged-down tracks that hit you like an earthquake in a brick factory that had brought me to the music right from the beginning, relationship songs, cheating songs, heartbreak in three chords and a throaty vibrato. It's no pleasure to have to admit it, but that was the sort of tune I wound up inhabiting in real life, because Mary wasn't who I thought she was, and I couldn't do anything about it. (And yes, she did a killer version of "I Put a Spell on You" too, more Screamin' Jay than Creedence, her vocals carrying a full payload of rage at the world that had tried to keep her down because she was a woman, a fat woman, two strikes against her before she even laid eyes on a microphone.)

My first intimation of that came maybe two weeks after the non-incident at Gabe's. I'd been out someplace that afternoon, I don't remember where—that might have been the period when I'd picked up a secondhand bike from an ad in the paper and rode it all over town for a couple of weeks till that grew old, or maybe not, maybe I'd been out getting a buzz on and playing chess at the sunny table in front of Gabe's with whoever happened by on the sidewalk while Mary slept in, something I periodically did when the air smelled a certain way or my blood felt like it was boring new channels through my arms and down into my fingertips till it was dripping out from under my nails—and when I walked up the stairs to the apartment I didn't hear the TV going or the low thrum of a record but voices, two voices, Mary's and somebody else's.

The other voice was Donald's. That clicked with me just before I opened the door and saw him there on the couch, bare chested but with his Rasta tam clinging to his head like some sort of fungal growth and his feet in their dirty sandals splayed across the pillows. I didn't get excited over much. Musicians are chill, that comes with the territory, that was how we were, and as far as it went I was no different from Stuart in that regard—or Muddy Waters, who after his doctor told him hard liquor was going to kill him, switched to champagne. Poker face. Show nothing.

Everything's cool. Still, to see Donald stretched out there as if he owned the place, and Mary sitting in the chair across from him, smoking a joint and sipping a beer in her plus-size robe with the black half notes running up and down the sleeves that I personally had gone out and bought her was just too much to process. I didn't nod or say "Hi" or "What's happening" but just stood there with my hand on the doorknob till the words came clear in my head. "Correct me if I'm wrong, but aren't you the fucker that punched me in the mouth?"

He let his eyes roll, but he didn't say anything. Mary didn't say anything either.

The next thing I said was addressed to her. "I don't want him here." And then, because I could feel something coming up in me I didn't like and the point seemed important to clarify, I added, "This is my place, remember?"

"You are one sorry racist motherfucker," Donald said, and that was all it took. In the next instant I was on him. Never mind that I hadn't been in a fight since junior high or that he was sitting down and I wasn't, I balled up my fists and tried to do what damage I could, and whether that was cool or not I was beyond caring. There was something primitive going on here, he in his bare skin and Mary in her robe and the roach in the ashtray and two bottles of beer set out on the coffee table like bishops in a game of chess.

He tried to fend me off with his feet, but my forward motion and his backward thrust knocked the couch over and suddenly we were wrestling on the floor in a scramble of limbs, both of us punching and slapping and grabbing, my breath in his face and his in mine. The whole thing couldn't have lasted more than half a minute, and then I had him pinned down, his neck doubled back and his head jammed against the wall, and if he hadn't spat in my face I would have stopped right there. But he did and I didn't stop. I punched him till my hands started to hurt.

That was when Mary stepped in. "Get off him, Doke," she said, her voice stark and hard and contained by nothing. "Can't you see you're hurting him?"

I didn't care. I punched him again and then again until Mary, Big Mary, who'd never lost an arm-wrestling match in her life, pulled me off him and held me there with my arms pinned back so he could come up off the floor and spit in my face all over again.

Talk to me about authenticity, about who has the right to play whatever kind of music no matter what they look like or where they come from—I say you're authentic if you play with the kind of feeling that takes you out of yourself to the point you don't even know you're playing anymore. It's a trance. It's getting into a trance, which is what all good musicians do, and nobody has dibs on that. Culturally, I mean. Or racially. Does that make me a jerk? Or a racist? What sort of music should I be playing, "Nights in White Satin"?

The upshot of that little incident in my own living room was that Mary walked out the door with Donald the Rastaman and came back just once, once only, to get her things—when she knew I wouldn't be there. It was the middle of October by this point, the days winnowing down to the bleak months ahead, stubble in the fields, the hogs you saw when you drove by the farms going into their hog barns, pumpkins piled up at the supermarket and apple cider on special. Normally, I would have fallen right into it—Halloween, how can you beat Halloween?— but this year was different. For one thing, I wasn't playing music, for the simple reason that I no longer had a band to play in. Mary just quit without saying a word and moved in with Donald and cut me out of her life. I didn't understand why back then, and I don't understand now.

She didn't come into Gabe's anymore, and he didn't either. I heard they were hanging out at a place on the other side of town, down by the river, a place that didn't even have live music, just a jukebox, which was pretty pathetic the way I saw it. I still put in my time at Gabe's, afternoons and nights too, along with Jeremy and Richie and some of the other people we knew, but they weren't any happier than I was because they weren't doing anything either. We talked about putting a new band together, but the key to any band is the singer and we were fresh out of those, weren't we? I even put in a call to Stuart to see if anything was happening there, only to discover he was in L.A. after all, which was a surprise, as was the news that he was close to signing a deal with Warner Brothers. Or so he claimed.

"That's great," I said, hating myself. "Really great. Any word on when that's going to happen?"

"Soon," he said. "Soon."

"Be sure to let us know," I said. "And if you come back"—I was going to say, "we're waiting," but I knew in that moment he was never coming back no matter what Warner Brothers did— "the first pitcher's on me."

He laughed—give him credit there—and then he hung up.

I got a job at the record store a couple days a week, just to pay the rent, and that was all right—it gave me something to do—but the manager didn't want to hear any blues over the store's speakers because blues wasn't what people were buying. What they were buying was rock and roll and, yes, reggae, which had gone big with white audiences in the wake of Bob Marley's *Natty Dread* album the year before. So I had to hear that all day. And then, nights, it was the bar, which meant that I was drinking more than anybody who has any interest in staying alive ought to, especially on weekends when some band that wasn't us was playing Gabe's. I'd stand there at the bar mocking them under my breath, and I danced with one girl or another, but nothing came of it and all I felt through that long stretch of sorry, windblown days was loss.

Then Mary put her own band together, with no one in it I knew except the bass player, who, you guessed it, was Donald, and speaking of authenticity and commitment, he cut off his dreads, greased back his hair like Muddy Waters, canned the patois, and picked up that beat he'd had to drop when he was Mr. Rastafari. I didn't like any part of it—why would I?—but when I saw the flyer announcing their gig at Gabe's, I knew I'd be there. I knew I'd be drunk too. And, forgive me, angry, though I so wanted to be above it all, to be cool and unconcerned and shining with my own light.

Mary was good, great even—how could she not be?—and she had a keyboard player, which we'd never had, an older guy with hippie sideburns who created a lot of drama around her and spurred her to come in raw and powerful over these big chunky chords he was laying down. Donald was Donald, competent enough, but to my mind totally out of his element, but then what do I know? What I do know is that during the break, when Mary was being her big preening queenly self, accepting praise and free drinks and every sort of ass-kissing available to the royalty of this earth, Donald got feeling possessive and starting hanging all over her to the point where some of the thicknecks at the bar began to make comments.

Understand that this was a college town and everybody was cool with everything, or that was the pretense anyway, but still it was the Midwest and the experience of black on white was sliced pretty thin. There was some heckling, some back-and-forth, beer bottles jabbing like pointers at a chalkboard, and everybody trying to talk at once. People began jostling for position around Mary's table and the three or four tables next to it, the tension building till it was like the moment before a thunderstorm breaks on the hottest day of the year.

Somebody said something somebody didn't like, and in the next moment chairs got overturned and drinks spilled, and then people were swinging at each other in a stew of drunken animosity and the worst kind of preprogrammed hate, and Mary tried to defend herself as best she could, and so did he, so did her Rastaman, but somebody threw a pitcher of beer down the front of her dress and got in close, where all you could smell was sweat and blood, just to punch out Donald's sneering, twisted little bloodsucking Rastaman's face, but it wasn't me, it wasn't me at all.

The Hyena

That was the day the hyena came for him, and never mind that there were no hyenas in the South of France, and especially not in Pont-Saint-Esprit, it was there and it came for him. The truly mystifying thing, the thing he never could quite manage to assimilate no matter how many times Maxime Bonnet, who read the newspapers from beginning to end every day, tried to explain it to him, was how a hyena could emerge from a loaf of bread. It made no sense. And what of Marie Lavigne, whose hyena was a two-headed serpent as big as a man and uncoiling to its full height right there at the foot of her bed, so that she had to jump from the second-floor window and break both her ankles to escape it? Was that made of bread too?

"No, no, Henri, you're not following me—what you saw was an illusion," Maxime insisted, against all the evidence. He'd seen its teeth, smelled its breath. He knew its claws and the heat of its intention. And he'd heard it speak in perfect French, even if it did have an Algerian accent. "As I've told you, over and over, the flour was contaminated with an agent that makes you picture things that aren't there. Don't you see?"

He didn't see. And he shook his head.

"Think of it like a fermenting agent. Like wine. Drink too much wine and you get drunk, isn't that right?"

The first time they had this conversation was a week after he'd come to himself in the *asile de fous* in Avignon and rode back to the village in the passenger seat of Dr. Veladaire's Peugeot, only to discover that five of his neighbors had died of complications in the interval and just about everyone else was staring out of eyes that looked as if they'd been replaced with light bulbs, and he said the same thing to Maxime then as he said now, "But bread doesn't get you drunk."

Like all the other shopkeepers in town, Maxime Bonnet rolled down the steel gate and closed up shop promptly at twelve noon each day, reopening at three when all the artisans, mechanics, plumbers, and carpenters had enjoyed their lunches and post-prandial *siestes* and would be in desperate need of whatever odd or common item he stocked on his shelves and happened to be indispensable to the job at hand. On the day in question, he and his wife had gone to their usual café, and they both had a salad and the *moules marinières*, but the bread had an odd look, more gray than white, and it smelled musty, as if it had come from a wine cellar rather than the bakery, and they'd pushed it aside and ordered *frites* instead, which was a shame because he liked nothing better than to sop up the broth with a heel of bread. He didn't even bother to complain to Mme Doumergue, the proprietress, because this was the way things were six long years after the war, with the controls still in place, so that the bakers were at the mercy of the millers who adulterated their flour with anything they could get their hands on, bone ash, chalk, slaked alum, and God knew what else. And they were the true criminals, the ones who should have been held accountable for the madness that was to descend on the village that night. "Stand them up against a wall and shoot them," was what Paulette said in the aftermath, but there'd been enough shooting in the war, and the millers were victimized too because it had been an unusually wet spring and summer, which caused the wheat—and the rye, the rye especially—to become contaminated with ergot, the fungus that was at the root of the problem. But nobody knew that yet. It was a summer's day. Life progressed. And if Henri Sardou was a bit slow mentally, as great a shame as it was to have to say it, he was going to be slower still once that bread had gone to work on him.

That morning, before the sun had put the color back into things, Henri had been out in his rowboat at the confluence of the Ardèche and the Rhône, as he was every morning except Sunday— as he'd been all his life, for that matter, at least since he'd left school at twelve to help his father haul the nets and offer up their daily catch in their stall on rue des Quatre Vents. His father was dead now, dead ten years, and his mother, after her second stroke, had moved in with her sister in Nîmes, an hour away by car, and he didn't have a car. He talked with her on the phone every week or so, but it was difficult because her condition had garbled her speech, and he couldn't always make out what she was trying to say. No matter. He was content with his solitary life, though if he could have found a wife—or if a wife could have found him—he would have been happy to give it up. He was forty-seven. He smelled of fish. He was slow with figures, and when he talked to people, women especially, he was slow in finding his words. Still, he lived in nature, out on the water, and he was strong and dedicated and he savored the way the light caught the wings of the herons as they lifted off into the sky. He knew the intimacies of the weather, he was a scholar of the catfish, zander, barbel, and sturgeon, and he was self-sufficient and true in the core of himself.

The morning wore on, but it wasn't a particularly good day for him. His gill nets held little—and one was torn where something big, catfish or sturgeon, had bulled right through it—and the bait was picked clean from the hooks of the trotline he'd stretched across a usually profitable cove he knew upriver, which meant a whole lot of rowing for very little reward. He too took his lunch at the café, and because it was so hot already, even at noon, he ordered just a salad and soup, and if the bread wasn't up to par, at least it was filling and he realized as he ate that he was hungrier than he'd thought, so he called for more bread, and when Mme Doumergue came round with a second carafe of wine, he accepted that also and sat there at his table smoking a cigarette over dessert, and if he felt the faintest bit unusual, he chalked it up to the wine. He went home for his *sieste* and was back out on the water by four, checking his nets and trotlines.

He drifted, he smoked, he watched the sky. The sun was an egg yolk, the birds chattered like a hundred radios tuned to different stations, and as he rode the current back down in the evening he began to notice that everything moving along with him—sticks, bottles, an automobile tire, a child's faded rubber duck—was infused with hues he'd never seen before, as if a technicolor film were being projected somewhere beneath the surface. This was odd, odd in the extreme. He'd seen spills, spewing drains, oil and gasoline from motor craft, and every sort of storm runoff conceivable under every sort of sky imaginable, but never anything like this. The river seemed to be aflame with licking tongues of fire. Baffled, he dipped his hand in it, cupped the water in his palm, and let it dribble between his fingers, water as cool and fresh as it always was, but it wasn't transparent and it wasn't gray—it was the color of the viscous blood in the belly of a perch when you slit it open . . . and what did that mean? He didn't feel frightened, not yet. He blinked his eyes rapidly, blinked them hard, but each time they snapped open, the river was still flowing past him in ribbons of flame. That was when he looked over his shoulder, and there it was, the hyena, perched in the bow and showing its teeth.

It was just past six when Paulette came to him, white-faced and wringing her hands. He was sitting at his desk in the back of the store, sipping an espresso and going over the books for lack of anything better to do—the day had been such a slow silent creep he might as well have been running a mortuary. To this point there'd been only one customer all afternoon, Piero Ponticelli, the Italian *garagiste*, and all he needed was a pair of linchpins that were hardly worth the bother of ringing up. "Come quick," his wife said, and he followed her to the front of the store, where the door stood open because of the heat. There seemed to be some sort of commotion in the street, a gabble of shouting, moaning, the knife-edged cries of a woman gone hysterical, and when he stuck his head out the door, he saw two of his fellow shopkeepers running awkwardly up and down the pavement as if they were in a sack race at the spring fête, but even stranger and more alarming was the sight of a vintner they knew well—Jean Cullaz, whom they'd patronized since they'd got married ten years ago and moved into the apartment above the store—crawling on his belly in the middle of the street as cars shunted to the curb and bicycles shot past in a shimmer of spokes.

"Oh, God help me!" the woman's voice cried, and he glanced

up to see Marie Lavigne hanging out her window on the far side of the street, flailing her arms as if she were being attacked by hornets. "The claws!" she shouted. "The claws won't retract!"

But here was Jean Cullaz, crawling right up to him on chafed elbows and seizing him by the ankles with both hands. The vintner's face was bloodless, his pupils so enlarged it was as if his eyes had been poked out. "I'm dead," he sobbed, "dead, and my head is made of copper and all I can think of is potatoes and I don't like potatoes and I don't want potatoes but I'm dead and my head's a copper pot and the potatoes are boiling in it! Boiling, boiling, boiling!"

Maxime didn't know what to say. What could you say? *No, your head is not made of copper and you are not dead, not in the slightest*? It was as if he'd stepped into a movie theater halfway through the first reel—of a horror picture—and the only response was to say, as the hero always did, *But you're mad!* Instead he turned to Paulette and said, "Call the doctor."

The way he escaped the hyena was cleverness itself, though it got him soaked through to the skin and cost him the evening's catch. Terrified, expecting at any moment to feel the crush of its teeth that were designed to break down even the most durable bone of the carcasses dotting the savannas of Africa, he swung hard right, against the current, and tipped the boat a hundred yards from the quai. Down went the animal, shrieking and frothing, and as he clung to the hull of the overturned boat, he watched it go down again, and then a third time, but then—horribly—it bobbed back up like a buoy and cut a vicious trench through the current as it made for shore. The water was fire, the water was blood, but he was at home in it for all that, and he kicked out his legs and guided the boat to the quai, where he made it fast, though it was still upside down, and then he looked up into the face of the architecture he'd known all his life—the colorless mass of stone that was L'église Saint-Saturnin and the equally colorless two- and three-story buildings crowded in beside it—and watched them morph into huge pillars of orange, green, and cherry ices on wooden sticks the size of plane trees. He began to shiver violently, and though he had no intimation of it at that point, he wouldn't stop shivering for the next seven days. He wrapped his arms round himself. His clothes clung wet to his skin. He knew one thing only: he had to get home.

Yes, of course he did. The world might have become alien and unfathomable, and his gut ached and his head too, but home was home and he would be safe there because he could bar the door against the hyena and wrap himself in a blanket and build a fire, a real and actual fire and not one made of water. The only problem was, he didn't recognize anything. The buildings loomed and shrank back again. Everybody seemed to be running and so he started running too, his heart pounding to break free of his chest, and why weren't any of them who they were supposed to be? Why were they all wearing masks? Why were their bodies cobbled together out of odds and ends—scraps, just scraps of people? He ran till he was exhausted, and still he couldn't stop shivering. Suddenly it was dark and the lights of the houses and shops were fierce yellow eyes boring into him, the eyes of hyenas, whole packs of slavering, chittering hyenas just waiting to work their jaws and tear bloody gobbets from the limbs and torsos of his neighbors—and him, from him especially, and what had the animal said to him as it perched on its reeking haunches in the bow of the boat? *The flesh is weak, the flesh punctures, the flesh is delectable.* And then it laughed.

He was frightened now, deeply frightened. His fear was every-thing, as big as the world that was spinning beneath his feet as if he were a thousand miles tall and riding it like a bicycle. He didn't have the perspective to know that he was poisoned and hurtling into the madness that would drive him to the asylum in Avignon, where he would be strapped down on a bed for seven sleepless days and nights while every hyena in the world gnawed at his guts and his privates and the soft spongy lobes of his brain. No, all he had was the immediate and present fear that jerked at his legs and drove him careering headlong into the night. Things could have ended badly for him right then and there, as they would for so many others that day, but it was luck and luck alone that all at once gave him a stiff shove and brought him to the doorstep of his own house, even as people ran screaming past him and sirens tangled themselves in the densest shadows of the streets.

Paulette never ate between meals, which was one of the reasons she'd retained her figure even now that she'd turned forty, but on this day, of all days, she'd felt peckish around five in the afternoon—and maybe that was because they'd had the *frites* instead of bread at lunch and *frites* just don't fill you the way bread does. Nothing was happening in the shop, so she told him she was going upstairs to the apartment to make herself a *jambon-beurre* sandwich with the baguette she'd picked up that morning at the bakery and asked if he wanted anything, which he didn't—it was too hot even to think about eating. He read through the newspapers and a magazine devoted to auto racing and forgot all about her till she came down the stairs and alerted him to what was happening in the streets, to Marie Lavigne thinking she could fly and Jean Cullaz slithering on his belly like an adder and half the rest of the town raving like lunatics. At first he thought it was some kind of elaborate joke, as if it were the first of April all over again, but when he saw the look on Jean Cullaz's face, the torn knees of his trousers and his bloody elbows, he knew it was no prank.

While Paulette went to the phone to call the doctor, he tried to help Jean Cullaz to his feet, but Jean Cullaz was having none of it, and he was too heavy to lift, so, his heart racing, Maxime dragged him in over the threshold to get him out of the sun— was it sunstroke?—and raced upstairs for water and a wet towel. When he came back down, Paulette was kneeling over the man while he writhed on the floor and kept repeating, "Potatoes! Potatoes!" over and over, and the screams and curses of a whole mob of people echoed off the buildings and in through the open door. That was when Jean Cullaz turned violent. In his delirium he kept insisting that his head was a copper pot and he tried to remove it, to pull off his own head by the ears, which were instantly bloody and ragged, so that he and Paulette had to sit on the man's chest and pin his arms down to prevent him from mauling himself. When Dr. Veladaire came hurrying through the door, black bag in hand, he took one look, drew out his hypodermic syringe, and injected the patient—who was now foaming at the mouth—with a powerful sedative. Which had no effect whatsoever. Cullaz kept screaming about copper and potatoes and the boiling heat of his brain, and now the doctor was obliged to sit on him as well for fear he'd break loose and do real harm to himself or someone else.

It was a challenge. It was terrifying. A man they hardly knew—a farmer from downriver—burst through the open door, snatched an ax from the shelf, and raced shrieking back into the street while Jean Cullaz writhed under them and tried to tear his own ears off. "What is it?" Paulette gasped, riding Jean Cullaz's midsection like a cowboy on a steer in the newsreels. "What's happening? What's wrong with him?" she demanded, and all the doctor, who was bucking along with her while Maxime held fast to Jean Cullaz's kicking feet, could say in a clenched voice was, "Rope. Get rope."

One of the signs of the madness was dilated pupils, pupils so enlarged they entirely engulfed the sclera of the eyes, and it was at this point that Maxime noticed Paulette's eyes getting darker and darker till they were as black as the inside of a closet, and he was afraid all over again. More afraid. Freshly afraid. So afraid he could have been back in the war again when every waking moment vibrated with the icy tension of death.

The fire leapt and roared and he couldn't stop shivering. Never mind that the evening was stifling and all through the day he'd been sweating like a *cochon*, he was cold, colder than he'd ever been. The thought came to him of heating something up on the stove, coffee, soup, anything for the warmth, but the idea nauseated him, and even so, as if to mock him, the stove suddenly turned into a block of ice as massive as the Glacier Noir, with its hard glaring face and the scattered acne of its crevasses. He pulled his chair up as close to the fire as he could. Time erupted, flowed like lava. He clung to himself. Everything was alive, everything in motion, and there was the oddest smell about the place, an odor of dead mice, mice poisoned and rotting in the walls with the slow creeping stench of death, and after a time he realized the odor was coming from him, from his own body, which was alternately shivering and sweating as if it were two different bodies in one. He shut his eyes fast, but that did no good. He rocked back and forth, beat at his thighs to warm them, but that did no good either. And then, in the middle of everything, he heard the first harrowing scritch-scratch of claws at the door.

It was the hyena. Of course it was. It had come back for him so it could finish the job it had started out on the river, and was he going to allow that to happen? No, he wasn't. Instantly he was on his feet, the blanket dropping from him atop the pile of wet clothes he'd shrugged off on first coming through the door, and wasn't it the American Indians who whooped naked into battle, wasn't that how they did it, how they'd defeated the best-equipped armies the English could throw at them? He snatched up the poker from the fireplace, tore open the door, and there it was, the hyena, its eyes fixed on him.

In the aftermath, he was solemnly assured by everyone concerned—the doctors, Maxime Bonnet, Mme Doumergue, even Paulette Bonnet, who should have known better—that the hyena was a delusion fomented in his brain by the poison infesting the bread, but none of them were there in the moment he slammed the poker down on its skull and kept raising and dropping it till the animal's face was bright with its own blood, and none of them were there to follow him into the street, where he lashed out at everything else he saw until he was tackled and pinned down and fitted with the straitjacket.

He did what he could. In a world of madmen—and women—he was one of the few sane ones, and once the doctor had rushed off to the next emergency and Jean Cullaz had stopped tearing at his own ears and against all remonstration crawled back out into the street, he shut and locked the door. The phone got him nothing—there was a busy signal at the police station, the same at the hospital, the fire department, the mayor's office, and the mayor's mansion too. Outside, the shrieks rose and fell as regularly as waves beating on the beaches of the Côte d'Azur, and when he poked his head out the window, he saw the town's single ambulance pull up beside Marie Lavigne, who was at this point crawling across the pavement like Jean Cullaz. He watched as a pair of orderlies lifted her onto a stretcher and the rear doors of the ambulance gaped to receive her even as the two men he'd seen earlier came lurching back up the street, still struggling with the invisible sacks round their legs.

It grew dark. And here was his own wife, thrusting a fist in her mouth and biting down on her knuckles, all the while staring at something he couldn't see, her pupils fully dilated and her clothes giving off a peculiar odor. They hadn't eaten dinner. He hadn't checked inventory or swept the floors or wiped the counter. He put an arm round her shoulders and drew her to him. "What's wrong?" he asked.

"I don't know."

"You're feeling a little under the weather, is that it?" When she didn't answer, he said, "Well, who wouldn't be with all this"—he waved a hand to take in the street outside, the river, the church, the whole town—"this craziness. Right?"

She just stood there, biting her knuckles.

He took her by the hand, though she held back, whimpering inconsolably, and led her up the stairs, where he put her to bed despite her protests. When finally she settled down he went into the living room and sat by the radio, hungry for news. There was none. The news was in the street below them, and what was propelling it no one knew, though the doctor had said it must have been some sort of mass poisoning, an insecticide in the air or something in the town's water supply, but how could that account for the lunatic ravings of otherwise mentally stable people? What kind of poison could that possibly be?

He was pacing back and forth, at a loss, every so often thrusting his head out the window to see a scrum of hectic figures loping by in the street, Henri among them—naked and brandishing some sort of weapon—when he heard Paulette call out to him. He went to the bedroom door. "Yes?" he called softly, focusing on the pale globe of her face hanging there in the darkness as she propped herself up against the bedstead. "Can I get you anything? Tea? Would you like a cup of tea? Or something to eat?"

"There are six panes in this window, Maxime," she said in an unnatural voice. The room reeked of dead mice.

He stood there, waiting. She hadn't seemed as affected as some of the others, as Jean Cullaz or Marie Lavigne or the man who'd stolen the ax, and he'd hoped that it was only a touch of the grippe—when he put her to bed she'd complained of an upset stomach, of a headache, of heartburn, all commonplace complaints, and that was all it was, he told himself. She'd be better in the morning, after a good night's sleep.

"Yes," he said, "yes, of course, there are six panes in the window."

"One, two, three," she said, counting them, "four, five, six." And then she started over, "One, two, three, four, five, six," and then over again. And again.

By midnight she'd counted the panes in her steady unwavering voice at least a thousand times, two thousand, who knew? And every time he tried to distract her, to make a joke of it, she paused just long enough for him to get the words out, then started in again. Eventually, he was able to get through to the doctor, who came trudging up the stairs half an hour later, in the final stages of fatigue and looking like a madman himself, to give her an injection, just as he'd done with Jean Cullaz. And just as with Jean Cullaz, it had no effect. She counted while he inserted the needle, counted while he withdrew it, counted as he packed up his bag and started down the stairs, and after he himself had fallen asleep out of sheer exhaustion, he kept jarring awake to the rhythm of her indefatigable voice, counting and counting again. "One," she breathed. "Two. Three . . ."

No hyena came for Maxime Bonnet's wife, or not that anyone would admit, and as far as Henri could see, she seemed to have been one of the milder cases among those who'd been stricken by the menagerie lurking in the bread. She tended to stare into space and move her lips silently, as if she were talking to herself or counting out change over an invisible register, but she was pretty still, the prettiest woman he knew, if you excepted Marie Lavigne, whose face seemed to be lit from within and whose legs, stretched out before her in the wheelchair as if being presented anew to the world, were all the more shapely and inviting despite the plaster casts she was obliged to wear. Or maybe because of them. All he knew was that he couldn't take his eyes off her every time she wheeled by in the street. Of course, he went back to fishing as soon as he was able, and he was grateful for the catch, which was better than he could ever remember for this time of year, as if the hyena's savage strokes had stirred up whole unimagined shoals of fish from the depths. The damage he'd done to the furniture of the house he'd inherited by default when his mother went into her sister's care was complete, but he'd managed to pick up a few items here and there to replace it, and there was a long future ahead of him, a happy future, because the events of that terrible day and night had, as it turned out, held an unforeseen benefit for him.

For the first two days after returning home he did nothing but sleep. All through the previous week he hadn't shut his eyes, not once, the bread relentlessly locking him inside his visions like one of the saints—like Jeanne d'Arc, whose holy visitations,

Maxime insisted, were strictly illusory and due to a version of the very same bread poisoning that had afflicted Pont-Saint-Esprit, which was to take nothing away from God, but you had to dwell in facts in the modern age, didn't you? When he did finally come back to himself, when the pupils of his eyes shrank to normal and the odor of dead mice blew away on the wind, he took up where he'd left off, setting out his gill nets and baiting his droplines. One afternoon, while he was sitting over a dish of *bouillabaisse* at his usual table in the café, his plethoric catch already on ice and no need to go back out after lunch, his eyes jumped to a sudden movement at the door, and he saw Marie Lavigne there, struggling to hold the door open and at the same time work the wheels of her chair over the threshold, and so, naturally, he sprang up and went to assist her. Naturally too, and without even thinking, he wheeled her to his table, where she opened up her smile and spoke more words to him in the next two hours than had been spoken to him in the past two years. No one there that afternoon, including Maxime Bonnet and his wife, whether they'd eaten poisoned bread or consumed a jeroboam of wine, could have doubted what was happening before their eyes: it was a match.

Within the month, Marie had quit her job behind the cash register at the *épicerie*, and on a breezy morning in October they were married, though she had to support herself on crutches during the ceremony. There was a wedding dinner afterward at the café, and Maxime Bonnet gave the matrimonial toast, and everyone ate the baguettes and *pain de campagne* accompanying the six courses Mme Doumergue served up and didn't think twice about it. That night, as they lay in bed, Marie told him again of the beast that had come for her and the horror that had driven her to leap out the window with nothing but desperation to support her. "I'll never get over it," she whispered. "Never. No matter how long I live."

He drew her close and hushed her and told her a lie—"It was all just an illusion"—even as he caught his breath and held it, listening, with every fiber of his being, for the scratch at the door.

The Shape
of a Teardrop

POLICE DOGS AND FIREHOSES

I'm not going anywhere. They can come in with police dogs and firehoses and I'll cling to the woodwork till I'm stripped to the bone—they'd like that, wouldn't they, their one and only child who never asked to be born in the first place reduced to an artifact in his own room in the only home he's ever known? A memento mori. A musculoskeletal structure without the musculo. Shouting matches? If they want shouting matches, well, I'm more than equal to the task. They're old and weak and ridiculous and they know it, with their stained teeth and droopy necks and faces like masks cut out of sheets of sandpaper with two holes poked for their glittery, hypercritical eyes to blaze through. You want to call them duplicitous, unloving, conniving? Check, check, and check. But what a fool I am—I'd thought the final straw was when they dropped me from the family plan and I woke up one day with no cell-phone service and really, knock-knock, how can they expect me to get a job if I don't have a phone? Is that so hard to figure out? Does that take higher reasoning? The application of logical thought processes? Putting fucking one and one together? But then there was the next final straw, when they brought in Lucas Hubinski, who used to be in high school with me back in the time before time, and had him put a lock on the refrigerator and the pantry too, as if they were display cases at Tiffany's. You think that was extreme? How about the final straw, the one that could have filled a whole barn full of ungulate fodder bound up in bales eight feet high? You ready for this? They went out and got an eviction notice and taped it to the door of my room, as if that was going to mean anything to me, as if I could care what the Danbury Superior Court has to say about anything. Or them either. Them either.

EVERY ADVANTAGE

He had every advantage. We loved him, we still love him, our only child who came to us as the sweetest and truest blessing from God when I was forty-one and so empty inside I was staring into the void through my every waking moment and in my dreams too that used to be so full of wonder but turned rancid on me as if my brain was rotting right there on the pillow while Doug snored the night away because he'd given up, he really had, worn out from working overtime so we could afford the in vitro treatments, which was just money thrown down the drain, because nothing ever came of them except heartache. But I don't give up so easily—I'm hardheaded like my mother and her mother before her. I went to Victoria's Secret for lingerie, got Doug drunk on champagne when the calendar said I was ovulating, posed for him, sat in his lap and watched porn till we were both so hot we practically raped each other. Still, nothing happened. Months dripped by like slow poison. I told myself there were other ways to be fulfilled besides bearing children, though when you come down to it, God and heaven aside, the whole point of life is to create more life. Then, in the way of these things, the mysterious way, I mean, the way the world turns whether you think you're in charge of it or not, I missed my period. One morning I woke up feeling sick to my stomach. I knew right away. I was elated. I took off like a rocket ship. And my baby was more beautiful than beauty itself.

THE DOCUMENT IN QUESTION

The document in question is just a paragraph long—pithy, to the point—and was drawn up by some lower life-form with a J.D. degree they knew from the bar at Emilio's, where they used to take me in happier days, before, in my father's words—no joke, my own father—I became an embarrassment to them. Ha! *I'm* an embarrassment to *them*? Have they looked in a mirror lately? Anyway, it was a day from hell, first week of February, a cold needling rain harassing me all the way back from the mall, which is a 2.3-mile walk, one way, and of course to get there in the first place, I had to walk the 2.3 miles and forget sticking your thumb out because nobody around here's picked up a hitchhiker since the first *Star Wars* movie came out or maybe even before that. Who knows? That's a matter for the social historians. But why didn't I drive? Because my car, a Japanese piece of shit, needs a new front end, and it's been up on blocks in the driveway for the past eighteen months because my parents refuse to loan me the wherewithal to get it repaired, and again, their thinking is beyond stupefying, because, even if I do manage to find a job *without a cell phone*, how do they expect me to actually *arrive* at my place of employment?

But I needed to get out, if only for my own mental and physical well-being, because you can only reread your creased and moldering paperbacks you've had on your shelf since you were fourteen, play video game retreads, and stare into the fish tank so many hours a day before you start feeling like Dostoevsky's Underground Man and poisoning yourself to the outside world, so I decided to take the trek. In the rain. I'm not much of a drinker, and since my unemployment ran out, I don't have a whole lot of money to throw around, but there's a bar there where I like to sit over a pitcher and watch the barmaid go briskly about her business (the way she moves her elbows, wow, as if they're rhythm machines with a whole separate function from the rest of her body), which mainly involves polishing the bar top and flirting with the male customers, a subset to which I belong. Her name is Ti-Gress, or at least that's what her name tag says, and after what I have to put up with at home, it's beyond refreshing to sit there and watch her while the sound system delivers electronica and the patrons jaw at one another and the TV redirects its pixels till everybody's in a trance. Plus, I wanted to stop at Pet Emporium to pick up a pair of convict cichlids for the big tank (fifty gallons, freshwater, strictly Central and South American species because that's my method, not like these so-called "hobbyists" who promiscuously mix Asian, African, and South American in a way that's an outrage to nature, if you think about it, because what you're creating is a world, an ideal world, and perfection is within your sights if you know what you're doing). Anyway, I watched Ti-Gress and exchanged a comment or two with her as her elbows flew and she slid like a big silk kite up and down the bar, finished my beer, picked out the convicts, and had the stringy-haired sixteen-year-old pet shop nerd put them in a bigger-than-normal plastic bag with an extra shot of O2 (which I tucked inside my jacket to keep warm for the 2.3-mile walk home), and reversed direction.

It had gotten colder. The rain turned to sleet. Nobody this side of an asylum would even consider stopping to offer me a ride, and no, I don't have the money to waste on Uber, if that's what you're thinking. Then I walk in the house—nobody home, they're still at work, thank the tutelary gods for small miracles, and Jesus, Mohammed, and Siddhartha too, if they're listening—and there's this notice taped to my door. *You are herewith informed. Et cetera.*

BIRTHDAY CARD

I didn't even have a chance to get out of the car before he was right there in my face, waving the notice I'd come all the way home on my lunch break to tape to his door so there would be no mistaking our intentions, no more second chances or third chances—or twentieth, actually, if you want to know the truth of it. He was ugly in that moment, which I hate to admit, but what adult stamps around in the slush of the driveway throwing a tantrum like a two-year-old on a day so bleak you just want to break down and cry anyway? And with the neighbors watching too, Jocelyn Hammersmith across the street foremost among them, whose stone face I could see poking through her parted blinds? Oh, he was so put-upon, so abused, and I was inhuman, the most unfeeling mother in history, who'd never understood him, never supported him, never given him a break. Doug called him an embarrassment, which was cruel and wrongheaded, but in that moment, with his face contorted and the unkempt snarl of a beard he never trims or even washes, so it's flecked with dandruff that he looks like a fur trapper in a snowstorm, and all the weight he's put on feeling sorry for himself in the room I haven't been allowed to enter since he moved back home after he broke up with his girlfriend seven years ago, I can't help seeing the truth of it. Would he ever think of opening the door for me? No, he just wants to rave. "You're killing me, is that what you want? You want me to be homeless? You want me to sleep outside in this shitty weather and get what, multiple-drug-resistant TB from all the bums? Huh, would that make you happy?"

Does he notice that my arms are full or wonder why I'm bringing home a bouquet of pink roses and white carnations or why my eighth-period honors class went out of their way to surprise me with them? Does he even know it's my birthday? And what about a card? What about a birthday card, even a generic one—or a handmade one like he used to give me when he was in elementary school? Am I being petty to want some kind of recognition that I'm alive and breathing, if it's only one day a year? Who is this person? What have I made? What has he become?

The door of the car—a Jeep Grand Cherokee Doug insisted I get for the four-wheel drive—is heavier than the door of a bank vault, and even in the best of times I have to push hard to get it open, but now, juggling my purse and briefcase and trying to protect the flowers, it's a real trick. Somehow I manage, and now I've got a foot on the pavement, in the slush, and I'm so angry I'm afraid of what I might say, afraid I might lash out, reminding him of all the "loans" over the years and the fifteen hundred dollars we gave him for Christmas to get himself an apartment, which he says he spent on "expenses," so I just match my expression to his and say, "It's my birthday."

That stops him, if only for an instant, the hand that's been flailing the notice like a doomsday flag dropping to his side and his face softening before it snaps back to the habitual look of umbrage he seems to wear all day every day, even when he's out in

the yard by himself or power-walking down the street to wherever he goes when he leaves the house. "You want me to die?"
he shouts, loud enough for Jocelyn Hammersmith to hear, even
through her storm windows.

I should bite my tongue. I should remember the way he once
was, the way life was before whatever happened to him—to us,
all of us, him, Doug, and me—wiped it all away. "Yes," I say, making my way past him, so close that the flowers in their crinkly
cellophane brush the black leather coat he insists on wearing
winter and summer, as if it's the skin he was born in. "If you're
going to die, go ahead and do it—but do it someplace else, will
you? Will you at least do that for us?"

I'm furious, I am, but he looks so pathetic in that moment I
just want to take everything back no matter what it comes to. "I
didn't mean that," I say. "Justin, listen to me, look at me—"

But he's already turned his back on me, stamping up the front
steps and slamming the door practically in my face.

A card. A birthday card. Is that too much to ask?

LORENA

What my parents, especially my mother, don't seem to understand is that Lorena is a miserable excuse for a human being and
a certified bitch to boot. I tried with her. Tried to "man up" as she
put it, and when she got pregnant in our senior year at the state
college that didn't have much more to offer me than a penal col-
ony, I even moved in with her in her apartment that was the size
of the sweatbox in *The Bridge on the River Kwai* (movie version; I
never read the book), and I put up with that till she got so big I
started calling her Godzilla Jr., and things that weren't so sweet
and loving to begin with became toxic to the point at which it
made me physically ill just to look at her. Yes, I had sex with her,

guilty as charged, but it was all her, because she knew exactly what men wanted and all the experience was on her side. I was her pawn. I barely knew what a condom was. And *please*, I never asked to have a child. A child is just a parasite growing inside an otherwise healthy organism—a female organism, thankfully, because if it was me I'd just shoot myself. Okay. I wasn't ready to be a father—so sue me. Which, of course, is what she did, and when I dropped out of school twelve credits short of a B.A. in Cultural Studies and got a job at Home Depot, they garnished my wages for child support. Whoop-de-doo! Welcome to the legal system of the U.S. of A.!

I made it short and sweet on the day I ran into her on the street with the kid after I'd been sleeping on the couch at Steve Arms's place for something like half a lifetime, my back rearranged to the point where I could barely straighten up and my boredom level right down there in the subbasement of hell, where everything's frozen like Antarctica in the long, black night of the soul. "Lorena, you're killing me," I said, and it was the literal truth.

Lorena might have been pretty if she had more style, but she didn't. She just looked like a big sack, and there was the baby, a little sack, propped up beside her on the bench waiting for the bus, and I just happened to have the bad luck of walking by at that moment. Five minutes before or after and she wouldn't have been there at all. "No, *you're* killing *me*," she said and gave out with one of her curdled little laughs, as if it were the wittiest thing that ever emerged from anybody's mouth.

I didn't know what to do. I was frozen there. I still had a car then and a job, and I could have done anything I wanted. The baby didn't look like me, but the DNA test her lawyer made me submit to came up bingo, and there he was, the baby, gazing up at me out of a pair of eyes that were as black as the empty spaces between the planets. "What's his name?" I asked, and she gave me a look as if I'd just slapped her and her mother and her mother's mother all the way back to the hominids loping across Olduvai Gorge.

"What are you *saying*?" She was looking down a double barrel of hate aimed right between my eyes. My legs felt weak. I felt weak. I was so far gone I almost sat down beside her. "You know his name as well as I do."

"I didn't give it to him."

"No," she said. "No, you didn't."

And that, right there, that encounter at a bus stop, of all places, was what started the rift between my parents and their only child, because if there was one thing they wanted, my mother most of all, it was to see this marvel, this grandchild ("grandbaby," as she put it), and if I'd decided against that right from the beginning, right from the moment Lorena announced her pregnancy to me as a fait accompli, I was more determined than ever to put a lid on that. Truthfully? I was ashamed. Ashamed of what I'd done and the black-eyed evidence of it staring up at me from the hard plastic seat of a bus stop bench in a place that was bleak and ugly and had nothing to do with me or what I wanted out of life.

ALEJANDRO

That was his name, my grandson, Alejandro Diaz Narvaez, and if my son had done the right thing by the child's mother he could have been named Alexander Dugan and brought into the family legitimately and not have to swim against the current all his life with a single parent who couldn't begin to give him the advantages he deserved. But my son refused to let us see him or have any contact with the mother, with Lorena, whom we laid eyes on for the first time a month after Justin moved back into his room, and she appeared on the front porch with the baby in her arms. "Mrs. Dugan?" she said, making it both question and surmise, and I said, "Yes?"

Neither Doug nor I have a prejudicial bone in our bodies so I can't imagine how Justin could have thought we wouldn't accept this child as readily as any other, and Lorena as our daughter-in-law, even if we'd all been deprived of a wedding (and more than that, the birth of the baby, the shower, the christening, getting to meet the other set of grandparents, shopping for baby outfits and toys and cribs and strollers, all of it). I was gracious with Lorena, of course I was—that was how I was raised. And as we sat over a cup of tea and a platter of shortbread rounds I found in the back of the cabinet and was afraid had gone stale (but hadn't, thankfully), I studied that baby like a genealogical sleuth, and whose nose did he have? Whose eyes? Ears? Hair? Even the bow of his legs and the dimples that creased his cheeks when his mother made him laugh, which he did readily, a little chirp of a laugh, and I could see right away what a good mother she was. He kicked out his legs and waved his arms, and when Lorena put him down on the carpet he showed off his ability to crawl at speed and even stand for whole seconds at a time without assistance, and the more I watched him the more I knew in my heart just who this child was and the thing I felt above all else was blessed.

ON A LEGAL FOOTING

So things are on a legal footing, as the expression goes, my mother, on her birthday, of all days, taping the eviction notice to my door where it would instantaneously awaken me to their machinations, like a verbal slap in the face, even before I could work the combinations on the three case-hardened padlocks I had to install to protect my privacy and get the convicts in the tank because the water in the plastic carrying bag wasn't getting any warmer and the O2 level was dropping by the minute. And guess what? When my father came home, though I refused to come out of my room and join in any birthday celebration—are you kidding me?—he went right along with the agenda. Because he's weak, a drudge, a drone who's toiled away at IBM his whole life and brings his lunch to work in the same scuffed aluminum lunch box he claims I gave him for Father's Day when I was five years old, which probably isn't even true, and if it is it's beyond pathetic.

Anyway, no sooner do I get the convicts into my ten-gallon holding tank to acclimate them and scrutinize them for disease—Ich, in particular, *Ichthyophthirius multifiliis*, that is, which can infest an entire tank and drain the life out of your fish till they're just tiny, bloated white corpses floating in little slicks of their own scum—than I hear my mother's car pull into the driveway and it just sets me off, her coming home like that as if today's no different from any other, and so I tear the notice off the door and run right out there in the driveway to confront her with it. Which, of course, is just another kind of disaster because we've reached the point where she doesn't care if I live or die, just as long as I vacate the premises. And she admits it, says it right to my face in a tense little choked voice, as if it's tearing her up inside, when the fact is she coldly contracted with her lawyer friend to draw up the notice and then went down to the courthouse and paid the fee to file it. You tell me—where's the excuse for that? It's like in that Russian story where the wolves are chasing the sled through the snowdrifts and they toss the baby out to distract them and save themselves—and the horses, don't forget the horses.

Later, after my father comes home, I hear him at my door,

though I've got the music going and I'm so furious I can barely concentrate on what I'm seeing on the computer screen, while I scroll through site after site about tenants' rights, most of which are telling me I have none because I never paid rent or helped with maintenance or entered into any kind of legal agreement *because they're my parents, for shit's sake*, and he's saying things like, "Come on, Justin, it's your mother's birthday" and "You knew this was coming and don't say we didn't warn you" and then adding a threat or two about cutting off the power (which he knows drives a knife blade right into my spinal cord because it would kill my fish inside of an hour in this weather) before he gives up. I hear them thumping around up there for the next half hour or so, and then they're slamming out the front door and into my father's car to go out someplace (Emilio's, no doubt) for a celebratory dinner without me, the embarrassment who's so embarrassing he's not even going to have a roof over his head anymore, but none of that works for me, and what I'm doing is putting things on a legal footing of my own, searching for the cheapest lawyer I can find.

TIT FOR TAT

The notice gave him two weeks to vacate the premises, and every minute of those two weeks was soul-wrenching for us, because after everything that's happened over the years, his disrespect and hostility, his slovenliness, his refusal to look for a job or offer to help out in the least bit, and the way he categorically rejects his own son and won't listen to reason or even consider our feelings as grandparents and bolts straight out of the house on the rare occasions when Lorena and Alejandro do make the effort to pay us a visit, please understand that we love him, no matter what he might tell you. But he makes it hard, so very, very hard.

The night of my birthday, after that scene in the driveway,

we came home to a mess in the kitchen like you wouldn't believe. He'd managed to pry the door off the pantry and take a pair of bolt cutters to the lock on the refrigerator and make himself a big pot of the slumgullion stew he'll eat for days on end, just grabbing everything he could find, from the porterhouse steaks I'd picked out at Delforno's to the contents of the vegetable compartment to the French rolls in the breadbasket and the softening bananas I was saving for banana nut bread, and throwing the whole mess in the biggest pot we have, which, of course, disappeared into the basement, where he had his hotplate and microwave and whatever else I don't know. His door was locked, as usual. And when I went down the hallway to pound on it and yell my lungs out in frustration, the carpet gave like a sponge under my feet. Why? Because it was wet, soaked right through to the maple flooring, and I saw then that he'd taken one of his little ten-gallon aquariums, the first one I'd given him when he was still in elementary school, and just flung it in the hallway, plants and gravel and broken glass and all (but no fish—his fish were too precious for that, no matter what kind of gesture he thought he was making). I pounded on the door. Doug pounded on the door. But all we got back for the effort was the dismal artificial electronic music he listens to 24/7, which got progressively louder the more we pounded.

Happy birthday, Mom.

Two days later, when I got out of my car at school, a stranger walked up to me, handed me an envelope, and announced, "You've been served."

WHAT I REALLY WANTED TO SUE THEM FOR

What I really wanted to sue them for was for having given birth to me in the first place, which had happened without my knowledge or consent and resulted in my having to live a shit life on a shit planet and all because they wanted to have sex (all right, all right, so I fell into the same trap, but if they hadn't irresponsibly brought me into the world I wouldn't have been here to have Lorena take hold of my tool and stick it inside her as if that was where it belonged), but the lawyer I talked to on the first-five-minutes-free hotline said that would never fly, despite the guy in India who's suing his parents for the exact same thing, so I settled on breach of contract and drew up the complaint myself, alleging that by virtue of their giving me my room in the house since I was an infant and freely letting me move back in after I broke up with Lorena and Steve Arms got tired of seeing me there on his Cholula-stained couch, they had entered into an unwritten contract to provide me with shelter, and that even if it was in their power to evict me, they at least had to give me six months' notice, because you can't just throw somebody out in the street unless you're in some country where they randomly kick down doors and put people in concentration camps.

They didn't take it well. My father, the drudge, got somebody with a tow truck to come and haul my car away, leaving me to contemplate the bleached-out car-shaped blotch on the blacktop driveway and the bill for a hundred twenty-five dollars that arrived in the mail three days later, along with the address of a garage where I could pick it up (after shelling out twenty-five per day in storage fees). Which meant, in essence, that I no longer had a car, because I wasn't about to pay anybody anything for having misappropriated my property, and why couldn't I sue *them*, along with my father? Or better yet, just call the police and report it stolen? That would make them squirm.

As it turned out, I didn't get around to it because other problems arose. Specifically, Lorena and Alejandro. Time might have winged by, but Lorena was pretty much the same, sack-like and shapeless and without a clue as to style (unlike Ti-Gress, who absolutely rocked every outfit she wore and was the only one I knew who actually got my jokes). It was different for the kid. He'd grown, as I'd had a chance to observe through the window on the occasions when Lorena came to visit my mother, hoping no doubt for some kind of handout, because I wasn't paying child support and never would, which was why I wasn't about to go out and get a job, *Mom, if you're interested,* just to see my wages garnished, and for what, this skinny, hungry-eyed blur of motion who was something like seven years old and still didn't look anything like me at all no matter what the spit-in-a-kit DNA test said? Oh, my mother would stand outside the door of the room *from which she was evicting me* and tell me my son was here and how much he wanted to see me, and I'd just crank the music till the house shook and look hard for my chance to slip out the door. And I'm sorry. But I am not going to be forced into any kind of relationship with anybody ever—I've got enough to deal with as it is when my own flesh and blood want to throw me out in the street as if I'm no more to them than trash.

Yeah. Right. Call me naïve, because I had no idea in the world the kind of cabal I was faced with here or what they were scheming together, my parents and Lorena and the kid too, but let me clue you in—they wanted me out. And if I was out, that left an open question: what was going to become of my six-hundred-square-foot room with its own private entrance, full bath, and the knotty-pine paneling I'd measured and cut and nailed up myself when I was a junior in high school and busting my hump over the college prep classes I was taking just to please my parents, including the true ballbusters, pre-calc and French? *French,* Lorena, not *Spanish.*

DAY IN COURT

He had his day in court, which was what he wanted, what we all wanted, lacking an alternative. We served him notice three times before we finally got to stand before a judge in the public court-room where our family differences were going to be aired as if we were the lowlifes and toothless rednecks you see on the reality shows I never really had the stomach for, and the whole experi-ence was as humiliating as anything I've ever been put through in my life. We retained a friend of Doug's boss at IBM to repre-sent us, and Justin, looking the way he truly could look if he ever put any effort into it—dignified and handsome, dressed up in a sports coat and with his beard trimmed and his wavy hair pulled back in a ponytail—represented himself, because ultimately he was too cheap to hire a lawyer, which Doug knew all along would be the case.

But listen to me, I sound as if I'm my own son's adversary, as if I want to denigrate him, and I don't—far from it, I want to build him up, want to love him and respect him, but here we are, in a courtroom, and everybody present, from the judge to the court reporter to the onlookers with nothing better to do, are just having the time of their lives with our public ignominy, as if we're back in colonial times and sitting in the stocks in the town square. We're suing to evict our own son from our family home, where he's lived all his life, because he's become a burden to us, an impossible person, lazy, venal, and abusive—yes, an embarrassment—and he's countersuing us on the grounds that we've failed in our parental duty, reneging on the parent/child bond we made in the hospital on the day he emerged from my womb and Doug cut the umbilical cord and the doctor handed him to me to clasp to my breast. That hurts. Lord, how that hurts.

SO THEY NAILED ME

I pleaded with the judge (this balding meringue-faced automaton who could have been a clone of my father) and made my case with all the authority and ironclad logic I had inside me, and believe me, I'd done my homework online and cited a precedent in which the evictee—somebody's daughter who was in the same figurative boat I was—got the court to side with her and grant her a six-month extension, which was really all I wanted at this point, because the level of animosity and tit-for-tat-ism at home was just beyond belief, and I *did not want to live there anymore* or really ever see my parents again, but the judge came back at me as if he were the prosecuting attorney in some tabloid murder case on cable TV, just grilling me and grilling me. Did I have a job? Was I paying child support? Had I ever contributed anything toward rent at my parents'? (Which was bogus, because I happen to know they own the house outright and mortgage-free, so blood from a stone, right?) Was I aware that a parent's legal responsibility for his or her child ends when that child turns eighteen and—here he shuffled the papers on the bench and made a show of clamping a pair of reading glasses over his niggardly little upturned lump of a half-price nose—it says here that you're thirty-one years of age, is that right?

Well, I was. Simple fact. Do your homework, dude. But the relevant fact here was that whether I was six or sixty, I was the one getting thrown out in the street, and I tried to make him see that, tried to make him understand what it was going to take for me, with no money, no prospects, and let's face it, no hope, to get it together to move, and did he have even the slightest notion of what moving six fish tanks is like, including the fifty-gallon? Did he know how big that was? How much it weighed? Did he know that water weighs 8.34 pounds *per gallon* and the tanks would burst unless they were drained first, and if they were drained, where did he expect me to put the fish, which required, life or death, a pH factor of 7.1 and a steady temp of 78 to 80 degrees or they risked getting the Ich and the Ich could kill them? *Would* kill them?

But the judge was the judge and I was a minute speck on his docket, a blot, a nuisance, nothing. He set down his glasses, looked first to my parents, then to me, and pronounced his verdict. The case I'd cited, so he claimed, had been superseded by a more recent case and the weight thrown back on the parents' side, who had the absolute right to evict anybody from their own domicile, and in respect to that and his own determination in the case before him, he was finding against me and giving me forty-eight hours to vacate or face forcible eviction at the hands of the county sheriff who—and here he looked me right in the eye—really had better things to do. Understood?

And then there was the scene in the hallway, when I was so blind with fury I couldn't have told you my own name if you asked me three times in succession, and before my parents could get to me and gloat or jeer or threaten me or whatever they were going to do, I was confronted with Lorena and the kid, who were standing there practically blocking the exit, Lorena in a burlap-colored dress that showed off her fat knees and the kid in a miniature Mets cap and jersey, as if that would mean anything to me, since I gave up on baseball forever when I was thirteen, the year that the Mets, far from doing anything meritorious or even noteworthy, just crashed and burned. She looked from me to the kid and said, "Alejandro, say hello to your father."

PYRRHIC VICTORY

The silence that night in the house was almost insupportable, as if the air had been sucked out of us and we were just waiting for permission to breathe again. For the first time in as long as I could remember, the floorboards were not reverberating with the pulse of our son's music, which, as dreary and insistent as it was, had nonetheless become the heartbeat of the house, a filial rhythm I absorbed through the soles of my sandals and the arms of the chairs in the living room and could detect even in the faint rattle of the dishes in the sideboard, and if I wasn't always consciously aware of it, it was there, letting me know my son was alive and well and present. But why wasn't he playing his music? He was down there, wasn't he? I'd sat at the window watching since we'd got back from court, feeling nervous and guilty, hating myself, and I hadn't seen him go out since Steve Arms had dropped him off hours ago.

I asked Doug that question over dinner, which was a homemade paella with clams, mussels, and shrimp fresh from the seafood market, which Justin used to love when he was still Justin. "I don't know," Doug said. "Maybe he unplugged the stereo—maybe he's packing up." He bent forward to dig a wedge of the *socarrat* out of the bottom of the pan. "All I can say is it's a relief to be able to sit here and eat dinner like normal human beings without that constant goddamned thumping. You know what I say? It's time. It's about fucking time."

Of course, Justin is Justin, and that meant he ignored the court order and Doug had to call up and have them summon somebody from the sheriff's department to come by and enforce it, which was a trial all in itself, watching my son put through that on top of everything else. I wanted to go out and interfere, but Doug wouldn't let me. Here was this young man no older than Justin himself, in his pressed blue uniform and gun belt, standing outside the basement door and Justin pleading with him for just a little more time while Steve Arms backed his truck up to the door and the two of them started putting black trash bags full of his books and games and clothes into the back of the truck, and the sheriff's officer pointed at his watch, got in his cruiser, and drove off. Mercifully. But the process had started and whether the officer had given him an hour or three hours or five I didn't know—all I knew was that by the end of the day there'd be a new lock on the door and my son wouldn't be allowed back inside ever again, whether he'd got all his things out or not.

I watched them work, watched them drive off with the first load, then the second, and then finally come back for the fish tanks, the two of them maneuvering gingerly round the big one that still had half an inch of water in it, and the fish batting around in the bulging clear plastic bags they laid carefully in the tanks after they'd secured them in the bed of the truck, and I knew they didn't have long before they had to get those fish where they were going and back in the tanks with the heaters and the filters up and running—that much Justin had taught me over the years. But where *were* the fish going? That I wasn't privy to. I wasn't privy to anything, not anymore. I used to have a son and now I didn't.

THE SHAPE OF A TEARDROP

People congratulated me—Steve, Ti-Gress, a couple of dead-heads I knew from the bar—and they all said the same thing, *You're better off, don't you feel better off?* and I had to seriously wonder if they were joking or being sarcastic or just radiating their own hostility and insecurity, as if bad vibes were the rule of the day. Better off? In a Section 8 shithole infested with addicts and ex-cons and welfare mothers with their shrieking welfare brats hanging off their necks like tumors, and my tanks crowding the room so I can barely turn around? The tanks I had to move *twice*, incidentally, first to Steve Arms's garage literally under the gun of some fascist stormtrooper and then to this place, and if I lost half of them in the process, what's that to anybody, least of all the judge or my parents? Or Lorena. Who—you guessed it—moved in with my parents, *temporarily, strictly temporarily*, because her place was being renovated, or so she claimed, and that was six months ago, and every time I walk by at night I wind up peeping in the window, even though I don't want to, and I can see them in there, one big happy family, and my mother smiling and laughing and the kid bouncing off the walls like a Ping-Pong ball, and Lorena looking pleased with herself, as if she's finally settled the score with me once and for all. My father I don't talk to. But my mother put me back on the family plan out of the bigness of her heart, and I do get to hear her voice once in a while—all right, daily—and she has one theme only now: Alejandro. As in, when am I going to take him to the park or a movie or show him my fish tanks, because he's crazy about fish tanks and he loves you, he really does, and I'm saying, how can he love me when he barely knows me, and she counters with *It's in his blood, don't you get it?*

You can only live with resentment for so long, I know that. Of course, that doesn't mean I can do anything about it. I'm free of that place, free of my parents, and yet every time the phone buzzes in my pocket it's my mother or sometimes Lorena and even, with their prodding, Alejandro. They had him do some artwork at school, which my mother sent me via the U.S. Postal Service, pictures of fish in tanks, squirrels and dogs and cars, the usual sort of thing, except for one that said *Dad* on it in big red bleeding letters and showed a kid's face, his face, obscured by a swarm of floating misshapen blobs that I finally figured out were teardrops, as if he was sending me a message, which he was, no doubt at the prompting of Lorena and my mother, but the thing was, the kid was no artist and you couldn't really tell what they were supposed to be.

Dog Lab

For Joe Purpura

The flight he was on ran into heavy turbulence when the pilot started their descent, the kind of turbulence that brought up images of sheared metal, flaming jet fuel, and scattered body parts. Everybody aboard instantaneously went from the vague unease of airplane mode to full-on panic. The girl sitting next to him—a young mother he'd been flirting with after he'd put his anatomy text away—snatched the baby to her chest and molded her body into a shield. The plane dipped violently and shuddered through the length of it. Something thumped to the floor and rolled under his seat, the sound of it lost in the scream of the engines. He felt his heart rate spike and found himself fiercely gripping the arms of his seat as if he alone could steady the plane and bring them all home safely. "We're encountering a little rough patch here, folks," the pilot crooned redundantly from the cockpit. "Make sure your seat belts are securely fastened."

Afterward, when the plane was on the ground and the rain

lashing down as if they were parked under the Iguazu Falls, the girl turned a ghostly face to him. "God, that was . . . I mean, I thought . . ." she managed before the baby supplied the rest with a single lung-rattling shriek. He said, "Yeah, me too," and he was still trying to recover his equilibrium, never happier to be alive than in that moment. The pilot's voice came to them again, and it was a voice he could have listened to forever, the voice of salvation, but what it had to say was utterly pedestrian, not to mention anticlimactic—there was an aircraft ahead of them at the gate and there would be a brief delay. In the next moment, the engines shut down on a vast collective silence riven only by the hiss of the rain. No one said a word. They were all still in shock.

That was when they heard the barking. From below them, in the hold, came the harsh insistent complaint of a dog that had been caught in the same maelstrom they had. With the difference, of course, that the dog couldn't conceive of what had just happened or where it was or why. The dog had known only the lump of ground meat containing the sedative, then the last touch of its owner's hand, then the cage, then the drowsiness. And now it was awake to something else altogether, strange smells, darkness, the mechanical groans and whimpers of the plane settling around it.

Jackson was feeling the same sort of disorientation himself, they all were, but they'd boarded the plane voluntarily and their cage was the aluminum shell sculpted overhead, familiar to them, expected, confinement a part of the price you had to pay to get where you were going. Not that it would have mattered to the dog—it was frightened, it was uncomfortable, it was caged. It barked and kept on barking. He pictured a big animal, deep-chested, a German shepherd or Rottweiler or some such, its head thrown back, jaws snapping open and shut with each furious breath. Its distress preyed on him, especially after what he'd just gone through, what they'd all gone through. And why couldn't the pilot or the flight attendant or whoever take the initiative and switch on some music, anything, even the inane pop drivel they usually inflicted on their passengers?

The pilot came back on the intercom then to inform them that he'd gotten word it would be another twenty minutes and admonish them to remain seated with their seat belts fastened. His voice overrode the dog's and momentarily distracted them all from the animal's discomfort, which was different from theirs only by degree. But as soon as the intercom switched off, the dog's barking was right there again, front and center, working like a drill at their nerves.

"Poor dog," the girl said.

Beyond the rain-smeared window, somewhere inside the long, low terminal building that appeared as a dim glow against the night, was Juliana, who'd come to pick him up with the prospect of dinner and bed in their immediate future. She knew nothing of the near-death experience he'd just been through, or of the young mother with her milk-swollen breasts and birdlike shoulders transforming herself into impregnable steel, or of the desolate dog that just couldn't stop barking. "Yeah," he said, lighting and extinguishing a quick smile. "Poor us too."

One minute you're alive, the next you're dead—those were the conditions of the world, and even to attempt to assign any logic to them was to fall into the deep, dark vat of religion and other associated forms of voodoo. The plane could have crashed, transmuting himself, the young mother, her baby, and the bewildered dog into so many scraps of scorched meat, but it hadn't, and once he'd hugged Juliana to him and told her the story—it took all of thirty seconds—he forgot about it. Life was expendable, wasn't it? And it hadn't expended him yet, so what was the problem?

He thought he'd put it behind him, but when he went up the steps to the teaching hospital three days later, the barking of the dogs in the basement brought the scene back to him. The sound, faint and tympanic, was heavily muffled by the storm windows and the ancient stone walls, and it was so familiar it had long since become a kind of background noise to his daily progress up and down those steps, no different from the rasp of tires out on the boulevard or the chatter of the birds in the trees or the screech of brakes, but now it separated itself and he pictured the dogs down there in their cages, awaiting their turn in Dog Lab, as uneasy and impatient as the dog in the cargo hold, except that that dog was going home and these weren't. He was in his third year of med school, and his rotation had taken him through ob-gyn, pediatrics, and internal medicine, and surgery was next up on his schedule, which meant he'd be in intimate contact with those dogs soon enough. When he'd first mentioned it to Juliana a month ago, she'd made a face and said, "What you mean, *Dog Lab*? You're not going to be a veterinarian, are you, Jax?"

They were at her apartment, on a study date, she at her desk in the corner, he on the couch, hunched over one of the twenty-pound texts he had to lug around with him everywhere he went, lest he should miss out on a precious undirected moment in which he could be studying. They'd been dating for the better part of the past year. Her apartment was a model of order and tasteful arrangement, like a stage set before the actors drift in from the wings; his was not. She cooked for him sometimes and sometimes he spent the night and they'd talked of moving in together and consolidating expenses, but because of their madhouse schedules (she was student teaching and working af-ternoons at Burger King, and for his part he couldn't tell the difference between med school and what the Marines had to go through in boot camp, except that boot camp was a whole lot shorter), they hadn't got around to it.

"No," he said, "I told you—it's part of the surgery rotation?"

She had her own massive text spread open before her, the gloss of its thick, coated paper redirecting the light of her desk lamp every time she turned a page. "What do you mean?" she asked, glancing up at him. He could see from the way her eyes clicked like counters—one beat, two beats, three—that she was doing the math. "You're not going to . . . I mean, you don't *practice* on them, do you?"

If he'd had his own qualms, he was well past that stage now. He'd had a dog when he was a kid and a cat too, and he'd never intentionally inflicted pain on any creature, not even the cockroaches that erupted from the drain every time he turned the shower on, and that met their fate quickly and decisively, but he nonetheless did what was required of him—and this was what was required. "How else are we going to learn physiology, I mean, outside of cadavers and a textbook? It's not like we can just take the elevator up to the OR and start doing heart surgery on somebody . . ."

She was silent. Behind her, on the flickering screen of the TV she kept going through every waking hour, as if it were her own personal life-support system, the massive lumpen head and vacant eyes of Gerald Ford advanced and receded as he took questions at a press conference, his mouth moving in dumb show because the sound was muted. Thankfully. He thought she was going to say something more, something along the lines of *Doesn't that bother you?*, but she didn't. She took up her turquoise marker and highlighted a passage in her text that was already highlighted in yellow. From the apartment above came the repetitive thump of the bass line to a tune he used to play with the R&B band he was in back in the days when he had the time to devote to anything other than *Basic Neuroanatomy* or *Harrison's Principles of Internal Medicine*, and that pulled him out of himself long enough for her to drop the next question into the vacuum. "What happens to them when, you know, they've been, what, operated on?"

What happened was that they were euthanized and their blood was drained for use in veterinary clinics. He said, "I don't know."

"They kill them, don't they?"

Professor Ciotti had addressed the issue in Medical Ethics by pointing out that there were too many irresponsible dog owners in the world and too many unwanted dogs—the shelters couldn't begin to keep pace with the numbers they were daily presented with. If a dog wasn't adopted in two weeks, it was euthanized. Why not, Professor Ciotti asked, use them to benefit humanity?

He gave her a weak smile. He didn't like it any better than she did. "Yeah," he said, "I hate to say it, but they're going to put them down in the shelter anyway."

"So they're expendable, is that what you're saying?"

Behind her, President Ford had been replaced by a Ford Mustang, a convertible, red with black upholstery, a car he'd love to get his hands on someday. He watched it eat up S-turns on a deserted blacktop road, then sighed and slapped the book shut. "You know what?" he said. "I don't want to talk about it, I really don't."

The dog he was assigned—or rather, his group of three was assigned—was a beagle. It didn't have a name, or not that he knew of, anyway. There was no point in names. The dogs had been selected at the pound by one of the lab techs, an acromegalic giant by the name of Reggie who everyone called Lurch behind his back, after the character in the TV show, and if at some point they'd lived with families and worn collars and tags with their names engraved on them, no one knew about that either. They'd been abandoned. They were lab animals now, and that was all anybody needed to know. "Don't think of them in terms of your family pets," Dr. Markowitz, the resident overseeing the surgery rotation, told them the first day. "Think of them in terms of a problem to be solved." He'd let out a low chuckle. "Which, if any of you do go on to become surgeons, is more or less how you'll have to think of your patients. Emotions have to be compartmentalized and you shouldn't have to think about your first incision any more than your last. Practice makes perfect, and that is what this lab is all about."

There were three dogs laid out on separate operating tables, each attended by three students who would take turns rotating between prep, assisting, and operating. His group consisted of Jerry Katz, whom he liked and respected and had even once or twice played pinball with at Herlihy's, a dive bar that was equally divided between med students and neighborhood types busy blackening their lungs and concretizing their livers, and Paul Sipper, who'd gone to Yale and never let anybody forget it, and was about as likable as a sealed jar on a high shelf.

The dogs had been prepped by Lurch and the other tech, an equally inimical figure who'd worked at the hospital for the past decade or maybe even longer, nobody knew, not even the nurses, and the nurses knew everything. His eyes were like drill presses—he'd seen every sort of fuckup imaginable, and he wasn't shy about letting you know it. All three dogs had been anaesthetized, intubated, and draped, the area to be operated on ready to be shaved and painted with Betadine, so that the main grunt work was done by the time the students walked in the door—all they had to do was try to avoid slashing themselves with their scalpels and doing irreparable harm to their patients. The effect was that you really didn't see the dog, not in a holistic way, but only as a square of cutaneous membrane, under which lay the internal organs. That made it easier, and he supposed the administration had contrived it that way so as to eliminate any possibility of attachment to an animal that was destined, after four weeks and four procedures, to give up its being in a higher cause.

On the first day, he'd felt absolutely nothing beyond the usual fatigue. His breakfast consisted of a bowl of the sugary granola he'd bought at the health food co-op and as much coffee as he could get down in the twenty minutes he budgeted for showering, shaving, eating, and caffeinating before running for the 5:00 a.m. bus and starting his rounds at the hospital. Dog Lab met on Wednesdays, eight to eleven a.m., and when he humped down the concrete steps to the basement it was just in time to see Lurch and the other tech sidling out of the room after delivering the prepped dogs. They didn't nod to him, and he didn't nod to them. That was the way it was—they were the working class, and he the overeducated and underqualified med student for whom this was just one step up the ladder to something a whole lot better, or at least that was the way they saw it, and the way they saw it set him on edge enough to fit right into the role.

The first day's procedure was to make a midline abdominal incision, wait till Markowitz inspected it, then disinfect it and sew it back up. Jackson was surprised to see that there was no autoclave for sterilizing the instruments, just a dishwasher, but then if an infection should crop up, it wasn't all that momentous given the end result of all this—and, presumably, the students could gain experience in treating the infection in any case. Sipper, who'd been chosen to do the surgery while Jerry assisted and he himself cleaned the incision and stitched it up, even made a joke about it. "Not exactly the most sanitary OR I've ever been in, but then we really don't have to worry about saving lives here, do we?"

"No," he said, nodding in agreement, or at least in acknowledgment, "but if we're gloved and masked and following procedure, you'd think they'd spring for an autoclave, right?"

Sipper's eyes, isolated in the slit of flesh between mask and cap, jumped with amusement. "Dream on," he said, and somehow—maybe it was the coffee or the fact that he had unresolved issues with all this—Jackson heard himself say, "Yeah, well somebody's got to say it, right? Or else we might as well be working behind the meat counter at the A&P."

Dr. Markowitz, who was leaning in to inspect the work of the group closest to them, glanced up at the tone of his voice. Jerry said, "You're right, of course you're right—but Jax, in the final analysis, it's just a dog."

Suddenly, he felt himself grinning, all the tension evaporated in that instant. "What would Gertrude Stein say?"

"Oh, I don't know," Jerry said, and here came Markowitz to see what this was all about, because this wasn't playtime, gentlemen, was it? "A dog is a dog is a dog?"

The second week, he was chosen to do the surgery, which involved opening up the dog's abdominal cavity, finding and identifying the gallbladder, and removing it, after which the dog would be sewn up—in this case by Sipper—put back in his cage, and given a week to heal before the next procedure. He was feeling as exhausted and compensatorily caffeinated as he'd been the week before, but when it came to it he was steady and precise and everything went without a hitch. Dr. Markowitz, who leaned toward the critical side and doled out praise in an almost homeopathic way, inspected his work and said, "Good job," which was about as much as you could hope for.

Still, the praise felt good, and since the next day was his day off, he took Juliana out for pizza at the place around the corner from her apartment, and they shared a bottle of Chianti while she told him about her day and he told her about his, without going into too much detail—what mattered in the telling was that he'd controlled his nerves, done a bang-up job, and received praise from a doctor who didn't dispense it lightly.

"What's a gallbladder do?" she asked, idly licking a strand of mozzarella from her upper lip. Roxy Music was on the jukebox with "Love is the Drug," a tune he found hypnotic—when he had time to be hypnotized, that is.

"Stores bile and lets it out when you're digesting your food."

"But you can live without it, right?"

He shrugged, dropped his eyes to the pizza, and separated a slice. "Yeah, of course." He would have pointed out the obvious— "The dog's got to last four weeks"—but didn't want to get her going on that theme again, so he concentrated on easing his slice away from the body of the pizza with its tentacles of cheese intact. "My mother can testify to that. She had hers out when I was a kid and for years it was there in a jar of formalin on the bookcase, propping up Steinbeck and Sinclair."

Juliana made a face. "I don't know, but that's grotesque, isn't it?"

"Not especially. It's physiology, that's all. I used to love to shake up the jar and watch it float around in there, thinking that thing was inside my mother—and there's one inside of me too. Inside of everybody."

"And the one you took out of the dog, is that in a jar too?"

He shook his head. After they'd examined it for pathology, it had gone into the bin for medical waste.

"What, you didn't think to bring it home for *my* bookcase? It's like a trophy, right?" He didn't like the way this was going, didn't like her tone or the way she was looking at him. Wasn't this supposed to be a celebration? Wasn't he supposed to be happy?

He just shrugged—again—and then he was eating.

Two nights later, he was on call and making the rounds of the patients he was overseeing, one of whom he'd stitched up himself after kidney surgery, when the image of the dog came into his head. If he was checking up on the human patients, then why not see how the canine ones were doing? He got himself a Sprite—no more caffeine; his nerves were in a jangle already—and went down the basement steps to the converted storage room where they kenneled the dogs. As soon as he turned the doorknob, they began to whine, and then he flicked on the light and the room jumped to life: the dogs, the cages, bowls for food and water, a chart on the wall, a bucket, a broom, a mop. The cages were standard transport units, which were manageable, yet gave the dogs sufficient room to turn around and change position if they were experiencing pain. For obvious reasons the school favored medium-size animals—they were easier to work with, especially when somebody (Lurch) had to haul them around after they were sedated.

Well, okay, here they were. The other two, mixed breeds with whiskery faces and flag-like tails, stopped whining the minute he came through the door. The looks they gave him were without expectation—they sank down over their front paws and gazed steadily at him, as if they saw him for what he was, a functionary of the system that locked them away in cages and made them hurt.

"Jesus," he murmured, "it's okay, good dogs, it's okay," and then he was bent over his dog's cage, and his dog was licking his hand and he was rubbing its ears—or *his* ears, that is, and how could he not even have known the animal's sex? Was it really all that abstract? No, it wasn't—he was a dog, a living sentient being, an individual, a male, and that made him present in a way he hadn't been three mornings ago, when he was nothing more than a problem to be solved. That was the beginning of it, he supposed, that simple touch, the dog's hot, abrasive tongue exploring the back of his hand, and his fingers stroking the silk of its ears, a moment that wasn't disinterested or scientific but something else, something that felt very like connectedness, like pity, like love.

The next night he brought treats for all three dogs, and when nobody was looking he put the beagle on a leash and walked him up the steps and out the door so the dog could feel the night air on his face, sniff at the bushes, lift his leg. The whole thing, beginning to end, was no more than the fifteen minutes he allotted himself for his break, but as he stood there in the middle of the darkened flower bed, all the frenzy of activity—the ambulances, the ER, the silent procession of headlights endlessly entering and exiting the lot—seemed to exist in another dimension. His pulse rate slowed and he actually looked up and saw that there were stars in the sky.

Every night that week, he took his break in the basement, and every night he took his dog out for a sniff around the lawn and the flower beds, careful to stay in the shadows in case anyone should question him, though he'd already worked up an excuse along the lines of they'd operated on this one and he was having urinary tract problems and since the techs had all gone home and there was nobody to oversee things, he'd taken it upon himself, et cetera. And wasn't he a good med student? Wasn't he caring? Didn't he see to every least detail all by himself and without having to be told? He found himself calling the dog "Dog," which in this case made the generic specific and to that extent became a private joke between himself and the little animal that never complained, even when he lifted his leg against the tug of the stitches in his abdomen. He wasn't self-pitying like the other two, and when he did his business and scratched around in the rich loam of the flower bed, he did it with a brisk efficiency and then looked up at Jackson as if to say, "All right, what next?"

When Wednesday came around, he woke before the alarm went off. He was feeling cored out and vacant, as if he'd developed a touch of the flu, but after jumping in and out of the shower and gulping down his coffee and cereal, he realized that wasn't it at all—no, he was nervous. Not on his own account, as he'd been the week before—Jerry would be doing the cutting today, he'd be assisting, and Sipper would prep—but nervous for the dog. For *Dog*. Any operation was a risk, and things could go wrong, radically wrong, but he kept telling himself it didn't matter, because the dog was meant to be sacrificed in any case, wasn't that right? Wasn't that the way it was?

He did his morning rounds, and at eight a.m. he was in the lab, the dogs sedated and intubated, and the instruments laid out and gleaming from the dishwasher, and did they use rinse aid to make them shine like that? Sure they did. They at least had to maintain the illusion that this was the real deal and the outcome mattered to anyone. Markowitz was there already, hovering. There were brief greetings all around, and then there was the intense silence of concentration as the three groups focused on the task at hand: opening up the abdominal cavity, resecting a loop of small intestine, waiting for Markowitz's inspection each step of the way, and then stitching up the incision.

Markowitz called out the steps of the procedure, as usual, and all three groups operated in concert: Prep the skin. Make a midline abdominal incision. Dissect down to the peritoneum. Enter the abdominal cavity—*carefully*, so as not to perforate the bowel . . . Jerry worked confidently and well. There were no screwups. For whatever reason, maybe because he'd used up his quota of praise the previous week, all Markowitz said was, "Fine. Now sew it up."

That night he brought a box of frozen lasagna over to Juliana's, and they watched a made-for-TV movie that was idiotic in the extreme, but soothing because it was somebody else's idiocy for a change, almost as if it were a prescribed dose. He'd checked on Dog before he left the hospital, and the patient was groggy still, but roused himself enough to give a dedicated lick or two to the hand presented to him, though he left his treat untouched.

"So we operated again today," he said during the commercial break, which featured a Dodge Ramcharger pulverizing a streambed in a tree-choked forest somewhere. "Jerry this time. He did a great job, very efficient and sure-handed, but for whatever reason Markowitz didn't praise him the way he praised me last time around . . . which I think means I'm going to be the one he picks to do the big one next week, the heart procedure?" He ended with a rising inflection, as if he were asking a question, which in a way he was.

She looked up from her plate. They were eating at the table, the TV turned around so it was facing them. "What do you want me to say—that's nice?" She picked up the spatula, cut a square of lasagna from the pan, and lifted it to her plate. "It's not the same dog, is it? I mean, how can you—?"

"Yes, I told you—there are three dogs and each team gets their own one, beginning to end."

She didn't have anything to say to this. She chewed, staring into his eyes a moment as if she were about to say something more, but she didn't. On the TV screen, oversize tires flung ribbons of water at the banks of the stream.

"He's really a brave dog, you know that?" he said.

"Brave? What's brave about being strapped down on a table and getting, what, cut up by a bunch of med students?" Her mouth compacted. "He'd be brave if he bit you."

"You're not hearing me. I like him, I really do—I even named him . . ."

"What's the point?"

"I named him 'Dog.'"

"'Dog?' Why don't you just name him 'Nothing'? Isn't that what he is, *nothing*? Trash for the incinerator?" That was when she got up from the table and went into the bedroom, slamming the door behind her. There was silence, into which the return of the movie fed itself, line by banal line. He felt bad, worse than bad—she made him feel like a criminal, as if he were the one who made up the rules, as if it were all on him. What was happening here went against everything they were trying to teach him, and he resisted giving into it—where was his discipline, his detachment?

When she wouldn't come out to watch the rest of the movie, he cleaned up and washed and dried the dishes himself, feeling resentful now—she wasn't going to chase him away. He was going to sink into her couch and watch the inevitable shoot-out at the end whether she was in there brooding or not. A week from today Dog Lab would be over and they could forget about it and go back to the way things used to be, because he had enough hurdles to jump as it was without her digging into him all the time.

Going to the refrigerator for a beer, he noticed that she'd

torn a sheet of paper from her notebook and stuck it squarely in the middle of the door with four reinforced strips of Scotch tape, as if it was meant to last. She'd inscribed a quotation on it in her careful back-sloping script, attributed to an animal rights activist whose name was basically anathema in med school. "We have to speak up," it read, "on behalf of those who cannot speak for themselves."

The days ticked down, everything a blur, but no matter how crazy things got, he made time each night to visit with Dog and make sure he got his walk out in the world of sounds and scents and lights that got up and moved across the horizon. One night a cat came stalking around the margin of the flower bed, and Dog growled and tugged at the leash, and on another, a girl hurrying by with her book bag stopped a moment to bend and pat his head. "He's cute," she said, straightening up and giving Jackson a smile. "What's his name?"

Then it was Wednesday. As he'd hoped and dreaded in equal measure, Markowitz picked him to do the procedure, a right auricle resection, which involved cutting the muscles between the ribs, and then, using rib retractors and longer instruments, removing a portion of the right auricle, after which the patient would be patched up and sent back to his cage for recovery. When Markowitz called his name, he was so wound up he almost jumped. The dog was prepped and ready to go, but this wasn't some generic lab specimen, not anymore, and the last thing he wanted was to inflict pain on him—more pain, unnecessary pain, since as far as anyone knew the dog's heart was getting along just fine as it was—but then he didn't want anybody else to do it either. If it had been Sipper—or even Jerry—he would have been screaming inside. But it wasn't Sipper and it wasn't Jerry—he was the one with the scalpel in his hand as Markowitz called out the steps, and he was the one who was going to have to make this as near to flawless as humanly possible.

When it was over, when the stitches were in and Markowitz had made his final inspection, he was so overwhelmed he could barely speak. Markowitz hadn't said "Good job," but he'd smiled and patted him on the shoulder, and Jerry was right there for him, like a teammate when the winning basket swishes home at the final buzzer. He should have felt jubilant, but he didn't. He wasn't going to be a surgeon. He'd known that before he started the rotation, and if he'd told himself to keep an open mind, which was the whole point of experiencing each of the specialties in turn—it was closed now. Oh, he had the strength and the fine motor skills, but did he have the heart for it? Even as he asked himself the question, he had to laugh—the dog had a resected right auricle, but he had nothing there but a gaping hole. That night, late, when he was on call, he went down to check on the dog and found him lying on his side, all but inert. The dog didn't raise his head, but when Jackson called softly to him, his tail began to thump, as if in absolution.

During the course of the next week he visited the dog when he could—secretly, of course, because if any of the techs or his fellow students had caught him at it, he'd be an object of derision, if not outright mockery. There was the ear rubbing, the patting, the delivery of treats—and not just for his dog, but the other two as well—and when Dog had perked up toward the end of the week, the leash and the walk round the flower bed ensued. What he was wondering—and was afraid to ask—was how long the dogs would be allowed to recover before the terminal procedure, which certainly wouldn't involve any more consideration or skill than would have been required of an abattoir. The thought depressed him. Every time he slipped down the stairs and opened the door, he expected to see the three cages standing empty, and it came to him that he just couldn't bear that, and whether it violated protocol or for that matter was flat-out illegal, he wasn't going to allow it to happen.

From the pay phone in the lobby, where he could be sure no one would overhear him, he called Juliana and asked her to pick him up in her car. Right away. Now.

"What's up?" she asked. "Is there some kind of problem?"

"You'll see," he said. "And don't pull into the lot—just park around the corner on Elm, where the drugstore is?"

For the next month they switched off on keeping Dog either at her apartment or his, but it was problematic, what with their schedules and the inescapable fact that both their leases specified, in bold letters, No Pets. Dog was well-behaved, as far as that went, housebroken by whoever had selected him as a puppy from a kennel or an ad in the paper and then given him up in circumstances that could only be guessed at, the move out of town, poverty, sickness, death. Or indifference. A dog was a responsibility, a burden, as he was beginning to discover despite his best intentions. The landlord got on his case, and he took the dog to Juliana's till her landlord stormed up the stairs and threatened her with eviction. And though Dog was house-trained, the gallbladder removal meant that he was getting a continual drip of bile in his digestive tract, which tended to give him the runs. He was always apologetic about it, because he was a good dog, the best, the dog whose life he himself had saved, but there it was, shit on the floor, night after night. So now came the true point of reorientation: what was he going to do? Put an ad in the paper? Take the dog to the pound and start the cycle all over again?

No one at the hospital said a word about the dog's disappearance—for Lurch, he supposed, it must have made things all that much easier—but there was no way he could confide in anybody there, not even Jerry. He tried to talk it out with Juliana one night as they huddled over the cluttered Formica table in his kitchen, because there had to be some way around this, didn't there? They were eating tepid cheeseburgers she'd brought home from Burger King, while Dog waited stoically for the scraps and the record on the stereo channeled the down-and-out heartbreak of the blues. "I don't know," she said, "but I can't take him, that's for sure. Billy, my landlord? He just about goes through the roof every time I bring him over—you know that." She took a delicate bite of the burger, working her teeth like precision instruments to separate a piece for Dog, then leaned over to feed him from the cupped palm of her hand. When she straightened up, she said, "What about your mother?"

His mother lived four hundred miles away, in the town on the Hudson where he'd been raised. She'd retired the year before, just after his father died, and she was all by herself in that three-bedroom tract house with the fenced-in yard and big, rolling emerald lawn. He could have been a better son, could have called more often or even visited once in a while, but his life was hectic and it was difficult, increasingly difficult, and she had to understand that. And she did, he was sure she did. She was his mother, wasn't she?

"Yeah," he said, "I'll bet she's lonely, I mean, since my father died," and he bent down to where the dog was gazing up at him expectantly. "And what about you? Could you go for a little country living? Huh, boy? Huh? Does that sound good?"

He didn't call ahead. "We'll surprise her," he said. Juliana drove. They spent two days with his mother, who, the minute they walked through the door with the dog, knew exactly what was coming. "'Dog'?" she said. "That's no kind of name. Come on, Jax, you can do better than that, can't you?"

She named him Freddie, and when he died of natural causes fifteen years later, she wept for him.